BEST FRIENDS

Carys Jones

About *Best Friends*

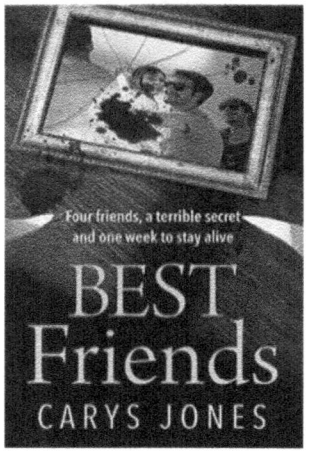

Four friends, a terrible secret, and one week to stay alive...

Grace doesn't have a family. That was taken away one dreadful day when she was just six, and her twin brother Peter was killed. Instead she has her best friends and flatmates – Jasper, Franklin and Aaron – and nothing can tear them apart.

Living in London, and trying desperately to make a living, the four friends are rapidly running out of money and hope. So, when they find a discarded suitcase in a skip, they can't believe their eyes when its contents seem to answer all their prayers.

But then a there is a knock on their door, and a very disgruntled thug with revenge on his mind, gives them one week to return his belongings, or they will pay with their lives. Soon the fractures in their friendships begin to show, and when one of them ends up fighting for his life, the stakes are raised even higher.

Will any of them get to the end of the week alive, or will the best of friends become the deadliest of enemies…

For my Best Friends who I'd simply be lost without;
Emma, Hannah,
Laura, Louise, Sarah and Ruth. You mean the world to me.

Prologue

It rained the day Peter was buried. Not a gentle, soft rain but a fierce lashing which soaked the grass of the cemetery and coated ebony headstones in a glossy sheen.

Grace did not trust the water. Nor did she trust the stranger standing at her side who kept her leather gloved hand around the little girl's upper arm in a vice like grip. They expected Grace to run. But where could she go? She longed to climb into the wooden box that contained her brother, to lie beside him and join him in his eternal slumber. Was he still cold to the touch as he had been when the police arrived, bursting through the door and prying the dead boy from his distraught mother's arms?

Those cries. They still lingered in Grace's memory along with the screams. An endless echo forever bouncing off the inner walls of her skull.

A crow landed in a nearby tree and then hopped along the lean branches as though trying to garner a better view of the grim scene below. Grace watched the bird, watched how the rain washed over its black feathers. Twice the crow vigorously shook itself and then it opened its dark beak to speak.

"Ashes to ashes," lamented the priest. Mrs Darden from flat fifteen was holding a large umbrella over him, shielding them both from the icy penetration of the rain.

Christmas was close. In less than a week children would be waking up from a restless night spent waiting on magic, running down the stairs of their homes to see what delights waited beneath a glittering tree.

There were no stairs in Grace's home. Not unless you counted the general staircase which ran up through the block of flats like a spine.

The call of the crow was shrill. Its rough squawk carried over the whisper of the rain and the words of the priest. Grace continued to look up at its black feathers, listening to the rasp of its cry.

"Come now, focus," the owner of the gloved hand instructed tersely. "This is your last chance to say goodbye to your brother."

Peter – forever small and pale with hair as jet black as the crow's plumage, just like Grace's. She always saw so much of herself in him. They had the same slight bone structure, the same hazel eyes and soft smiles.

"Adorable," strangers would stop to stare at the twins in the supermarket, tilting their heads as they issued the obligatory 'oohs' and 'ahhs.'

Would anyone stop now that Grace was alone? The abandoned half of a pair.

"Focus," the voice beside her demanded. Grace imagined that they were gritting their teeth and narrowing their eyes but she wouldn't look up to confirm it. She kept staring fixedly at the crow, at its beady black eyes. It kept calling out, the haunting sound carrying over the crowd gathered at the grave side. Grace looked at the crow and she knew; it was death. And when she left the cemetery that rainy December day it would follow her, follow her home, follow her through life because she had seen death, looked it square in the eye and now it was never going to let her go.

1

Fifteen Years Later

It was raining. The streets of London were awash with water. It gathered in rivers beneath the kerb and dripped down from gutters. Grace stepped out of the tube station and smiled as the first wet drops splashed against her. She walked boldly down the street, head held high, savouring the sensation as the rain soaked through her thin trench coat and began to damply settle against her skin.

She moved as her name suggested – with poise and elegance. With the measured steps of a prowling cat she wove her way through the congested street, dipping beneath low hanging umbrellas and skirting around the larger puddles. Grace was like the water; fluid with her motions and able to fit through the smallest gap. Her body was slight and lithe and when she walked her feet were always turned out, the telltale mark of a dancer.

To Grace the rain was glorious. She laughed to herself as she tilted her head up to meet the pewter sky above.

God's tears.

That's what her mother believed rain to be. And whenever the sky darkened she'd pluck the twins from their beloved swing set in the local park and hurry them back to their cramped flat. It was a sin to get wet.

"The sorrow," she'd lament as she closed the curtains and turned up the heating, "you can't let God's tears and sorrow touch you else it'll sink in."

As she moved further away from the station the bodies swarming along the street thinned and Grace was able to stretch out her arms. The rain washed against her, purifying and icy. Her hair that was held in a tidy bun became sodden, the tan shade of her coat darkened. Still Grace dawdled, stretching out every step on her way back to her flat. She was never in a rush, especially when it rained.

"You'll catch your death acting like that," a stern faced woman with a northern accent commented as she scurried past, shielded beneath her Radley umbrella. Grace wanted to laugh in the woman's face. It was people who brought death, not water. But it wasn't the stranger's urge for caution, but her Manchester twang that made Grace begin to hurry home. She had once spoken with a similar cadence but during her years spent at a prestigious ballet school she'd learned to phase it out, adopting a more clipped, formal accent.

She didn't need another reminder of home. Nor had she wanted to give the rest of the girls in her class another reason to see her as an outcast. Grace was already strange in their eyes. They came from homes with front doors, back gardens, places where parents came in pairs.

Up ahead a battered blue door flung open and a handsome dark haired guy burst out. He headed directly for Grace, extending his arms which made his long wool coat fan out behind him like a cloak.

"Jesus Christ," he exclaimed as he reached her. "What have I told you about your damn rain fetish? Now get your ass inside."

"I don't have a fetish, Franklin," Grace assured him as she followed him into the small communal hallway which led up to their two bedroom flat.

"Yes, you bloody do," Franklin feverishly shook off the miniscule cluster of raindrops which had landed on him during his short time outside. He behaved like the dark clouds lingering over London were releasing acid rather than water. "Whenever it rains I find you swanning around outside like you think you're Kate Bush. Now get in, hurry."

"I *am* hurrying." Grace ascended a steep staircase, made a sharp right turn and found her front door. It was of bare, unvarnished wood. She gently kicked the base and it opened without protest. Franklin followed her inside and paused to secure the many deadbolts on the inner side of the door.

"I've been waiting for you to get back," shedding his coat Franklin vaulted over the sofa and then dropped down against its flattened cushions. His dark eyes regarded Grace as his full lips curled with impatience. The liquid eyeliner he'd carefully applied that morning made his expression seem even more severe.

"I told you I'd be back for two." Grace cut a more demure path to the sofa and sat beside him.

"It's nearly three."

"It is?"

"See," Franklin pointed at her and pouted. "Rain fever. You get it every time. Makes you delirious. Now you're losing track of time."

"I guess I just ran late at the studio."

"And they'll charge you for it," Franklin rolled his eyes and raised his fingertips to his forehead. Slowly, carefully, he checked the peak of his moussed hair. Satisfied it was intact he dropped his hands. "I don't know why you pay to practice there when you could do it here for free." He gestured at their little flat and then made a blunt sound in his throat.

Their living space was tiny. Grace, as the only girl in the flat share, was fortunate to have her own room. Franklin and Aaron shared the second bedroom which worked on a rotational system. Since

Aaron was in a struggling rock band he was generally out most nights. As an out of work actor Franklin was always home, he could sleep whenever Aaron wasn't around. Their final flatmate, Jasper, made his bed on the sofa. Grace was forever offering her room to them but they were all stubborn in their gentlemanly ways and refused to let her give up her girly sanctuary just for them.

"If I did one pirouette in here I'd risk knocking over the TV," Grace remarked.

"And we can't risk you hurting Tina. She's too precious."

"Tina," with a smirk Grace stood up and headed over to the small kitchenette. It was attached to the living area and three doors led off to the bedrooms and bathroom. Life in the flat was cramped but they all referred to it as cosy.

"Everyone names their television, Grace," Franklin stated haughtily.

"I don't think that they do." In the kitchenette she turned on the kettle. The chill against her bones which had been pleasant outside was now verging on unsettling. She needed to warm up.

"You've not asked yet." Franklin turned to rest his arms against the back of the sofa and watch her. He'd kept his fingerless gloves on as part of his protest to Aaron that the thermostat for the heating was being kept too low. During the Christmas holidays, just a month ago, the temperature of the flat had been hotly debated. Franklin yearned for a comfortable twenty degrees but collectively they could barely afford to keep the place at seventeen.

"Asked..." Grace dragged out the word as she mentally went through a rolodex of possible responses. Franklin had been waiting on her return which meant that he'd been somewhere, rather than been sleeping off his latest tequila hangover or binge watching *The Good Wife* on the sofa. But where had he been? Grace berated the rain as she watched the plastic kettle tremble as it reached the boil. The rain was always so distracting. "The audition." She released a breath she hadn't intended to hold. "How was it?"

"Kudos on remembering," Franklin flexed his fingers and stared at his nails. The cuticles were all pushed back, neat and trim. Franklin insisted on perfection. He was forever cleaning the flat, bustling across the floor space with a hoover or flicking his feather duster around and up into hard to reach corners. He definitely considered cleanliness to be next to godliness. "And the audition was shit."

"What?" Grace's shoulders dropped. "Seriously?"

"It was a big, fat pile of stinking shit. Like I went, took my CV, my headshot, sang an achingly good rendition of 'Stay With Me' if I do say so myself."

"So, what went wrong?"

"I kicked my bloody arse off." Franklin raised his arms and then sullenly dropped them at his sides. "I kicked so high and so hard that I nearly did myself a mischief."

"It sounds like it went well, then?" Grace countered as she made them both a mug of tea.

"They said they'd get back to me."

"Okay."

"*Get back to me,*" Franklin spat out the words with sudden venom. "If you get the part they say they'll call. *Call.* But no, I got," he adopted a cheesy American accent, "so great, Franklin we'll get back to you."

"Maybe they will."

"No, absolutely not."

Grace carefully carried the two drinks round to the sofa, passing the yellow Pokémon mug to Franklin.

"It sounds like it went better than you thought it did."

"I need this," Franklin nursed his tea between his hands and sagged against the worn out sofa. "Like, I *really* need this."

"I know."

"I've been out of work for *eight months.* Eight fucking months, Grace."

"You could try getting, you know, a regular job. I saw that Pret are hiring."

"See you there, then," Franklin remarked sharply. "Because you and I both know that we're not going to get some regular job, not when we came here on a dream. Getting a job would be giving up, admitting defeat."

Grace couldn't argue with his point. Since graduating from her dance school she'd drifted between jobs, failing to land a coveted permanent place at a company. With each failure, each unsuccessful audition, a little voice chirped in her ear like a bitter bird;

You're not good enough. You need to go home. You need to give up.

When those thoughts came she thought of Peter. Of the little boy who'd never be a man. She fought for him. For all that he might have been because, since the day he died, she'd been compensating for his loss, trying to cram two lifetimes into one.

"Maybe we're just gluttons for punishment," Franklin sighed.

"Maybe we just believe in our dreams."

"I should be on the stage," his eyes glistened as he imagined it. "I should be front and centre, taking my bow every night in front of an adoring crowd. There'd be roses, cheers. Everyone would love me."

"You should add modesty to your list of talents on your CV."

"And then one night a studio executive would be in the audience," Franklin dreamily continued, ignoring her. "She'd see me, see me shine and know, just know, that I was destined for greatness. She'd cast me in a breakout part where I play Leonardo DiCaprio's lover and I'd take home the Oscar for best supporting actor the following year."

"Because Leo takes the Oscar for best actor, I've heard this fantasy a million times, Franks."

"It never gets old," Franklin whispered reverently. "One day I'll be there. One day I'll have my star on the Hollywood walk of fame and people will know my name."

"Do you remember what Aaron said about the walk of fame? That it's in a really seedy area of Los Angeles and next to really famous names are like porn shops and brothels. He said it was horrible."

"His actual words were *soul suckingly awful*," Franklin recalled with a wave of his hand, "but we all know that dear Aaron is prone to theatrics of his own, though the brooding bassist would never admit as much."

"I just mean that sometimes the reality doesn't live up to the dream."

"Please," Franklin scoffed, "you're telling me that your fantasy of being a principal at a ballet company wouldn't be every bit as wonderful as you've imagined? That your pulse wouldn't race as you take that final bow before a rapturous audience?"

"I mean…" Grace tucked her legs up beneath herself and picked at the hem of her dress. "Time isn't on my side anymore," saying the words made her feel like her whole body had turned to wood. Rather than being nimble and graceful she was suddenly stiff and awkward. "I'm…" she drew in a pained breath. "I'm getting too old."

"Bollocks."

"Franks, it's true."

"Margot Fonteyn danced into her sixties. You told me that when we first met at that shoddy bar in Shoreditch."

"I know but…" Grace looked into the depths of her mug of tea. She'd tried to swirl the milk the way her mother used to do. She'd expertly twist her spoon in the mug so that a light circle of foam gathered atop the hot drink.

"There's my tuppence worth," she'd say to the twins with a wink.

But Grace had failed. The top of her tea was flat and uniform in colour.

"Margot, she was the exception," she hated the way her own words were cutting against her. "What if I'm just the rule?"

"What if that's true for both of us?" Franklin placed his tea on the cluttered surface of their coffee table and laced his arm around Grace's shoulders. "What if when I audition they don't see a star in the making but some pathetic wannabe?"

"Franks, that's—"

"You'll tell me that I'm wrong. That I am a star. Start talking to yourself how you'd talk to your friends and you'll be a lot better off. Trust me." He kissed her forehead.

"What about the rent?" Grace mumbled with dismay. "I'm short this month and now you will be too."

"We'll discuss it with Jasper and Aaron when they're back."

"Things are seriously tight though, Franks. We might have to sell Tina."

"Hush!" Franklin desperately clamped his hands over Grace's mouth. "She might hear you," he dropped his voice to a theatrical whisper. "Tina is family. You don't sell family."

Grace forced his hands away from her face and hoped he'd hadn't smudged her red lipstick. She couldn't afford to apply it more than twice a day, she was running low on makeup supplies as it was. "Tina is a television and if it comes to it we'll sell her. It."

"Don't listen, baby," Franklin gestured at the large screen. "She's lying. We'd never do that to you."

"What's the issue? Just watch Netflix on your laptop."

"Can't," Franklin remarked grimly. "I pawned that last month to cover my share of the rent."

"Shit."

"Shit indeed."

2

"So," Aaron's voice was deep, like it had been forged in iron. "We need to discuss the rent."

The rain was still pelting against the windows of the small flat. Its wet touch lingered like whispers at the edges of the room.

"Rent," Franklin threw his head back as he sat with his arms spread along the spine of the sofa, feet resting on the coffee table.

"Yes, rent," Aaron stiffly confirmed. "It's due in three days."

Grace was on the sofa beside Franklin. Aaron stood across from them, still wearing his leather jacket which glistened with raindrops. He unfolded his arms to gently stroke the closely cropped chestnut beard which crept up his jawline.

"I'm short," Jasper was perched on one of two stools in the kitchenette. His thick blonde hair fell into his blue eyes in shaggy waves. He was dwarfed by the blue cable knit jumper he wore which was two sizes too big. "My freelance work this month hasn't been all that lucrative."

Aaron rolled his green eyes, eyes which always reminded Grace of a damp spring meadow. He grunted in her direction.

"I…" she chewed her lip and squirmed beside Franklin. She was worse than short. She was broke. She'd withdrawn the last ten pounds from her bank account to treat herself to a caramel latte. She blamed the rain for making her uncharacteristically hedonistic. She was usually so good with money. When she had it. "I have that audition tomorrow."

"Audition?"

"You know," Franklin crossed and un-crossed his long legs against the coffee table. "She's auditioning for Matthew Bourne's company. It could be her big break. *Remember.*"

"We went to see *Sleeping Beauty* last year," Jasper piped up from behind them. "And *Edward Scissorhands* the year before."

"The guy is a visionary," Franklin gushed. "If Grace lands this job then she won't have to worry about rent again. She'll be off touring the country in some chic performance of a fairy tale, being front and centre no less."

"Off touring?" Aaron narrowed his eyes and resumed his initial stance of having his arms tightly crossed against his chest.

"Yeah," Grace peered up at him, smiling softly. "It's a big opportunity."

"Hm," he made a non-committal sound. "If you get the part it doesn't help us in the short term. We still need to pay the rent."

"Where's your contribution, Mr Rock Star?" Franklin demanded with a condescending air. As usual his tolerance for being talked down to was wearing thin. Aaron always assumed the role of reluctant leader amongst the group, largely due to him being the eldest. "You've been doing gigs all month," Franklin continued, crossing his arms to mimic Aaron's posture. "You dragged us to that god awful place in Camden to watch you guys play. Surely you can manage the lion's share of the rent."

"Again," Jasper added, unhelpfully.

"Actually, I can't," Aaron clenched his jaw and doused them all in a disdainful glare. "Most of those gigs we… we played for free."

Grace pushed her body down into the sofa. She wanted to get up, wanted to wrap her arms around Aaron and hold him close. He was a wolf, proud and solitary. Even to the rest of his band he was an enigma. He existed within two clear packs; his musical group and his flatmates, but he managed to remain detached from both. Grace knew what the true cost of playing for free would do to him; it would wound his pride.

"We're trying to get exposure," Aaron insisted. "We have to do these gigs to build up a following."

"Three years," Franklin lowered his voice but not enough to avoid detection by the others. "If you've not built up a following in that time it's not going to happen."

"I've yet to see your name in lights!" The beast was unleashed. Aaron's words were a roar. He pointed a calloused finger at Franklin. "You're hardly pulling your weight around here."

"Hey, hey, let's not fight," Jasper had abandoned his stool and now slid between the coffee table and Aaron, facing the sofa, slim arms raised. Beside the bassist he looked especially small, a sparrow in the shadow of a hawk. He was twenty-five but could pass for fifteen if he wanted to. He stood a little over five foot three and could fit into most of Grace's clothes. It was Jasper who had convinced her to join the flat share when she'd first moved to London. He'd reminded her so much of her late brother that she couldn't say no. There was a gentleness within Jasper that she was drawn to.

"Some people are still water," her mother would say. "Peter is still. You… you are a tempest."

Grace saw the truth in the statement. Peter was always measured, always kind. He never lashed out, never screamed with frustration or punched a wall. Once Grace grew so mad at his placid nature that she bit him during a fight, hard enough to draw blood. As punishment her mother made her sit in the bath for three hours, long enough for her skin to pucker like a prune and grow white and weak.

"We'll figure something out," Jasper told the others, voice calm. "We always do." He shifted to glance behind him, not at Aaron, but at the television.

"Oh no," Franklin was on his feet. "She's going nowhere. We'll sell that damn Mac book of yours before she goes."

"I need my laptop to work," Jasper countered, shoulders still lowered, expression still devoid of agitation. Fireworks were exploding all around him yet he behaved like he was on an empty beach enjoying the serene image of a setting sun. "If I sold that I couldn't make any money at all."

"You're a writer," Franklin threw up his arms as he wedged himself defensively in front of the television. "Go old school, get a notepad and pen, write longhand, it'll be fun. You can pretend you're Dickens or something."

"If he wrote eighty thousand words by hand he'd risk his fingers falling off," Grace shrugged apologetically at Franklin. "He needs his computer."

"Eighty thousand words?" beside the TV Franklin put his hands on his waist and stared between his friends in disbelief.

"That's what makes up a book," Grace confirmed.

"Christ," Franklin shook his head at Jasper, "no wonder you never want to go out, you must be bloody knackered all the time. I could barely write the five thousand words required for my dissertation."

"Rent," Aaron threw the word in amongst them like a verbal grenade. "We need a plan and we need it quick."

"I know," Franklin playfully lodged his thumb and finger against his chin, "let's write a musical about our struggles to pay rent. It could be like a year in our lives. We could call it," he paused for dramatic emphasis, "*Rent.*"

"That's been done," Jasper remarked flatly.

"I know," Franklin rolled his eyes and returned to the sofa, landing heavily next to Grace. "I was being funny. Did you sell your sense of humour for last month's rent or something?"

"We're not getting anywhere," Aaron paced away from the television towards the kitchenette. "Everyone, go get what you have," he pulled several twenty pound notes out of his jeans back pocket. "And do it now. No excuses. I need to see where we're at."

Ten minutes later and the results were grim. On the cracked counter in the kitchenette was laid out a measly one hundred and twenty pounds. Way off the seven hundred that they needed for their rent. Grace pressed the tips of her nails against the inside of her palms, loathing how she'd put down six pounds and seventy-five pence. She felt like she was mocking the rest of them with her lack of earnings. Everything was riding on tomorrow's audition. If she got the part she could risk going into her overdraft because she knew she'd soon be able to pay it off. If not…

"I can't call my parents for help again," Jasper looked at the money, hands resting deep in his pockets. He'd put down sixty pounds. The other fifty-four came from Aaron. Franklin had failed to contribute at all. "Jessie has just started university and they are paying for her tuition. Mum is already pulling double shifts at the hospital. I can't put upon them, I really can't."

As Jasper was one of five, his parents were being pulled in a myriad of directions when it came to finances. He didn't like to approach them for a hand-out, especially when all his siblings were doing the same thing. Two were still in education and of the three that had graduated from university two were unemployed; himself and Jenny. Only his oldest brother, Jackson, was doing well. He lived in London and worked in finance but he'd only give his siblings a hand-out at the expense of their dignity and Jasper had said before that nothing was worth that. He was determined to match his brother in level of success.

"We need money," Aaron stared squarely at Franklin.

"Do not look at me!" Franklin instantly raised his hands and stepped back from the counter. "I'm broke. Skint. I'm whatever the cockney rhyme is for completely poor. And *no,* I am not calling my parents. They're still recovering from my coming out."

"Wasn't that ten years ago?" Jasper dusted some strands of hair out of his line of sight.

"Yes," Franklin nodded. "And they're *still* recovering."

"Sounds like your parents are as dramatic as you are," Aaron began to gather up the presented money.

"I have to get my flair from somewhere. It's about the only decent thing they've ever given me."

Grace felt Jasper's eyes on her. He was looking but not pleading. She knew he'd never do that, never come straight out and tell her that it was her turn to phone home on a begging mission. Over the last year the guys had all done it, swallowed their pride like a bitter pill and asked for financial support from the people that had made them. They'd exhausted those avenues for themselves but they thought that Grace's path back home remained paved with yellow bricks. She never spoke about where she came from, about her mother. They knew about Peter but not the details. Or maybe they did. A quick internet search would reveal the truth about what had happened. But if any of them had figured it out they said nothing which only made Grace love her flatmates even more, and hate that she couldn't contribute to the rent.

"I'm going to nail my audition tomorrow," she told them with a confident smile. "And then I'll be okay to go into my overdraft and we'll be sorted."

"There, see," Franklin patted her on the back, "problem solved. Now let's fire Tina up so I can get my daily Will Gardner fix."

Grace declined the invitation to watch *The Good Wife*. She retreated into the fairy lit cave she called a bedroom and sat cross legged on her bed looking through old programmes of ballets she had been to see whilst in London. Her flannel pyjamas were a soft shade of rose, almost the same colour as the first pair of ballet shoes Grace had ever worn.

She'd never danced before Peter died. Afterwards a group of adults sat around a table and tried to decide what would be best for her. A focus. A purpose. They threw abstract ideas around amongst themselves until someone mentioned ballet. They commented on her slight figure and dainty movements. They stumped up the initial cost for Grace's first year of training themselves. Yet she didn't know their names. Didn't know how to thank them for introducing her to the love of her life. They were just people on a board. She didn't even know if they were male or female. Not that it mattered.

"Hey," the door to her bedroom cracked open allowing in a slither of golden light. It illuminated the clutter on the floor, a medley of pink tights, dance shoes and hairpins scattered over piles of unwashed clothes. Franklin would always literally shriek when he came in and saw the mess. He'd disappear and return clad in garish yellow marigolds demanding she vacate the room while he cleaned.

But it wasn't Franklin peering in. It was Aaron. He awkwardly cleared his throat and lingered in the doorway.

"Come in," Grace instructed, patting the space beside her on the bed. "You know you can always just come in when you want."

"I know but..." he rubbed his hands against the back of his head and came over to the bed but didn't sit.

Grace forced herself to smile as she looked up at him. Her dark hair was loose and fell in lazy waves down to her shoulders. "We're still friends, right?"

"Of course," a look of hurt washed over his strong features.

"Good," she patted the bed again. "So sit."

"I can't," he shrugged in the direction of the door which he'd made sure to leave ajar. "I'm off out in a minute. Another gig."

"Oh," Grace's smile began to wilt like an unloved flower. There was so much he didn't tell her any more. It extended far beyond his musical schedule.

"I just wanted to say good luck for tomorrow."

"Thanks."

"And…" slowly he did lower himself against the bed. "Don't put too much pressure on yourself, okay?"

The open door was letting in more than light. A cold draught stole its way in, causing Grace to shiver. A thousand tiny wounds opened up across her skin as though she were covered in paper cuts. She didn't want to think about the past. About—

"If you don't make the audition tomorrow it's fine. We'll figure something out with the rent. We'll," he lowered his voice, "we'll sell Tina if it comes to it."

"So now you're naming the television too?" Grace arched an eyebrow at him.

"I'm just going along with Franks." Aaron blushed and Grace had to sit on her hands to stop herself from reaching out to stroke his cheek. "But yeah, don't let tomorrow become a big thing. Okay?"

"Don't you think I'll get it?" the cold from the draught had slid into Grace's voice.

"That's not what I'm saying," with a grimace Aaron stood up. "I didn't come in here to fight. I came in here to wish you luck."

"Right. Well. Thanks."

"Grace, don't be like that."

"Have fun at your gig."

"Grace—"

"And if you bring someone back please be quiet. I've got an early start."

"I wouldn't do that," Aaron went through the door and closed it behind him, sealing her in the dark twilight of her messy room.

*

Grace was nine when she was in her first show. She wore a tutu of sugary pink taffeta and had to spin her way across the stage in a solo. It had been thrilling, exhilarating to wait for the rise of the curtain, the strident note of the piano and her cue. Grace had twirled with perfection, not missing a single step. The audience clapped, some people cheered. As she tottered off stage she looked out at them, their faces concealed by shadows cast by the blinding stage lights. They were just ghosts, phantoms. And she knew none of them. No one had come to see just her dance.

The next morning the rain had eased. Grace wasn't sure if she was grateful for that as she hurried down the steps towards the tube station. Her dance bag was clutched to her side, stuffed full of spare pairs of tights and shoes. Beneath her jogging bottoms and hoodie she was already wearing her leotard. The schedule of the day had been etched into her brain. She'd stared at it on her phone the night before as her eyes became heavy and her mind numb.

Her audition commenced at 9 a.m. sharp. It meant navigating the tube system at peak time, something Grace usually tried to avoid.

"You'll be fine," Jasper had muttered sleepily as he rolled over on the sofa as she bustled around him, grabbing a glass of juice and shoving a handful of nuts into her mouth. "Try and enjoy it."

Franklin was still sleeping in his room which meant that Aaron had yet to return from his gig. Grace tried not to think about him as she tussled her way through the crowds. Her heart was already pounding and she wasn't even at the studio yet.

You're not good enough. You need to go home. You need to give up.

Her song of self-doubt began to play in her mind. She wished she still had her iPod so that she could drown it out with some classical music. But the iPod, like so many other valuables, had been sold to cover rent.

Rent.

Just thinking about it made Grace break out in a cold sweat. Aaron had told her not to worry but everything was riding on this audition. She'd failed to get paying work for months. Dance jobs were scarce and every time she went for one she saw the same desperate faces, dozens who'd danced their way through prestigious schools just as she had done. If only dreams provided sustenance they'd all be fine, but instead they were being worn down by the city they'd so eagerly come to just a few years ago.

"You can do this," Grace whispered to herself as she flexed her hands and pointed her toes within her trainers. She'd spent all the money she had left on rehearsal time at her local dance studio. She'd twirled in front of the large mirrors until her toes bled. Still she feared she hadn't done enough.

A horrible feeling spread through her, one she knew she needed to ignore.

Phone mum.

Because that's what most people did when they were stressed or afraid, they called home. They called the person who'd brought them into this cruel world for reassurance that it actually wasn't so cruel and they still were the cherished prodigy they'd been brought up believing that they were.

But if Grace called home there'd be no answer. She bit down on her lip so hard that her mouth filled with a coppery tang. She had to do this. She had to nail this audition. She needed to pay her rent.

3

Where was the rain when she needed it? Grace walked slowly up the street, her steps heavy with regret. She needed the rain to cleanse her, to soak through to her skin, to make her feel numb. A pale winter sun hung low in the sky, surrounded by wisps of ashen clouds.

"Dammit." Grace pulled up the hood of her jumper and bowed her head. When strangers shouldered their way past her she didn't look up to disdainfully catch their eye.

She'd fallen. In the audition. Just when the eyes of the company director were upon her scrutinising every lift, every extension. Grace had misjudged a pirouette. She blamed her eagerness, her desperation. In her haste to execute the move she launched herself into it too hard, too fast. She knew she was going to fall before the smooth floor of the studio slammed against her cheek.

No one had moved. The director and several senior dancers watched on, unflinching, as though they were cast in stone. Grace had scrambled back onto her feet with all the elegance she could muster and continued her routine but her heart had been hollowed out. She knew as she swept her way across the floor, feverishly twisting in time with the music, that she had failed. It was over.

Now she was left to return to the flat empty handed with no contribution to the rent. Another dream lay in tatters around her feet. Grace wanted to weep. To scream. She wanted to get soaked in a rain storm so furious that it drowned her.

*

"It's okay," Franklin sat beside Grace on the bed, stroking her head as she lay in the foetal position, the cushions beneath her wet with tears. "You did your best. That's all you can do."

"I *fell*." The word felt dirty in her mouth. Shameful. "Right in front of everyone. I fell. It was humiliating."

"But you got straight back up, right?"

"Right," Grace croaked, her voice as sore as her ego.

"Then, so what if you fell?" His voice was bright, almost bright enough to banish the sorrowful shadows that clung to Grace. "You got back up, you showed tenacity. Professionalism. One fall won't cost you the audition."

"It will," Grace pressed her face against her pillows, muffling her voice. "It will because no one else will have fallen. Everyone else will have been perfect."

"You don't know that."

"I'm not good enough. I need to go home. I need to give up."

"Hush!" Franklin instantly demanded. Grace shuddered as she realised that she'd uttered her mantra of self-loathing aloud. More tears came, a thick stream that seemed to have no end. As she wept Franklin continued to stroke her head, continued to stay close. "It's really not as bad as you think. I promise. And you can't go home. I won't let you. We're here for the long haul, remember? We vowed to help each other achieve our dreams."

"What a great job we're doing," Grace remarked bitterly. "And the rent." She rolled onto her back and blinked away her latest batch of tears. "What the hell are we going to do about the rent?"

"Fuck knows," Franklin smiled at her tenderly and stroked her damp, puffy cheeks. Then he playfully prodded her in the side. "How are your kidneys? Reckon you've got one to spare?"

"Oi!"

"We could fetch a nice price on the black market. Between all of us we can offer four kidneys, not bad going."

"I'm not sure Jasper and Aaron would go for it," Grace sniffed.

"We'll convince them. Either that or drug them and let them wake up in a bath tub of ice minus one kidney."

"Like you'd go through with it," Grace nudged him with the heel of her foot. "You squealed like a pig when you had to have the flu jab because of your nan."

"It *hurt*," Franklin declared emphatically. "And I had a bruise, remember?"

"That tiny dot on your arm?" Grace gasped dramatically. "Oh yeah, I remember. You must have been in *agony*."

"I was."

The door to Grace's bedroom opened and they both went quiet.

"Hey," Aaron leaned in, his hair askew and his eyes red. He wore an Iron Maiden t-shirt and oversized boxer shorts. He stepped into the room, careful to skirt his bare feet around the debris. "You okay, how did today go?" His voice was clotted. Grace could tell that he'd just woken up. "Wait," he moved deeper into the room. "Have you been crying?"

"I'm fine," Grace sniffed loudly and sat up, frantically dragging her fingers across her cheeks to hide any lingering tears.

"What happened?" Aaron looked between her and Franklin.

"I said I'm fine."

Aaron focused his stare on Franklin.

"She fell."

"Franks!"

"Well," Franklin shrugged and climbed off the bed. "He'd find out sooner or later." Then facing Aaron, "she fell and she thinks she's fluffed the audition, but I told her not to be so silly. She got back up, that's the main thing."

"You fell?"

Grace met Aaron's gaze. He was always so hard to read. He seemed to carry an invisible shield behind which he hid all his emotions. When she looked in his eyes all she saw was the dwindling fatigue from the night before, but she knew there was more there. She'd seen glimmers of it before.

"I fell and now…" her shoulders dropped with defeat, "now I'm worried about the rent because I can't pay my share and—"

"Get dressed," Aaron clicked his fingers at her.

"I'm…" Grace gestured at clothes she was still wearing from the audition. "I'm dressed. You're the one walking around in your boxers."

He grunted. "I mean properly dressed. Going out dressed."

"Going out?" Franklin leaned towards the door with interest.

"Yes," Aaron scratched at his beard and began retreating through the door. "We're going out. All of us."

"And we'll pay for our drinks with what? Good intentions?"

"She needs to be cheered up," Aaron nodded at the bed, at Grace, "so clean yourselves up. Drinks are on me. We'll figure the rent out tomorrow." With a grunt he returned to the main flat, letting the door click closed behind him.

"Ooh," Franklin dramatically dropped back onto the bed and looked at Grace, smirking. "He still loves you. He does!" He began to raise his voice "So *get dressed. We're going out.*"

"He's just trying to be nice."

"Because he cares, Grace. Because he never stopped caring. Aaron is a man of frustratingly few words and those that he does utter tend to relate to you."

"You're wrong."

"I'm not."

"Trust me," Grace freed her hair from its bun and ran her fingers across her scalp. "You are."

"Whatever," Franklin waved his hand at her, a white flag of submission. "Let's just do as the man mountain says and get ourselves tarted up. And…" he looked longingly at the floor. "Maybe I could…"

"Fine," Grace sighed. "Clean. Knock yourself out. Go mad."

Franklin leapt forward and kissed her on the cheek. "Thank you. Thank you, thank you, thank you. You've no idea how your room has been driving me crazy while I've been in here."

*

They started drinking at noon, huddled around a table in a bar where Aaron often played free gigs. It meant that the owner was willing to let them drink all the beer they could stomach for a nominal price.

"I don't even like beer," Grace protested.

"Then that can come my way," Aaron had eagerly taken the drink from her and claimed it as his own.

Once a few beers had been downed, shots were bought. Tequila. It burned as it slid down the back of Grace's throat. She knew she shouldn't be drinking. She should be using her overdraft to buy more rehearsal time at the studio. She needed to get better, sharper. She needed to never fall again.

"You were lucky not to hurt yourself," Jasper had quietly told her as they walked through the city towards the bar.

Lucky.

Grace wanted to laugh at the word. She had no luck. It had deserted her long ago, choosing to leave when Peter did.

As the day dragged on the bar became busier. People in suits, weary from work, came in to chat and banter amongst themselves. The scented smoke of e-cigarettes hung in the air. And somewhere between her third shot and second beer Grace ceased caring about her botched audition. About the rent. About anything. Instead, she started to actually have fun.

It was dark outside when Franklin felt ready to unveil his karaoke repertoire. He always liked to begin with a powerful rendition of Seal's *'Kiss from a Rose'*.

"No," Aaron tugged him back towards their little table by the cuff of his purple silk shirt. "Not tonight, Franks. It's a flatmate night. We're here to cheer up Grace."

"Grace," Franklin tugged his arm free and placed both hands on his hips as he stared at her from across the table, "will hearing my *beautiful,* oh so very soulful voice, cheer you up? You know it will. You don't need to say it. Your eyes tell me everything." He clicked his fingers and sashayed over to the karaoke platform. It was seven in the evening and no one else in the bar had yet felt inebriated enough to take centre stage. Grace knew that Franklin didn't need the beer and tequila in his system to perform. He was a born entertainer, he truly came alive when all eyes were on him.

"Here we go," Aaron muttered into his beer. "Don't say that I didn't try to stop him."

Out of the four of them Aaron was the only sober member of the group. Somehow, despite all the beers he'd downed he remained lucid, his words still singular and not slurred together. Grace already knew how much he liked to drink, remembered all too well the nights he'd steal into her bed stinking of beer and whiskey.

"Woo," Jasper applauded loudly. His cheeks were rosy, his eyes misty. He'd twice fallen off his stool. The first time Franklin had laughed so hard he spat out his beer.

"Look," he'd exclaimed as he pointed down at his fallen friend, "look, Grace, it's contagious. Everyone is falling."

Luckily Grace was drunk enough to also see the funny side. As she and Franklin clutched their sides as they giggled uproariously, Aaron got up with a groan and bent down to scoop Jasper off the sticky floor.

"Lighters up," Franklin commanded everyone in the bar as the first few notes of his favourite song came on. "Or… phones," he leaned heavily against the microphone stand. "Light up whatever the fuck you've got. Just... light... yeah."

Grace drained the last of her beer and listened. Franklin could sing. Whatever the note, he could hold it, harmonise with the best of them. With his sculpted cheeks and individual sense of style, he was born a few decades too late to be a New Romantic. He would have been adored in the eighties. Now he looked like a man out of his time. But he was still so heartbreakingly beautiful to listen to.

"Come on," the song hadn't finished when Grace felt strong arms lifting her from her stool and pulling her through the crowd which swayed around Franklin, phones held up towards him as he crooned through the final parts of the powerful melody.

"What... the?" She was outside. The cold night air slammed against her, knocking the air from her lungs and bringing her to her knees. Coughing, she peered up at Aaron who loomed large at her side, one hand protectively placed on her back.

"You're wasted," he told her.

"I'm... not." She tried to stand but the floor beneath her kept shifting unpredictably as though the pavement had been switched with sand.

"You are," Aaron looped an arm round her waist and held her against his side, supporting her. "You were crying while Franks sang."

"He has a... beautiful... voice."

"Hmm."

"I'm fine… really."

"I'm taking you home."

After a few stumbled steps down the street Franklin and Jasper came rushing out of the bar.

"Hey!" Franklin reached them first. "You missed the end of my song, *and* I had to decline the crowd's demands for an encore."

"Where's Jasper?"

Grace felt herself getting spun around in the direction of the bar. She saw Jasper wilting over the side of the kerb, head angled towards the gutter.

"Crap," Aaron released her and hurried over to their other friend, just as Jasper leaned forward and vomited into the road. Franklin's laughter bellowed out from behind.

"Ooh, J's overdone it."

"You've all overdone it," Aaron scolded as he knelt beside Jasper.

"*We* are fine," Grace felt a new pair of arms lock around her and begin guiding her further down the street. "I saw you adoring my performance," Franklin said to her, his voice warm with pride. "You've always had good taste."

"Does that extend to… *him*?" Grace's feet weren't working. She focused on launching one foot forward and then the other but it was like the final stages of building a house of cards, everything kept threatening to come tumbling down. She swayed uneasily beside Franklin.

"It most definitely extends to *him*," he confirmed. "He's gorgeous and he's complicated. The most tempting of combinations. Just like you," he tapped a finger against the tip of Grace's nose.

"I'm not… er… complicated."

"You are," Franklin steadied her sway and together they sauntered further down the street. "You keep your cards close to your chest but I know a messed up deck when I see one. Birds of feather flocking together and all that."

"The rent," Grace lamented. She was letting down her flock. If only she hadn't failed her audition, hadn't fallen then—

She slipped out of Franklin's grasp and landed on the ground with a dense thud. She felt something scrape and jar but she didn't know what. Come dawn there would be fresh wounds to inspect once she was home safe and in bed.

"Shit," Franklin bent down to retrieve her. "You wriggled out of my grip like a little worm." He tried to pull her up with both hands but Grace's legs wouldn't co-operate.

"The rent," she kept repeating forlornly. "I've let everyone down."

"Fuck it," Franklin released her hands. "You're going to have to spend the night there, tiny dancer, since I simply can't get you up on those feet of yours." He turned away from her to survey the rest of the street. "And you're right," he stepped away from her, his voice rising theatrically, "we can't pay our rent. We need to accept our fate. We are poor. Dirt poor. We'll have to sell the clothes on our back. We'll have to—"

Grace heard the pound of something metallic. She scrambled forwards on all fours just as Franklin threw open a skip down an alley and scaled the sides. He teetered on the edge and began rummaging through bin bags and rubbish.

"Jesus, Franks, what are you doing?" Aaron stormed after him, a feeble Jasper at his side. He released Jasper when he reached Grace and then continued towards the skip. "Franks, get your ass out of there."

"Urgh," Jasper sat on the ground beside Grace and leaned his head back to look up at the street light shining overhead. "I feel like shit." His jumper was stained with his own sick.

"You smell like it, too," Grace told him honestly.

"Thanks."

"No problem."

"I think we drank away the last of our rent money." Jasper kept staring up, eyes wide.

"I think so too."

"Get out of there," Aaron ordered, reaching forward to grab at Franklin's silk shirt. But Franklin was quick, he jumped into the skip, letting the bin bags cushion his fall.

"I'm dumpster diving," Franklin insisted. "Since we're dirt poor this is what we're going to have to start to do."

"Franks, get out."

"Let's see what we have here," he continued to rummage through the waste. Grace looked on, amused. "Ooh, some out of date ready meals," he tossed some cardboard boxes in Aaron's direction. "A half-eaten tin of beans."

"Franks, come on, you're going to stink to high heaven when we get you back to the flat."

"Seriously, Aaron, it's a hobo's paradise in here. We could live like kings. Just let me—" he dug even deeper, disappearing from view.

Aaron kicked at the skip in frustration. "Dammit, Franks, stop dicking about. We need to get J and Grace home and cleaned up."

Grace looked down at herself. Her black tights were laddered and the skin beneath them grazed and bleeding. Her khaki shirt dress was bunched up beneath her and her beloved beige coat bore a beer stain. And it was dry clean only. She winced in frustration.

She willed there to be rain. It could wash away the grime which clung to her, could rejuvenate her ailing senses.

"Look, I'm counting to five, Franks, and then I'm leaving with the others, got it?" Aaron's voice was loud, commanding. The times when he sang solo for his band he shook the room. His was a voice of power, one that demanded to be heard.

"Stop being such a bore," Franklin complained from the bowels of the skip.

"One."

"You're all talk, Aaron."

"Two."

"You'd never leave me."

"Three."

"Ooh, a broken laptop."

The discarded piece of technology landed on the ground beside the skip with a loud crash.

"Four."

Jasper leaned against Grace and whimpered with sickly breath, "I don't feel so good."

"Four and a half."

"Hey," Franklin popped up out of the skip like a mole. "I've found something."

"Franks, come on. Five. It's time to go."

"Seriously, I've genuinely find something that could be interesting. Help me get it out."

Giving in to his curiosity, Aaron stepped forward to help.

"See," Franklin declared proudly. "This looks interesting, right?"

"Yeah," Aaron agreed as he helped his friend and his retrieved item of interest out of the skip. "It actually does."

4

Grace had an arm held round Jasper as he drooped at her side but her attention was drawn towards the skip. Franklin jumped out, landing on the street with elegance befitting his lean frame. He was a panther prowling the streets, every muscle infused with stealth.

"Let's take a look then," Aaron ordered, his back towards Grace and Jasper. She could tell from the pitch in his tone that something had intrigued him.

"First, apologise for being so rude," Franklin ordered.

"Franks—"

"Only then will I share my spoils with you."

"For—"

"What is it?" Grace had to shout to allow her voice to carry over to the skip. Both Franklin and Aaron edged out of the alley to glance back at her.

"I've found something," Franklin threw her a Cheshire cat grin. "Come see."

It took several attempts to get Jasper up on his feet. He kept swaying as though caught in an eternal breeze. "I'm…" he puffed up his cheeks and loomed forward and Grace instinctively recoiled in case he was about to throw up again. "Fuck." All he released was an expletive. "I feel like death."

"You look like it," they were now close enough for Aaron's quiet remark to be heard. He grabbed Jasper by his armpits and hauled him against his side, freeing Grace from the weight of her slender friend. "You okay?" Aaron's green eyes were on her which only added to the dizzying effect of the alcohol.

"I'm…" she kept drinking in lungsful of cool night air, trying to breathe herself back to sobriety. "I'm fine."

"From this day forth you must all call me Indie."

"Indie?" Grace blinked at Franklin as he grandiosely raised his arms.

"As in Indiana," he scoffed, his elbows sagging with disappointment.

"Indiana?"

"Jones, Grace. Indiana Jones. Because I'm a treasure hunter. I mean, honestly, did you live beneath a rock before moving to London?"

"Franks, just cut the theatrics and open it up," Aaron's voice was hard.

"Fine."

Grace looked down at what 'it' was. At Franklin's feet stood a briefcase. It was made of smooth tan leather and had golden clasps and a simple fastening that didn't seem to include a numerical lock. Aside from the odd scuff on its front it looked new. Against the drab contents of the skip it must have stood out to Franklin like a rose amongst weeds. He grabbed the briefcase with both hands and showed it off to his friends like he was a daytime TV sales man on some cable network.

"Notice the fine leather, detailed stitching and gold embellishments," he ran his hands along the case, highlighting its appealing features.

"Jesus, Franks, either open it up or leave it," Aaron ordered.

"I'm taking it home," Franklin insisted, clutching the briefcase against his chest. "I think it'll raise my audition game. I come in with this bad boy under my arm and I'll look so important that they'll have to hire me."

"Or they'll think you've come from another job and already have too many commitments," Aaron countered.

"Pfft," Franklin released one hand from the case to wave through the air like he was conducting an invisible orchestra. "You're just jealous that I found the briefcase. It's mine. My *precious*."

"That's it, we're going back," Aaron began to head back down the alley towards the main street. "Franks, Grace, come on. We're going home."

All of them were either too drunk or distracted to notice the figure lurking in the shadows at the far end of the alley who had been there for quite some time, silently observing their movements.

*

It felt good to be back in the flat. Grace slipped out of her shoes which during the walk home had morphed from fashionable items into medieval torture devices. Her toes throbbed and her heels burned as she sat on the sofa massaging them.

In the kitchenette the kettle shook as it came to the boil. Aaron was on tea duty. Jasper was already tucked up in Aaron's bed with a bucket, some pain killers and a pint glass of water beside him. Franklin had disappeared into Grace's room with his briefcase, stating that he wanted to open it up and try to find it on eBay to see how much it was worth.

"Here," Aaron came over and handed Grace a fresh mug of tea. "Drink this; it'll make you feel better."

"I feel fine." It was a half-truth. She felt better within the comfort of the flat but her head was stuffed full of cotton wool and her throat was raw, as though she'd been eating sand all night.

And then there was the fall.

As the alcohol drained out of her system, the memory of her awful audition came rising to the surface.

"I keep thinking about my bloody audition," she peered at the surface of her tea, at the spinning circle Aaron had been able to conjure in the amber fluid.

"Forget about it. It's done. You did your best." He sat down on the sofa beside her and leant one arm along the back of it. He smelt of the cologne she'd bought him for Christmas. Grace had to bite down on her tongue to stop herself from crying.

"I know but there's the rent and—"

"Don't beat yourself up over this, Grace," he turned to look at her. She saw her worried reflection in his green eyes. "We'll figure something out with the rent. We always do."

"I know but—"

His hand found her cheek and she forgot how to breathe. A freight train of feelings slammed into her. The strongest of them, love, brought back the dizzying sensation she'd felt out on the street, making her feel disorientated and delirious. Grace flinched, lips trembling.

"Look, Grace," Aaron's voice was soft, softer than it had been in a long time. Grace didn't dare move and risk breaking the spell of what was happening between them.

"Guys," Franklin was in the doorway to her bedroom and something was off. He looked and sounded stricken. Grace shifted to look at him but

Aaron seemed reluctant to move, his hand still cradling her cheek.

"What, Franks?" Aaron's question was more like a growl.

"We've got a situation in here."

"Look, Franks—"

"The case. I got it open and—"

"Can this wait?"

"No." Franklin squeaked. Grace scrambled off the sofa and stared at him, wondering what had turned her charismatic friend into a frightened mouse. "It can't wait. I need you guys to look at this. Now."

"Fine," Aaron launched himself off the sofa and prowled over to Grace's bedroom.

The briefcase was in the centre of the bed and it was open. There didn't seem to be any name or address inside indicating who owned it. But as Grace stared at the contents of the case her mouth fell open. Nestled within the main compartment was money. More money than she had ever seen. Twenty pound notes stacked together like a game of Jenga. Across the top layer she counted two hundred pounds and that was just what she could see.

"What the fuck?" Aaron surged forward, thrusting his hand into the case and grabbing a stack of twenties. He thumbed through them, his expression darkening. "You just opened it and it had all this money in it?"

"Uh huh." Franklin was standing back from the bed, treating the case like a bomb.

"No note, no form of identification, nothing?"

"Just the money," Franklin confirmed, his words still getting strangled in his larynx.

"How…" Grace wasn't sure if it was the drink or Aaron's burning touch but she wasn't thinking straight. She blinked at the money several times and cleared her throat. "How much do you think is there?"

"Couple of thousand," Aaron guessed as he replaced the stack of cash he'd been holding. "There's a thousand right there so do the math."

"That's a lot of money."

"It's a hell of a lot of money."

"So, what do we do with it?" Franklin finally stepped forward, chewing on his nails.

Grace knew. They had to hand it in to the police. Money like that was trouble. It had to belong to someone. "We take it to—"

"Police," Franklin whimpered. "We take it to the police, right?"

"Yeah," Grace agreed. "We take it, say we found it and—"

"We sleep on it," Aaron stepped forward and closed the briefcase, securing its gold clasps. "Right now, none of us are of sound enough mind to be making any kind of decisions and I don't think turning up at a police station completely pissed is in any of our best interests"

"But—"

"Besides, this is a flat matter. We all need to discuss this and right now Jasper is dead to the world. We'll talk about this more tomorrow when he's back in the world of the living."

Grace frowned.

"Aaron, look—"

"Sweet, sweet, Grace," Franklin grabbed her hands and pulled her away from Aaron and the briefcase which were departing from her bedroom. "The big man is right, we all need to sleep off our drunken states and thrash this out tomorrow with clear heads."

"Thousands of pounds," Grace hissed at him. "That case contains *thousands of pounds*. We can't just keep it here."

"It's only for tonight," Franklin smoothed down her hair and ushered her towards her bed where he began pulling back the duvet. "You sleep, sweet Grace, tomorrow we'll talk about the money. Until then, don't stress."

"We can't keep it," Grace's words were too big in her mouth, barely fitting on her tongue as she made her objections. When she lay down it was like falling against a cloud. Her whole body sagged with blissful contentment.

"There," Franklin sounded far away. "Just sleep, sweet Grace, have pleasant dreams."

It felt like he kissed her forehead but she couldn't be sure. And then she was gone, swept away on the wave of a dream.

*

Someone giggled. The pure, weightless laughter of a child. Grace sat up in bed. The air in her room was hot and sticky. Within the walls she heard the pulse of the heating system beating away.

Another giggle.

"Peter?" his name almost died on her lips as she said it. She looked towards her bedroom door which was open. The only light from within the main flat was the glow of the large television, Franklin's beloved Tina. Her screen frazzled with static. And in the doorway to Grace's room stood a little boy. He barely reached the height of the door handle and his dark hair was flat against his head, heavy with water. "Peter?" Grace climbed out of bed. Her bare feet connected with the carpet and she felt dampness within the fibres. Had it come from Peter?

The boy in the doorway giggled again and moved back into the main area of the flat. Grace followed.

"Peter, wait."

Like a pale imp the boy picked his way around the flat with speed, darting behind the sofa and then running across to the kitchenette. The way he moved, it wasn't real, he couldn't be real, but when he stood still Grace saw the eyes of her little brother, the same eyes that looked back at her each time she looked in the mirror. It was him. It was Peter.

"Stop," she ordered hoarsely, "what are you doing here? Stop, wait, please."

He kept bouncing around the flat as Tina hissed, the static on her screen warping to become a heart monitor in a hospital.

"Peter!"

The beats on the screen mirrored Grace's racing pulse. As she became more agitated they spiked.

"Peter, what's going on? Stop running away from me."

The boy bounced over to the front door and clasped bony fingers around the handle.

"Don't go," Grace pleaded. "Stay. Please."

He turned to look at her and as he did the amber in his eyes darkened until the blackness of his pupils overwhelmed everything else. When he spoke his voice was demonically deep. Tina bleeped shrilly with warning as Grace's heart rate became dangerously elevated.

"Death," Peter stated. "Death is coming." Then he moved through the door as though the wood and the numerous locks weren't even there. Grace fell against it, pounding her fists as the deadbolts rattled in protest.

"Wait," she screamed, before clawing at the locks, trying to get out and follow her brother. "Peter, wait."

She managed to throw open the door to see that the familiar shabby corridor was gone. Thick velvety shadows swirled in its stead, eager to absorb Grace. Behind her the television bleated a single, shrill note. A flat line. She could barely breathe. Where was Peter? What was this sea of darkness at her door? "Peter," she called out to him in vain. "Peter, come back."

*

"Grace."

Breath warm and laced with coffee blew against her cheek. She opened her eyes.

"Grace, you were having a nightmare."

Aaron was sitting on her bed, his arms wrapped around her shoulders. Blinking Grace peered up into his green eyes which swirled with sorrow and concern. "You were shouting out for Peter but it's okay, you're awake now."

"Peter," she pressed a hand to her temple. Her brother, he had been there, in the flat. She turned and freed her legs from the bed and pressed her bare feet against the carpet. It was coarse and dry to the touch. Grace choked against the sob trying to climb up her throat.

"You were shouting out so I came in. I was just sat on the sofa drinking coffee, waiting on the rest of you guys."

"Did I... did I wake everyone else up?"

"No," Aaron freed a hand to let his fingers stroke across her forehead. "Jasper is still dead to the world and Franklin is sprawled out next to him, drooling. I can't see either of them waking up for several hours."

"So, it's just you and me?" A feeling Grace had thought she'd forgotten about flittered in her stomach.

"It's just you and me," Aaron confirmed, his voice as warm as the coffee that lined his breath.

The stillness within the flat told her that it was still early. In an hour or so she'd hear the rumble of footsteps overhead as people woke up and commenced their day. But for now everywhere was quiet, the world was still holding its breath.

Grace parted her lips, considering what she was about to say when Aaron interjected with a question she hadn't expected.

"What happened to Peter?"

She tensed and then squirmed free of his touch.

"You often call out his name during a nightmare but you never talk about him. I know that he died but—"

"No," Grace was hurrying out of her bedroom, half hoping to catch a glimpse of her brother's ghost racing across the floor. Even Tina was still, her glassy face reflecting the closeted quarters of the flat. "We don't talk about that stuff, remember?"

"Grace," Aaron followed her out, easily keeping pace with her as she approached the kitchenette. "Why won't you ever let me in?"

She shook out her hands before filling up the kettle. "I'm going to make some fresh coffee, you want one?"

"Grace!"

"We're not doing this, Aaron. Not now, not ever."

"Why don't you trust me?"

Grace closed her eyes, stealing a moment of peace. It was too early for this kind of conversation.

"Coffee," when she looked at him again she hoped he saw the resolute glow in her eyes. "Yes or no?"

Clearly he did as he wilted against the countertop and gazed at her sadly. "Yes, coffee. And then we need to wake the others up to talk."

"Look, I just said—"

"Not about you. About the money. We all need to talk about the money."

5

"So how much is there?" Franklin stood in front of Tina, staring at the sofa which was now covered in neatly stacked bank notes.

"Twenty grand," Aaron confirmed from where he sat perched on the arm of the sofa, hands resting between his knees, head bent low.

"Fuck," throwing his hands up, Franklin paced back and forth. The silk kimono he wore swept behind him like an elaborate cape.

"Twenty grand?" Jasper was in the kitchenette, elbows planted on the counter as he cradled his chin in his hands. All the colour had left his cheeks and his eyes were hollow. With a grimace he cleared his throat. "You sure it's that much?"

"I counted it," Aaron flexed his hands into fists. "Twice."

Grace looked at the money. She could smell it. Its crisp odour had invaded the flat, smothering every existing scent. She imagined it was what the inside of a bank must smell like. Or a vault. Every note was immaculate. New. And she yearned to touch it. There was something alluring about the smooth surface, the flash of purple and the metallic image of the Queen.

"We need to get it out of here," Jasper scrambled away from the counter and stood behind the sofa, looking down at the bed of money. "Really we should just turn it in to the police."

"Yes," Grace pointed at him and nodded. "It has to go. This money… it's going to belong to someone. But do we give it to the police? Or do we need to put it back in the briefcase and return it to the skip?"

Franklin stopped pacing and placed himself between Grace and the sofa. "Wait a bloody minute," he diverted his gaze between her, Jasper, and the twenty thousand pounds. "Don't be so quick to just *give it back*. We found this money. Possession is like ninety per cent of the law, right?"

"Maybe in America," Aaron grumbled. "We're not in America."

"Right, well," Franklin stooped to grab a twenty pound note from atop a nearby stack. "Is this all even real? It may well be counterfeit." Delicately he spread the note between his hands and raised it up towards the bare light bulb which hung overhead. "Well," he pursed his lips and returned the note to the pile, "it's real enough, as far as I can tell."

"It's all real, I think," Aaron commented. "I checked the watermarks when I counted it. They seem to hold up."

"So, it's all real," Jasper sniffed and shifted from foot to foot, clearly still in the final throes of his hangover. "All the more reason to put it back or take it to the nearest police station."

"It's against the law to claim money that isn't ours," Grace informed them all, her skin prickling with the discomfort of flying too close to illegal activity. She felt pressure on her upper arm, a phantom gloved hand reminding her what was right and wrong, which direction she should be going in.

"Then we don't claim it," Franklin suggested with a grandiose sweep of his arms across the money. "We just spend it."

"Franks—"

"Look, Grace," he said her name like she was a five year old failing to understand the concept of Santa Claus and his present giving prerogative. "This money, it's a gift. And you can stand there and pretend to be up in an ivory tower but I'm just saying what we're all thinking. *We should spend it.* We could pay the rent. I could finally get some decent headshots done. Hell, I could finally buy decent shoes, no more Primark specials that can barely outlast a one night stand."

"Franks—"

"We are *hard up.* None of us are making any money. This," he kept pointing at the stacks of twenty pound notes. "This is our ticket to stay here, to keep pursuing our dreams. Don't look a gift horse in the face, Grace."

"Mouth."

"Whatever," Franklin brushed off her comment with a click of his fingers. "Bottom line is, we're spending this money."

"No," Jasper massaged his neck and tried to stand as straight as possible. "We're not spending it, Franks. We're going to do the right thing and either put it back or hand it to the authorities. It has to belong to someone."

"So, you're siding with Snow White, great," Franklin scolded his hung over friend. "Since this is the age of democracy let's put it to a vote shall we?"

"Fine," Grace crossed her arms against her chest. Franklin was in the wrong. Whilst it was undoubtedly tempting to spend the money, they just couldn't. It wasn't theirs. To spend any of it would be breaking the law.

"All in favour of keeping this money, this *gift*, raise your hand," Franklin ordered. His own hand instantly shot up.

"See," Grace declared triumphantly. "You're alone in this, Franks. We're taking the money back. We should never have brought it here in the first place."

"Been to Specsavers lately?"

Grace frowned at the question, failing to understand its relevance. Franklin loved to talk in riddles and indirect insults. With a roll of her eyes she turned to face him, arms still tight against her chest.

"Look, Franks—"

"There's another hand raised."

She looked over at Aaron. He was sitting on the arm of the sofa, head hung low but one hand very clearly raised. Her eyes widened in alarm. "Aaron, seriously? What are you doing?"

"He makes a valid point," he lowered his hand to indicate the money. "Without this we can't pay our rent. Which means eviction for all of us. If the choice is between sleeping rough and keeping some of this twenty grand then I know which side I'm on."

"Exactly," Franklin bounced over to his new ally. "Besides we didn't *steal* it. We found it. It's ours."

"It's not," Grace was so angry she feared her blood was starting to boil. "This money is not ours, we cannot spend it. It has to go back."

"Aren't you concerned about who it belongs to?" Jasper interjected. "Someone must have deliberately put that money in the briefcase and in the skip and they are surely going to come looking for it."

"Anyone who leaves this much money in a *skip* is an idiot," Franklin proclaimed like he was a preacher in a church. "How could they expect someone *not* to take it? The money stays. We pay the rent. We all live to dream another day in glorious London. This flat meeting is over."

"Franks—"

"Over!" With a whisper of silk Franklin glided out of the room and into his shared bedroom, taking care to loudly slam the door to confirm his departure.

"Fuck," Jasper clamped a hand over his mouth and dashed off in the direction of the bathroom.

"How can you side with him?" Grace demanded of Aaron who was slowly standing up. He wore a plaid shirt that had bobbled over time, the red of the stitching faded to a light pink. Grace remembered when the shirt had been new, when she'd throw it on to leave her bedroom and steal out into the kitchen for a late night drink.

"He makes sense."

"To spend this money would be a crime. You know that."

"I know that we need to pay the rent," Aaron stated fiercely. "I know that together we have nothing. We're all broke. Are you telling me you truly want to put this back and give up this flat, go back home?"

Home.

Grace felt her resolve crumbling. She pressed a hand against her heart and tried to stay strong. For her there was no home, no place to go. Something shifted in the corner of her eye and she thought she saw the flash of someone pale darting towards the door. She blanched at the echo of the memory from her nightmare. Peter had raced to her door and there had been only darkness there. And he'd spoken of death.

"The money has to go back," Grace eyed every twenty pound note with caution. "It's tainted."

"*Tainted?*"

"The money has to go. It will bring death here. I know it."

"Money can't be tainted, Grace," Aaron shook his head and moved past her, towards the kitchenette. "Nor can it be evil. People are evil. People do evil things *for* money. But money is just printed pieces of paper."

"Please, Aaron, you have to believe me," she shadowed his every step, suddenly keen to stay close to him, to stay away from the money. "If we keep this money then something bad will happen. Please, tell Franklin it has to go."

"It was just a nightmare," Aaron held her in a level look as he flicked on the kettle and waited for it to boil.

"No," deep lines formed in Grace's forehead. "It was more than that. It was Peter... it was a premonition. Please, I know it."

"Was his death connected to money or something?"

"No."

Was it raining outside? Grace needed it to be raining. Then she could wander the streets and try to clear her head, purge the remnants of the nightmare from her mind.

"Then what is this? You're making Franks sound like the logical one in this, which is a scary thought."

"I just," Grace grabbed his hand, felt the rough callouses caused by years strumming guitar strings. "I need you to side with me on this. I need you to trust me. Can you do that?"

Aaron drew in a tight breath and held it. Upon the counter the kettle hissed. "I'll talk to Franks later."

"Talk to him now," Grace pleaded. "Please, make him see sense. This money isn't ours, we can't spend a penny of it."

"He's in his kimono." The kettle grew quiet and Aaron let his hand stay within Grace's grasp.

"So?"

"It means he's having a Google hangout with that guy from Denmark and there's no way I'm walking in on that. Give him an hour. Then we'll talk, I promise."

"Okay," Grace squeezed his hand, felt the warmth pulsing beneath his skin, "thanks."

"I still think you're crazy," Aaron added.

"I know."

*

Dreams of Peter always made Grace nostalgic. In her room she knelt by her bed and from underneath pulled free an old shoebox covered in stickers and scribbled incarnations of her name. Thanks to Franklin's cleaning spree her bedroom floor was now debris free, all her clothes returned to her rickety wardrobe. Pulling the box up onto the bed she popped the lid and the familiar smell of old books and stale vanilla perfume wafted up to greet her.

Grace smiled. She loved her little box of memories. It contained photos, notebooks and planners from when she'd been at school. She began to delicately look through a stack of photographs in which she was a little girl at numerous dance recitals. At the top of the pile Grace was tiny and dressed in sugar pink tutus with a smile as wide as her tulle outfit. As she moved through the pile the pictures changed. Grace became slightly taller, leaner. Her ballet shoes became pointe shoes and she swiftly turned from a cherub faced girl to an elegant ballerina.

One of her favourite images was taken during her first performance of *Swan Lake* when she'd been awarded the honour of playing both the black and white swans. Her classmates were green with envy.

She'd heard them gossiping about her along the corridors of the dance school.

"Why even give Grace the part? It's not like anyone will even come to see her perform."

Their words were knives and they always cut deep. Sat on her bed Grace rubbed at her bare arms, feeling the scars beneath her skin.

She had been at her best when she was the infamous swan princess. Grace had effortlessly embodied both the light and dark characters. The audience had adored her, her teachers had spoken in hushed tones about her 'going on to great things'. People believed in her and even her most bitter classmates, who'd spent the last year looking like they were perpetually sucking on lemons, conceded enough to congratulate her on her performance.

Grace had never felt more alive. She was nineteen and she had the world at her well turned out feet. She was destined for stardom. For glory. She'd put in the work, danced down the path which had been laid out for her, never looking back. Never questioning.

But truth was like decay. It eventually found everyone. And it found Grace. The past she'd been pivoting away from came for her, drawn to the glory of her Swan Lake performance. People within the school, the academy, they began to talk. It was the kind of chatter that died when Grace entered a room.

"They don't need your kind of scandal," her own tutor had told her when her application for a position within the prestigious ballet company, which the school's students usually fed into, was declined. Grace wept. She cried so hard that her mascara rained black tears down her face. She begged for her tutor to be reasonable, to plead with the company on her behalf, to see her just for how she danced.

"This isn't even my scandal," she told them. "It's nothing to do with me."

"But it will follow you," her tutor warned. "These sort of things always do, they become a black mark against someone's name. A prima can't have a past like yours."

Grace slammed the lid of her box back into place, no longer feeling sentimental. She shoved her memories back beneath her bed, brushing away the stray tears that had fallen while she pored over pictures of the past.

In her little flat she was still safe, still amongst friends. She'd kept her secrets well hidden. She would not dishonour Peter by discussing his death. He had been so much more than his tragic end, he'd been a boy full of dreams, adventures. To let his final scandal mark his name would be the ultimate insult to her fallen brother. Besides, Grace flopped back on her bed and stared up at her cracked ceiling, she was certain she couldn't handle the shame of the truth coming out.

*

At some point Grace rolled onto her side and fell asleep. She slept off the lingering fragments of her hangover and awoke groggy but stone cold sober. Stretching her arms up over her head she pulled out all the knots in her muscles and then shuffled out of her room. In the heart of the flat the television was on. Jasper was sat on the sofa beneath a blanket eating a pot noodle. Grace was relieved to see that the money was nowhere to be seen.

"Hey," she went and curled up beside Jasper. "You feeling okay?"

He offered her some of his blanket which she drew up over her knees.

"I don't feel like death anymore," he gave her a thin smile. "So that's something."

"Where's the money?" Grace whispered her question. Jasper shrugged and slurped up a forkful of noodles.

"When I finally emerged from the bathroom everyone had gone. The money too. I figured Franklin must have seen sense and decided to take it back."

"Did you check his room?"

"God, no," Jasper furiously shook his head and then uttered quietly, "kimono."

"Hmm."

Grace tried to focus on the television, but Jasper was watching an episode of *The Killing* which she'd already seen so her attention wandered. She hoped that Aaron had kept his word and spoken to Franklin. Because Franklin would listen to him, he always did. If Aaron decided that the money needed to go back it would already be neatly packed into the briefcase and shoved into the skip, waiting for its rightful owner.

"You think he did it?" Jasper asked between mouthfuls.

"Do I think Franks took the money back? I hope so."

"No," Jasper jabbed his fork in the direction of Tina. "The teacher. You think he did it?"

With a knowing smile Grace said nothing. She'd already learned the hard way that Jasper didn't react well to accidental spoilers when it came to his favourite shows. She'd once made a flippant remark about a key character dying in *The Good Wife* and he'd been furious. He'd turned blood red and lamented about loose lips sinking ships. Jasper was addicted to good television. He defended his obsession as being research based.

"If I want to be a great writer I need to absorb great content." And so he did. Pretty much all of the day when he wasn't sleeping. Grace knew she was being a bit unfair. Jasper was trying just as hard as the rest of them to make his dreams come true. But like the rest of them, at times it felt like smacking his head against a brick wall.

The turning of locks in the front door pulled Grace's attention away from the television. She turned against the sofa to peer over its back as the door swung open and Franklin came in. He was all smiles as he bustled in with six shopping bags in his hands. Expensive shopping bags.

As Grace shoved the blanket off her lap and stood up she started to feel sick.

"Franks," she demanded. "Where have you been?"

Franklin draped his purchases against the countertop in the kitchenette and beamed at her. "Shopping."

"*What?*"

She clocked the labels on the bags; Urban Outfitter, Dune, Ted Baker. Places which were usually strictly off limits to their meagre clothing budgets.

"Relax," Franklin urged flippantly. "I picked up some things for you."

"Franks!" She squeaked his name and stormed over to the kitchenette. "You spent some of the money, didn't you?"

He pouted and then rummaged inside his Ted Baker bag. "I saw this gorgeous top with a ballerina on it and instantly thought of you, so—"

"You did it. You spent the money."

"Jesus, Grace, you make it sound like I killed someone."

"How could you do it?"

Behind them Jasper had turned off the television, more interested in the drama unfolding in his own flat.

"Grace, I—"

"It's not ours!" she yelled, her voice bouncing off the thin walls. "That money, Franks, it's not bloody ours! How could you spend it?"

"Because I'm a realist," with a scowl Franklin scooped up his purchases and began storming over to his shared bedroom. "That money is going to save us, Grace. Stop being precious and accept that I've done the right thing. Spending that money is a *good thing*. Now we can nail the rent and finally start actually living, actually enjoying the city."

Grace watched him leave the main area of the flat, a silk Ted Baker top left behind on the counter for her. She couldn't even look at it. Her heart ached with the knowledge that Franklin was wrong. The money wasn't going to save them. It was going to condemn them. All of them.

6

Grace knew what it was to be hungry. She remembered the ache, the way her stomach would feel cavernous and hollow. Tears gathered in the corners of her eyes as the hunger thumped inside her.

At Peter's funeral she had feasted. She had not delicately approached the buffet table as she should have. Instead she'd elbowed her way through the dense thicket of adults and started shovelling everything she could find into her mouth; cheese sandwiches, sausage rolls, pork pie, cream cakes, iced buns. She ate everything, barely pausing to chew, just swallowing.

"Urgh she's *feral*," Mrs Darden had commented, forsaking the polite pretence of lowering her voice. She wanted people to hear her, she had an insatiable inferiority complex which meant that she thought all her thoughts and opinions deserved an audience. Before the advent of the internet, all she could do to accomplish this was to talk loud enough so as not to be ignored. Women like Mrs Darden would later come alive in the endless echo chamber of social media.

Feral.

Grace didn't even know what the word meant. She just kept eating, kept stuffing everything she could reach into her mouth until the gloved stranger found her. And they did. She was biting down on a cinnamon bun, fingers sticky with jam, icing and cream when she was yanked back from the buffet table.

"No," the stranger told her. "You shouldn't gorge yourself, Grace. You'll be sick."

Their intervention came too late. The food hit Grace's stomach like a punch. There was too much goodness, she was drowning in it. Her body shook from sugary shock and then she purged on the stranger's shoes. It was all leaving her; the sandwiches, the buns, the rolls. All of it ended up on a polished pair of brogues. Heaving, Grace wiped her mouth and stared dead eyed up at the stranger. She was once again hollow. And very much alone.

*

"And now," Franklin stood on Oxford Street widening his arms like he was Willy Wonka inviting guests into his chocolate factory. "We spend."

The money was already tainted.

That was the logic Franklin used to get her through the front door. Logic backed up by Aaron who was with them, though his brow remained permanently furrowed. Even Jasper had pulled on his thick wool coat and stepped out, lured by the prospect of spending. Every brick in their moral wall had been pulled down by greed.

Grace had wrestled with her thoughts on the tube ride over to Oxford Street. It was wrong. All of it. She needed to stand her ground, needed to tell the others to stop.

"I've already spent some of it," Franklin insisted. "Might as well spend the rest."

"We need to spend it before it's found in our possession," Aaron agreed. "Cash transactions, spend the lot."

"We could still put it back." Grace suggested but her words weren't heard. For too long they had all had too little. Starvation had made them desperate, irrational. Now was the time to gorge, to feel the rush that came with an impromptu transaction.

The money wasn't going to be put back. It was going to be spent. All of it. Franklin had picked the hole in the dam with his initial splurge and now everything was coming out, there seemed no way to stop it. Aaron had paid five months' worth of rent. A cushion to enable them to all keep pursuing their dreams. The rest had been divided up between them. Grace had a few grand burning a hole in her pocket. She was so paranoid, she was certain her fellow passengers on the tube could see the curl of smoke rising up from her jeans.

Did everyone know? Did she wear the presence of the money on her face like a scarlet M? When she plucked it from her pocket would store assistants sense that it wasn't really hers?

"Guitar time for me," Aaron turned away from the main street, in the direction of a music store he often frequented. Grace watched the back of his head until he disappeared from view.

The lure of his one true passion, the bass, had been enough to encourage him to spend. Were they all going to fold on their principles so easily?

"He has already spent some," Jasper told Grace, his voice soft with acceptance. "I mean, we can't really put it back now. Aaron is right, we need to just spend it all, get rid of the evidence."

"And the briefcase?"

"Oh, I'm keeping it," Franklin sounded completely certain of this. "Like I said, I think it will add a little something to my ensemble when I go to auditions."

"I'm for Foyles," Jasper told them both. "Got my eye on a new Kindle and a hell of a lot of books. I bid you guys adieu."

His compliance had been bought. All it took was Franklin's initial spend for Jasper to come round to his way of thinking. That and the promise of copious new books to read.

"Grace," Franklin hugged her shoulders and turned her to look down Oxford Street. "Where will your buyer's instinct take you?" He was in his element. The glow from all the store frontages was in his cheeks, his voice. "New dance shoes, an elegant designer dress? What do you want?"

It was a question Grace was rarely asked. She looked down at her feet, at her worn out black ankle boots.

So, the rent was paid. Grace had money in her pocket and a question to answer.

What do you want?

Her head instinctively twisted in the direction Aaron had gone. There was so much that she wanted, but none of it could be bought. Fame, success, they came at a price that wasn't monetary.

"Come on," Franklin squeezed her against his side. "There has to be something you want. Stop being so obstinate and join the rest of us on the dark side."

"I guess…" Grace closed her eyes. If only it were raining. The rain would guide her. Its cold pressure against her skin would help her focus. "A laptop." She concluded, as Franklin leapt in front of her to clap his hands with delight. "I could use a laptop."

"Then to the Apple store we go," he declared as he gleefully led her down the busy street.

*

"I was hungry," Grace explained tearfully as she sipped on a glass of water. The stranger had placed her on a chair in the far corner of the function room. People continued to mass around the buffet table, a bleak collection of black clothes and pinched faces.

The stranger had removed their gloves to reveal hands untouched by toil or time. "I know. But when you're as hungry as you were you can't gorge. You need to eat little bits, until your stomach readjusts."

"Why?" Grace demanded, kicking her legs out from the chair and then swinging them back with force. "The food was just there."

"You overloaded your stomach. Little bits, then in time you'll be able to eat more. Have patience, Grace."

Even though her name was a virtue Grace didn't feel very virtuous. She definitely lacked patience.

"I want to go home."

"You can't."

"Why not? Where's my Mummy?"

A dark thought entered her mind like a loaded storm cloud, ready to rain down chaos. "Is she with Peter?"

Peter had gone to the place she could not go, a place from which there was no return.

"No." The stranger confirmed. "She's not."

"Then can I see her?" Grace asked, brightening with hope. So many faces at the funeral but none of them her mother's. Where was she?

"No."

"Why not?"

"I'll explain later."

"Explain now."

"Grace," the stranger said her name like it was doused in vinegar. "You must trust me, do you understand? I will tell you what I can, when I can. Today is about your brother, about saying goodbye."

"And tomorrow?"

"Tomorrow is a new day. Things will look better tomorrow."

"Will it rain?"

The stranger seemed perplexed by her question. "I..." manicured nails scratched against a curved jawline. "I don't believe so, no."

"I'm not supposed to go out in the rain," Grace explained. "Mummy says it burns."

*

The Apple store was glossy and oozed minimalist chic. Franklin waltzed through the doors like he had a million pounds on his person rather than several thousand. With shoulders back and chin raised he proceeded to scrutinise the array of gadgetry on offer.

"So," he glanced briefly at Grace. "What model are we thinking? Mac book pro? And then there's the colour. This, dear Grace, is a very important choice."

A computer almost the shade of copper caught Grace's eye. She drifted over to it and softly touched its dark keyboard.

"Rose gold," Franklin sidled up beside her. "An elegant choice. Subtle, understated beauty. Suits you perfectly, Grace. Go for it."

Computers were always hard to come by growing up. They were a luxury bought for children by their parents. None of Grace's dance schools gave her a computer of her own, just access to their libraries. She didn't own a computer until she was eighteen and her roommate gave her an outdated model after she'd updated her own laptop. Grace had cherished it. She didn't notice its sluggish running speed, having nothing to compare it to. It was on that laptop she'd sourced the area of London where she most wanted to live, a place in close proximity to all the best dance companies. A place where she felt she could thrive.

"This," Franklin was gesturing at a store assistant. "We want this." He tapped the rose gold computer that Grace was admiring.

"And the phone," she barely recognised her own voice as she made the request.

"The seven?" the assistant queried.

"Yes."

"Also in rose gold?"

"Yes. Please."

Grace was back at the buffet table gorging herself sick.

*

The flat was almost unrecognisable covered in shopping bags. Aaron had returned with a new guitar and amp. He was eagerly unwrapping it over by the kitchenette, pausing to admire the emerald body of his new instrument.

"And this," Franklin was in the midst of putting on a fashion show for them all. He kept disappearing into his bedroom and returning clad in one of his new purchases. "Silk bomber jacket. It's very me, no?" He spun around.

Grace's laptop and phone were charging in her room. She'd spent most of her money in one store, with just enough left for the few ballet books she picked up when she met Jasper in Foyles, and a couple of staple Ted Baker items which Franklin had helped her choose.

"It's lovely," she looked at the jacket and tried not to think what its price tag read.

"Wait 'til you see the shoes I got to go with it," Franklin hurried back into his room.

"The guys are going to freak when they see this," Aaron strummed his fingers across the strings of his new guitar, striking a soft chord which hung in the warm air of the flat.

"How will you explain it?" Grace wondered. Unlike the rest of them Aaron had another group he belonged to, people who would notice his sudden wealth. He shrugged his thick shoulders.

"I don't know. Say I got lucky on the horses or something."

"Okay, but—"

"These," Franklin burst back out of his room, pointing at his feet, "are a little tight but look at the detail. The gold stitching is to die for, it really is."

Jasper pulled his head up out of the large hardback he was reading. "Whose turn is it to cook dinner?"

"Cook?" Franklin looked like he was going to choke on the word. "Oh no, tonight we don't cook. We order in."

"Pizza?" Aaron looked up from his guitar as he made his suggestion.

"Sounds good," Franklin glanced at Grace for confirmation.

"Sure." What could she say? She couldn't protest now. Her hands were just as stained by the falsely acquired wealth as anyone else's.

"Order it on your fancy new laptop," Franklin dictated as he grabbed her shoulders and marched her towards her bedroom. "No more pilfering internet from the used book store next door, now you can hook up to your fancy new phone and enjoy," he paused for dramatic emphasis, "decent band width. Besides I want to hear that little kitten purr. And the phone, it's all set up okay?"

Grace felt sick. She wished she could purge her spend all over Franklin's new shoes. Instead she nodded and drifted into her room. The laptop was resting on her bed, a white chord snaking away towards the wall. She stroked it's smooth, pink hued surface and couldn't help but smile. It was a thing of beauty. And it was hers. Yes, she might have gorged, but the spoils were worth it, weren't they? And how would anyone find out what they'd done? They money had no name attached, no indication of an owner. It was lost, abandoned and they'd taken it in. Where was the harm in that?

*

Weak winter sunlight warmed the floor in the main room of the flat as it bled in through the window behind Tina. Grace tracked a bare footed route towards the kitchenette, keen to inject some caffeine into her system. The kettle was half way through its manic boiling dance when she noticed that Jasper was sat up on the sofa instead of curled up.

"Hey," she went over to him. "I didn't realise you were up. You want a coffee?" He released a brittle sigh.

"What's up?" Grace abandoned all thoughts of coffee to join him on the sofa. He tugged back his blanket to make space for her.

"Not had the best start to my day," Jasper admitted as he dragged his hands through his thick blonde hair.

"Oh?" Then Grace nodded with understanding. "I mean, I've been thinking about it too. How we spent all that money yesterday. We really shouldn't have, we should've—"

"Not the money," Jasper interrupted. "I woke up to a rejection from that agent I was really keen to work with."

He passed Grace his phone where the email in question was on the screen. She scrolled through it.

"Standard rejection," Jasper sighed again. "Not even a reason why they didn't like me. It's just 'not a good fit for my list'. What the hell does that even mean?"

"Hey, don't lose heart," Grace handed him his phone back. "Your work is good, Jasper. Really good. Like, *The Killing* good."

"You think so?" Hope sparkled in his blue eyes.

"I know so," Grace confirmed with a smile. "It's just a case of finding the right agent. Keep submitting, you'll get there."

"And if I don't?"

"What if I never dance professionally again?"

"Grace, you will," Jasper instantly brightened. "You're such a natural. The way you float, those turns you do, there's just no doubt that—"

"See," Grace squeezed his arm. "You see the star in me and I see the star in you."

"Sometimes I wish I could see the star in myself," Jasper leaned back against the sofa and craned his neck to peer up at the ceiling.

"Yes, but then you'd be an asshole."

"Franklin sees the star in himself and isn't an asshole."

"Franks is always playing a role," Grace got up and returned to the boiled kettle. "The real him is just as scared and insecure as the rest of us."

"Aaron isn't insecure."

He is.

Grace bit down on the truth and made them each a mug of coffee. It was better to let Jasper keep seeing the myth rather than the man when it came to Aaron. Like with a ballet dancer, he was best appreciated from afar. When you got too close you saw the strain in each muscle, the effort, the pain.

"Do you fancy another *Good Wife* marathon later?" Grace asked as she re-joined Jasper on the sofa.

"Thanks," he nodded as he relieved her of one of the mugs. "And yes, a *Good Wife* marathon is how I'd usually want to spend my Friday afternoon but I'm heading out."

"You are?"

"My brother's wedding, remember?"

"Oh, right, yeah." Grace recalled the thick silver envelope that had landed on their stained straw doormat some four months earlier. "Christ, is that tomorrow? It's come around quick."

"It's *Frozen* themed."

"What?"

"Like, you know, the Disney movie. Ellen is a huge fan so she'll be in a blue crystal dress and their first dance is going to be to 'Let It Go'."

"Wow, that sounds…"

"Tacky?"

"I was going to say sweet."

"You're not the one having to wear a blue suit."

"Blue, really?"

"Pale blue," Jasper shuddered at the prospect of what was to come. "I look ridiculous in it. The whole wedding is blue and silver. Even guests have to wear the colour theme."

"They do?"

"Uh huh," Jasper took a long drink from his mug. "It's going to be intense."

"It sounds like it will be fun. Quirky."

"Hmm."

"And maybe it'll make good fodder for a book one day?"

"True," Jasper gazed thoughtfully into his coffee. "I guess that's the upside of anything weird that happens in life."

"So, when's your train?"

"No train, driving."

"Really?" Grace was stunned. Cars were a very rare commodity in London. She didn't know anyone who owned one.

"Not mine," Jasper confirmed. "Picking up my brother's from his place in Kensington."

"Oh, okay."

"Because it's a baby blue Fiat 500 so it matches the theme."

"I see."

"And everyone else is already in Kent which just leaves me to play chauffeur."

"You going to be okay?"

"I'll be fine," Jasper drained the last of his coffee. "I'll spend the drive massaging my wounded ego. Whether it's from a girl or an agent, rejection sucks."

"You forget about from a dance company. Or a director. Their rejection sucks too."

"I bet," Jasper offered her a consolatory smile. "So, did they get back to you, Matthew Bourne's company?"

"Not yet, no," Grace nursed her mug between her hands, enjoying the gentle warmth that seeped through the ceramic onto her palms. "But I'm not holding out any hope with that. I fell. I made an ass of myself. They won't want me."

"Don't give up on them, Grace. Not yet."

"Well, you should try a different agent. Eggs in one basket and all that."

"I will," Jasper smiled weakly at her.

"Ooh," Grace released one hand from her mug to click her fingers. "Take lots of pictures at the wedding."

"So you can laugh at them?" Jasper wondered dryly.

"No," Grace admitted earnestly, "so I can look at a real life fairy tale. Sometimes you need to stop and admire something like that to help you deal with all the stuff that sucks."

"Not sure I agree," Jasper threw off his blanket and got up. "But I like the sentiment. Anyway, I'm off to shower."

"Enjoy the wedding."

Jasper was already humming 'Let It Go' as he slammed the bathroom door closed behind him.

7

"I don't know who keeps voting her in," Franklin glared at the television, his voice hostile. "She sounds like a castrated walrus."

Grace shifted her legs beneath the blanket. It was getting harder to find warmth in the small flat. Even though the heating continually creaked within the walls as the pipes expanded begrudgingly, the bite of winter was zealously gnawing at the thin single glazed windows, letting tendrils of icy draughts slip inside. Soon there would be snow. Grace felt it in the snap of the air. The cold was more than biting, it was frozen. If snow fell over the weekend then Jasper's brother would have a truly themed wedding.

"When did it get so bloody cold in here?" Franklin shivered beneath the blanket he was sharing with Grace and burrowed his back deeper into the sagging sofa cushions.

"Aaron says it's the windows," Grace glanced at the thin brown curtains which were drawn across their main peep hole to the outside world. The worn fabric swayed gently as though humming in a dream. "Really they need to be replaced."

"Then let's replace them. We're minted now, remember?"

"I'm not sure that we are," Grace countered. "And replacing the windows would be up to the owner of the building, not the tenants."

"And Skinflint Steve isn't about to cough up for some windows," Franklin frowned disdainfully and then swept back the blanket as though it were made of thick velvet. "I'll make us a fresh mug of tea. Try to warm us from the inside. We all know that Steve would happily have us all catch pneumonia."

"Not sure he would."

"No?"

"Because then who would pay his rent?"

Franklin clicked his fingers and laughed. "True. He wants us freezing but still breathing, I get it. Because he needs our dough to spend on all his online vices. Like he thinks we don't know where our rent money goes." With a scoff he turned on the kettle. "Did Jasper leave okay for his brother's wedding?"

"Think so." Grace had to shout back. Between the warbling woman on the television and the guttural chugging of the kettle, the main living space in the flat was filling up with sound. If it reached a more frenzied crescendo then the door to the second bedroom would fly open and Aaron would storm out, cheeks crinkled from sleep. He liked things quiet when he slept. And dark.

Grace had struggled with the absence of light which he insisted on. In her room she left the string of illuminations around her bed on at all times. It gave her comfort to see their gentle glow when she stirred in the dead of night and slowly opened her eyes.

"What did you say the theme was again?" Franklin was slamming a cupboard door shut after retrieving the cracked jar of sugar.

"*Frozen*."

"Like the Disney film?"

"That's it."

Franklin clapped his hands together. "That sounds utterly delightful. Shame all the whimsy will be lost on Jasper. He's almost as sardonic as sleeping beauty in there." He nodded towards the closed bedroom door and then scowled at the television, his mouth dropping open in disgust. "She's literally assaulting my ears right now," he declared with an exasperated sigh. "*Who* is voting her in? They must be mad."

The mechanical chime of the doorbell cut through all other sounds.

Grace muted the television and turned towards the back of the sofa, peering over at Franklin. He shrugged at her and shook his head. "No idea," he checked the time on his phone. "I'm not expecting anyone. Are you?"

"No."

"And his Lordship is definitely sleeping, right?"

"Right. I saw him slink in there around seven muttering something about a headache."

"Maybe it's Steve," Franklin rested his hands on his hips and stared at the front door, frowning like he was trying to see through the flimsy wood.

"Let's hope it's not Steve," Grace pushed back the blanket and got up. "Unless he's decided to be a decent person and has come to offer us new windows and a replacement cooker, which I highly doubt."

"I can't remember when the thermostat on that thing was last working," Franklin muttered heatedly as he followed her towards the door, curiosity guiding him more than concern.

Standing on her tiptoes Grace tried to look through the peep hole. It was something she rarely bothered doing since it was cracked and offered a skewed view of the corridor. In all likelihood whoever was standing on the threshold could be after a different flat. Franklin was convinced that 3B were running an illegal brothel and that a number of their johns accidently wound up ringing their door bell. The main door in what constituted the lobby downstairs was a joke. The locks had broken two summers ago and Steve had yet to initiate repairs. So anyone could wander in. And they often did.

"I think it's a man," Grace squinted at the blurred image beyond the hole. She could make out a tall figure.

"Then tell them to bugger off to 3B. We can't offer them anything here. Unless he looks like Jude Law. Then we might be able to work something out."

"You're terrible," Grace began to turn the numerous latches.

"You love it."

With a whine the door swung open revealing the heavy set man who had rung the bell. He was tall, easily over six foot and he filled the space. Grace quickly took him in, noticing the starched jeans, long leather coat and green turtle neck jumper underneath. Then she was looking into his eyes. He was completely bald, and it looked like it was through choice rather than genetics. With a gaze blacker than coal he looked back at her, his dome shaped head resting on a thick neck. He was bigger than Aaron. Perhaps even bigger than Aaron and Franklin combined.

Fear collected in the base of Grace's spine and tried to pull her back into the flat but she stood firm at the door, one hand resting on the frame as she peered up at the stranger.

"Hi," her greeting was honey coated. "How can we help you? Are you looking for flat 3B?"

"It's right there," Franklin leaned over her shoulder to point further along the corridor. "You can't miss it. Let the heady musk guide you."

Grace discreetly elbowed her flat mate in the ribs.

"I'm here for my money." The stranger's voice was deep. When he spoke he revealed the wink of a gold tooth. Grace's hand began to shake against the door and she had to grit her teeth to try to stay still.

"Money?" Franklin rested his hands on Grace's shoulders, protectively drawing up close behind her. "You're not Steve. We've already paid our rent."

"My twenty g's, where is it?"

"Twenty?" Franklin released one of Grace's shoulders to let a hand fly up to his throat. "Twenty *grand* you say? Look around," he briefly moved aside to grant the man a clear view of the flat, "we're hardly well off. I suggest you try 3B."

"I know you took it." The stranger barely moved as though every muscle was made of stone. He remained thick and impassable in the doorway, his dark eyes holding both Franklin and Grace in a single steady gaze.

"Look," Grace tried to sugar coat her words as much as she could. "I really think you need to try 3B. We don't know what you're talking about and—" She moved to close the door but the man's booted foot crossed the threshold, preventing her from doing so.

"You were seen," he told her flatly, letting his hulking mass do the threatening rather than his tone. "Three nights ago you took my twenty grand out of a skip in Shoreditch. That money isn't yours. I want it back."

Grace remembered being young and playing on the swings. She'd sit beside Peter and together they'd kick their legs out as straight as they could in their attempt to reach the sun.

"Careful," their mother was forever fretting as she stood close by. "Don't go too high."

Peter heeded her warnings but not Grace. Grace wanted to soar amongst the clouds, to touch rainbows. She kept kicking, kept flying. But then she was falling. One of the rusted chains supporting the swing had snapped free. She connected with the tarmacked ground in one flat movement. An egg breaking against a wall. Grace felt the warmth of her own blood dripping down from her nose, tracing down her chin. Her hands burned as she scrambled to stand up. Her mother remained close, watching intently, but she did not help.

"I told you to be careful," she hissed as Peter lingered at her side, his eyes watery. "And now look what you've done," her attention shifted skyward and she bared her gap teeth like a feral cat. "Rain, it's going to rain. Your foolish actions have brought rain, girl. We'll have to hurry home before it touches us."

Despite her wounds Grace had been forced to run. Both knees were torn open and her palms were badly grazed but none of her pain was tended to, not even when they were back in the flat and rain was splashing against the windows.

"You were reckless," her mother chided as she sent Grace to bed without dinner. "Recklessness breeds danger. Danger breeds death."

Grace thought she heard the snapping of the swing chain as she stood in her flat doorway. She fell back against Franklin who managed to keep her upright. He firmly gripped her shoulders and she had to admire that when he spoke there was no quaver in his voice.

"We don't know what you're talking about."

"You can't kid a kidder," the man told him sternly. "You have my money. You were seen. Four of you. You took it and brought it back here. And now I want it back."

"Look—"

"Let me be clear," the stranger leant in bearing all the menace of a cobra about to strike. "If I don't get my money back I'll start breaking bones. One for each thousand. That's twenty broken bones. How does that sound to you?"

Grace sucked in a breath, preparing to speak but the man continued. "And don't bother threatening to call the police. You're just a pathetic little bunch of thieves. You took money that wasn't yours, how do you think that will go down with the boys in blue? Not very well I'd imagine. Now just hand it back and we'll consider this whole unpleasant matter concluded, okay?"

"We don't have your money," Franklin bravely insisted.

"Yes, you do," the stranger smiled, revealing his gold tooth in all its glory. "I know everything that goes on in this city. My ears have ears. And I know that you took my money and now I'm demanding that you give it back." He raised a hand and cracked his knuckles. Grace noticed the letters tattooed across his sausage like fingers. They spelt out *rain*. She wanted to throw up.

"Jasper has it."

Spinning around Grace stared up at Franklin in shock.

"He… he has it," Franklin continued with his lie. "He has it and he was going to… to gift it to his brother at his wedding."

"So where is Jasper?"

"At the wedding. He won't be back until Monday."

"Then you give me my money back on Monday."

"Did I say Monday?" Franklin slapped the heel of his hand against his forehead. "I meant Friday. He's gone for a week. Catholic family, weddings take a while. Lots of standing on ceremony."

Grace felt dizzy and pain was searing through her body as though she were repeatedly falling from the swing and crashing against the ground. Each lie Franklin told jarred all her bones. And when she looked at the stranger's thick, tattoo covered hands she imagined what it would sound like to hear her own bones break.

"Friday," the man bared his teeth again, wearing an expression that so accurately mimicked her mother's that Grace almost fainted in Franklin's arms. "I will come back on Friday and either you give me my money or I start breaking bones. And don't go taking me for a fool," he was focusing solely on Franklin now. "You try to run, you whisper a word about this to anyone and I'll know. I know everything. I'll cut out your tongues if I have to. As I can see," he grunted as he briefly diverted his gaze towards the interior of the flat, "you're just a bunch of runts. Of nobodies. You end up floating in the Thames and no one will care. I suggest you proceed very carefully this week. And be sure Jasper returns my money to me."

"Oh, he will."

Grace had to clench her throat around the scream which was trying to get out. Why did Franklin keep lying? Why had he placed the blame on Jasper?

"Friday," the stranger pointed at them, the coal in his eyes threatening to ignite at any moment. "I'll be back and you'd best pay up."

The man stepped into the corridor to leave and with trembling hands Grace was finally able to close the door. Pressing her back against it she slid down to the floor, feeling the tremble in each and every bone in her body.

"Fuck," Franklin dragged his hands through his hair and kept staring at the closed door. "Fuck."

"You blamed Jasper," Grace looked up at him, tears burning behind her eyes. "How could you do that? You were the one who found the briefcase, who brought it back here."

"Don't put this all on me," Franklin raged at her. "We all spent that money, Grace. All our hands are dirty."

"Then why blame Jasper?"

"Because he's not here," Franklin kept staring at the door as though he feared it might suddenly be forced open. "Jasper isn't here so my lie buys us some time."

"Time to do what?"

"Oi."

It wasn't the front door that was thrown open. Aaron stalked out of his bedroom, hair madly askew, t-shirt crumpled. "What the hell is going on out here? I'm trying to sleep and all I can hear is you two shouting."

"We had a visitor," with a sniff Grace pulled herself off the floor.

"A visitor?" Aaron looked between her and Franklin, his eyes red and his voice hoarse. For a moment Grace wondered if he was sleeping off a hangover and resented the accompanying pang of jealously. If he'd been out drinking all day then who had it been with? His band mates? Someone else?

"Yes," Franklin drifted over to the sofa and fell against it like a broken puppet. "A big bloody brute came to the door demanding his money."

"Did you tell him to go to 3B?"

"*His* money," Franklin slapped the back of the sofa with his palms. "His twenty grand to be precise."

Aaron changed. In a millisecond his expression shifted from angry to fearful before settling on concerned. He looked at Grace. "A guy was here," he pointed at the floor, "at the flat? Asking about that money?" She nodded. "Fuck."

"I know," Franklin rolled his eyes and slapped the sofa again. "I mean, who would have thought that—"

"Fuck!" From Aaron the word was a roar, almost a declaration of war. Grace reached over to him, letting her hands rest on his forearm. He was still warm from sleep.

"He wants it back. All of it. He threatened us."

"He threatened you?" Aaron's voice became strained.

"Us," Franklin spoke up. "He threatened *us*, Aaron. As in all of us. There was talk of breaking bones and sleeping with the fishes."

"Franks, he didn't actually say—"

"He was a straight up gangster, and not in a popular rap video way," Franklin stared directly at Aaron. "This man was salty sea dog savage and I get the impression that he isn't messing around."

"But we can't pay him back," Aaron growled, pushing his fingertips to his temple. "We spent it all."

"Ever heard of a return?" Franklin arched an eyebrow. "We return all our ill gotten gains, get the cash back and boom, it's done."

"What about Steve?" Aaron challenged. "I can't see him willingly returning our overdue rent to us."

"Ah," with a knowing nod Franklin pushed himself off the sofa. "I already planned for that. Our rent totals several thousand so we need to acquire that somehow. By Friday."

"Friday?" Rage crept back into Aaron's voice.

"Don't be pissed off, I bought us some time. We've got a week to gather everything together, to sort it all out."

"How did you manage that?"

"I…" Franklin's confidence faltered. His shoulders slumped. "I told the brute at the door that

Jasper had taken the money to his brother's wedding."

"You did *what*?"

"Chill, Papa Bear, we needed time. And I got us some time. It'll all be fine, you'll see."

"How will any of this be fine?" Aaron shrugged off Grace's touch and crossed the distance between him and Franklin in a single step. They stood eye to eye with Aaron's chest rising and falling with every angry breath he drew in. "You've put us all in danger," he told his flat mate. "You brought that money here. You spent it first. You've put a big fucking bull's eye on our door."

"How was I to know this would happen?" Franklin cried. "He said we were seen. *Seen*. Who the fuck saw us?"

"Someone must have followed us home," Aaron was grinding his teeth together. "If I hadn't been looking after the rest of you who were half cut then maybe I'd have noticed."

"You were the only one in a reasonable condition, it's on you that you failed to spot our stalker!"

Grace wedged herself between the two men. "We're in this together," she told them both. "We all played our part. We all carry some guilt. The only way we're going to recover the money by Friday is if we stick together."

"Agreed," Franklin placed a hand on her shoulder.

"You sure he meant it?" Aaron kept his eyes locked on Franklin. "The threats. He might have been bluffing."

"Oh, he meant it," Franklin pouted. "I almost soiled myself when I stood there listening to him."

"I, for one, don't want to wait around and see if his threats were real or not." Grace told them. "Let's just sell off everything we bought and somehow find the rest. We need to give the guy his money back."

"How do we even know it's his?" Aaron challenged.

"He said that his *ears have ears*," Franklin tugged at his own ear lobe. "That's gangster for 'do as I fucking say'. We need to give him the money."

"You should have woken me up."

"And what would you have done differently?" both of Franklin's eyebrows flew up his furrowed brow.

With a grunt Aaron buried his hands deep in the pockets of his jogging bottoms. "Nothing," he admitted, head drooping. "I'd have done nothing differently. You were right to buy us some time. Let's just hope we can make up what we're short else we'll be out on the streets."

"Or worse," Franklin chimed, "sleeping at the bottom of the Thames."

Aaron grunted again. "I know where I'd rather be. Let's find and return the damn money."

8

There were crows in the sky. They gathered en masse, their glossy feathers turning everything black. Guttural shrieks throbbed against Grace's ear drums as she looked up and felt rain lash against her face like a watery whip.

Death was coming.

She knew it as the rain soaked through her coat, her jumper, made her hair stick to her scalp. She felt its presence in the frigid air. Turning she tried to run but the ground was shaking, pulsing like a heartbeat against the fevered pounding of the crow's wings.

The beating of the ground forced her to her knees where she knelt at the avian altar. Surging forwards she tried to crawl, pushing her hands deep into the wet grass. Her fingertips sank into the damp mud and she kept crawling, kept moving. The crows were growing in number. Grace felt the whisper of their beating feathers fan across her back. They were consuming not just the sky but the land too, inhabiting every single piece of air. Soon she wouldn't be able to breathe; she'd choke on their plumage, lungs blackening along with the sky.

Grace started to dig. She pushed her fingers deep into the wet ground and hauled back chunks of mud.

All the while the crows kept shrieking. The feathers against her back turned to claws. They were trying to claim her. But she refused to let it happen. Gritting her teeth Grace dug as hard and fast as she could. The mud was like clay; wet and heavy. Her arms were growing weak as she slowly sank into the damp ground.

"No," she panted with exhaustion as the crows pecked at her shoulders and ears. "No."

Something reached up out of the ground. A hand. It was alabaster white against the darkness, seemingly almost pure bone. Fingers closed around her wrist and pulled hard, forcing her deeper into the ground. She tasted mud. And decay.

"Join me."

It was Peter's voice. Grace's heart beat accelerated with a mixture of surprise and alarm.

"Join me," he urged again, his words a ghostly whisper. "We can be together forever."

The hand pulled harder and the scream that erupted from Grace's throat was silenced by the mud that slid through her lips. She spluttered against it as Peter dragged her down into his grave.

*

Grace was breathing hard. Her brow was speckled with sweat as she sat up in bed, sheets drawn up to her chin. Every bone was shaking. Sucking in air with a panicked desperation she took a moment to orientate herself. The nightmare had been so real. Slowly she released her sheets and looked down at her hands, surprised to see them clean instead of coated in wet mud.

With a shudder she recalled the sensation of Peter's hand around her own. She was dreaming of him so much lately. Much more frequently than usual.

Against the stillness of her bedroom something was chirping. Each chirp was accompanied by a rattle of vibration. It took Grace a moment to recognise the sound. Her phone was ringing. Outside it still appeared to be dark but her fairy lights glowed around the metal art deco headboard, guiding her to the bedside table where her phone had been left to charge. Grace snapped the white cable from its base and quickly clocked the time. 7 a.m. And someone was calling her from a number she didn't recognise.

After allowing herself a moment's hesitation, Grace answered.

"Hello?" Her voice carried the creaks of a restless night's sleep.

"Hi. Is that Grace?"

"Yeah." The person calling sound familiar but only vaguely. "Sorry, who is this? Your number didn't come up."

"It's Jackson. Jasper's brother."

"Oh, oh, hi Jackson," she did her best to sound as cheery as was humanly possible at such an hour on a Saturday morning. "How are you? Aren't you getting married today?"

"I am."

"Did... did Jasper forget something? I know he's an usher, was he in charge of the rings or something? If he's forgotten them I can—"

"He hasn't shown up."

"What?" Grace swung her legs off the side of the bed, preparing to stand up. Instantly she was alarmed. Jasper was as reliable as the tide. If he said he was going to be somewhere he'd be there, a good half an hour early at least. If the call had been regarding Franklin she could have understood him going wayward at the eleventh hour. But not Jasper.

"He was supposed to get here last night," her concern was echoed in Jackson's voice. "And I'm sorry to call you so early it's just that he should be here and for him not to be, well..." he grew quiet. "It's not like him."

"No," Grace agreed. "It's definitely not."

"Can you," there was an anxious sigh on the other end of the line, "can you just double check he's not still at the flat? I don't know where to look for him. He's not answering his phone, it just goes straight to voice mail."

"Sure, I'll check now."

"Great, are you okay to call me back? It's just…" Jackson cleared his throat. "There's like a million things to do today."

"I'll call you back in a minute, it's fine. Let me go and see if he's here." Grace kept her voice bright, perky.

The stillness from her bedroom extended to the rest of the flat. After debating their situation until the small hours everyone had finally conceded to their pressing desire to sleep. Grace had shut her door on Aaron and Franklin six hours ago and tried to dream away her concerns but all she'd found when she closed her eyes were crows. And Peter.

A shiver dropped down her spine like a falling cube of ice. Ignoring it, Grace looked around, letting the light from her bedroom guide her. The floorboards winced as she approached the sofa. She gasped with relief when she saw the lumpy form huddled up beneath the blanket.

"What the hell?" she tugged on an exposed foot draped over the side of the sofa. "I thought you were leaving last night. Your brother just called, he's worried about you."

"Christ, *get off.*"

Grace recognised the haughty indignation of the slumbering figure and pulled back the blanket for confirmation. Franklin scowled up at her from where he was huddled against the cushions.

"What the hell is this?" he demanded. "I'm *sleeping*, Grace. You know I need at least ten hours else it plays havoc with my complexion."

"Franks?" Grace stared at him. "What are you doing sleeping on the sofa? I thought you were Jasper."

"The master has the suite tonight," with a groan Franklin sat up and began dragging his hands through his thick black hair. "He was hardly going to let me cuddle up with him. I believe that's a privilege reserved exclusively for you."

"So Aaron is in the bedroom?" Grace looked over at the closed door. "Alone?"

"Urgh," Franklin let out a louder groan and flopped back against the sofa. "Don't you two start this up again. The whole tortured lovers' thing is getting *old*. Either give it another go or let it go. Seriously."

"No, I mean is Jasper in there."

"Jasper?"

"Yes, blonde guy, well read, lives here. Usually sleeps where you are."

"He's at his *Frozen* wedding," Franklin reached for the discarded blanket and drew it up against his shoulders. "You should heed the theme of that wedding and, you know," he began to sing, "*let it go*."

"He's not at the wedding. His brother just called me. Jasper didn't show up."

"Didn't show up?"

"Apparently not. Jackson asked me to look around here for him."

"But that's not like him," Franklin scrambled beneath the blanket until he was sitting up again. "He's normally early for everything."

"I know."

"He never misses an appointment. He keeps everything written down in that moleskin diary of his."

"I know."

"And today is his brother's wedding he certainly wouldn't—"

"Franks, I *know*. Hence why I'm so concerned. Now get up and help me look for him."

"Look for him?" Franklin eyed her warily. "Look for him where, Grace? Do you think he's hiding in a cupboard or lying in the dust beneath the sofa? He's not here."

"I still need to check. I told his brother I would."

So they checked. First the bathroom. With a flourish Franklin pulled back the mildew laced shower curtain to reveal one very empty, very grimy bathtub. Grace checked her wardrobe, beneath her bed. She even made Franklin lift up the sofa. Then she had to push open the door to Aaron's room.

It was dark inside. The curtains were drawn tightly and for a moment Grace thought she heard the flutter of crow's wings. Then Franklin turned on the main light and the small room was doused in garish yellow light. From beneath a chequered blue duvet Aaron groaned.

"Sorry to disturb you, sleeping beauty," Franklin sauntered over to the side of the bed and boldly drew back the sheets. Grace knew better than to poke the bear. Aaron was never at his best first thing in the morning. The air in the room was heavy and musky. She wanted to get out.

"What the fuck?" Aaron instantly snatched the sheets back and did his best to cover himself up. He wore only a faded pair of black Calvin Klein boxers.

"Just checking if Jasper was in there with you," Franklin explained before dropping to his knees and scrutinising the shadows beneath the bed.

"*What?*"

"He didn't show up for his brother's wedding," Grace stated calmly from the doorway.

"He didn't?" Aaron dragged both hands down his face and then sat up, massaging his temples furiously. Grace wondered if he'd slipped out of the flat after she'd gone to bed. His eyes were bloodshot and she smelt stale whiskey in the air. If he had gone out where had he gone? And with whom?

Shaking her head, Grace derailed the jealous train of thought that had been charging through her mind. Her main concern was Jasper.

"His brother just called asking me to check if he was still here at the flat."

Franklin spread his arms wide. "So here we are, checking."

"Well, he's bloody well not in here," Aaron announced gruffly. "So, where the hell is he?"

"That's just it," Grace felt her throat tightening, "we don't know where he is."

*

The return call to Jackson had been tense. Grace tried to keep her voice bright as though she wasn't delivering bad news.

"He's not at the flat, we've checked everywhere."

"He's not?" Jackson's voice was a cocktail of panic and annoyance. "Then where is he? Do you have any idea where he might be?"

"He…" Grace absently chewed on her fingernails. "He mentioned going to pick up your car. If you text me your address I'll go and check if it's there."

"Right. Okay."

"I mean, he's got to be somewhere," it was a battle to maintain the forced cheerfulness in her voice.

"I'm getting married in three hours," Jackson's voice softened. "It won't feel right to do it without him here."

"He'll be there," Grace gushed. "I'll… I'll find him and get him over to you. I promise. He'll turn up somewhere. Maybe he just got lost in a good book."

"Ha. He used to do that all the time growing up."

"So, yeah, maybe he's tucked away in a reading nook somewhere and he's lost track of time. I'll go and see if he picked up your car, that's a start."

"Thank you. Keep me posted?"

"Of course."

Jackson hung up and Grace stared across the sofa to Franklin who was sitting on the far end.

"Where could our boy be?" he asked tensely.

"Somewhere. He has to be somewhere."

Behind the bathroom door the shower hissed loudly. Aaron was up, soon he'd be dressed and ushering them all out of the flat. Because together they'd find him. They had to. People didn't just disappear into thin air.

9

"Okay, this is it," Franklin brandished an address book high above his head. "This is where Jasper's brother lives. Let's go."

"Grace, you stay here."

She instantly flinched at Aaron's command. "Here? No. I want to go with you guys. I want to help."

"And what if he comes back?"

"Then you stay," Franklin stared pointedly at his broad shouldered friend. "Grace wants to help. Let her help."

"I know but—" Aaron's voice was as rough as the stubble he'd not bothered to shave from his jawline.

"We've all got our phones," Franklin tapped his coat pocket, "they are all sufficiently charged. So, let's go find Jasper. If he was coming back here he'd be back by now."

Grace knew that Franklin made a fair point. With each passing minute the possibility of Jasper walking through the front door became less and less likely. The floorboards winced as she strode over to the threshold of the flat with purpose. "Let's go," she urged the men behind her. "First stop, Jackson's."

It was bright outside. A clear blue sky stretched across London. But the sun which shone was like a mirage because it offered no heat. There was still frost in the air which laced upon flowers gathered in window boxes.

Aaron was their guide. He had intimate knowledge of the underground thanks to his years spent busking along its tiled tunnels. He'd strum his guitar and rasp out a perfect melody as commuters tossed the change in their pockets into his open case. Some days he could surface several hundred pounds richer. Other days weren't nearly as fruitful. In the quiet of night he'd sometimes tell Grace about the stranger things people had left him in his guitar case, from business cards to used condoms. Nothing ever seemed to deter Aaron from his path, even when the world showed him its ugliest face he'd just grunt in response and keep playing his music, keep playing his songs.

After two changes on the tube they found themselves in an affluent part of the city. Terraced houses with white washed walls lined up together like rows of perfect teeth. Trees along the pavement were bordered by neat little black fences. But this was still London. Cars massed together along the kerb like ants waiting to march. Grace wedged herself between her companions. Despite her years spent in the capital, the hectic nature of it still had the power to bother her. If she closed her eyes she could still see the sprawling green fields that lay close to her childhood home.

"I don't think we're in Kansas anymore," Franklin commented as they nervously moved further along an opulent road. The street lights were no longer the regulation ones installed by the council, they were black and sleek, complimenting the miniature fences round the trees. "What does Jackson do again?"

"Umm…" Grace frowned. Her default answer was to say *something in a suit.* Whenever she saw pictures of Jackson he looked like a worn out, more smartly dressed version of Jasper. His hair was thinning and his eyes had lost their sparkle but there was no denying the similarity between the brothers. "A lawyer maybe," she guessed. "Or an MP. Possibly a banker."

"So, we don't know?"

"We don't know."

"Well, it must pay okay, whatever he does," Franklin swept his gaze along the rows of polished cars. "Why couldn't Jasper just ask brother dearest to dig deep into his vast pockets and cover our rent for us?"

"Hey," Aaron reached behind Grace's back to shove Franklin's shoulder. "Don't go judging him for not creeping to his wealthy brother for a hand out. We all know how complicated family can be."

Grace hung her head. She knew. She knew too well.

A familiar pattern of thought begun to form in her mind.

If Peter were still alive would he be successful? Would he live somewhere like Jackson? If she asked him for money would he help or would he look at her with sad eyes? Or worse – disgust?

She could answer most of her own questions. Peter had been a kind boy. She didn't doubt that the man he would have become would have been generous, would have given her his last penny if she'd asked it of him. Sorrow became a ball in her throat, merging with regret. Spluttering out a cough she leaned forward, hands pressed to her chest.

"Oh, hey," Franklin rubbed her back, his voice soothing. "I could choke on this capitalist air too, but we need to at least check for the little blue car before we do."

"Here." Aaron turned to stare at the black door of a uniform white house. The windows of the building were long and cast in a glare of sunlight, making it impossible to see inside.

"This it?" Grace swept a hand across her mouth and straightened.

"This is it."

"Casa de Jackson," Franklin stepped closer to the stone steps which led up to the front door. There was a brass knocker attached to the sleek surface. It was long and lean, like a nose. Above the knocker was the number sixty-nine. Grace waited for Franklin to make an inappropriate comment but if he was having any sort of impure thoughts he seemed to be managing to keep them to himself. "So, where's the car?" he spun round to face the others. "I see two black cars. A silver one. A red over there. Nothing blue."

Grace scanned the nearby street. Franklin was right.

A door opened and promptly closed with a polished squeak and they all jumped. Next door an ashen haired woman was descending her own set of stone steps, led by a pair of pugs who merrily trotted ahead of her, each dressed in Burberry.

"Can I help you?" she froze on the street to regard the trio, using leather gloved hands to tighten her fur coat around her shoulders. Her lips seemed overly plumped, were glossed a vibrant shade of red and the cadence in her voice hinted at Russian roots.

"We're friends of Jasper, Jackson's brother," Franklin eased forward, acting as unofficial spokesman. "Fabulous shoes," he shot a glance down at the woman's black stiletto boots.

"Thank you," she purred as though the spirit of the animal which had died to make her coat had infected her soul and made her part feline.

"Jasper was supposed to come and pick up his brother's car yesterday and we're just—"

"Something about a wedding," the woman waved a hand through the air. It was difficult to tell if she was frowning, or at least trying to. Maybe she couldn't frown. "Some *tacky* theme."

"Yes, *Frozen*," Franklin nodded. "I'd say it's more whimsical than tacky but hey. Different strokes and all that. So," he clasped his hands together and gave her his most sincere look. "The little blue Fiat which Jackson owns."

"*Wife* owns," the woman corrected. "No man drives that."

Franklin puffed out his cheeks but didn't comment. "It doesn't seem to be here. Did you see someone pick it up?"

"Yes. Small blonde boy. Yesterday. Seen him before. He's so slight, like pixie."

"That'd be Jasper."

"He came. Got in car. Left."

"Are you sure?" Grace blurted.

"Very," the woman narrowed her eyes. "I was out with Porsche and Prince," she nodded at her pair of pugs who were happily sniffing Franklin's legs. "It was my second walk of the day and I saw him. He got in car. He drove away."

"Thank you," Franklin smiled like he was auditioning to present a daytime quiz show. "You've been really helpful."

"Mmm," the woman gave a clipped order in Russian and her two pugs pottered after her as she strutted off down the street.

"So, he got the car," Grace stared at the nearest parked vehicle. "But then where did he go? Why didn't he make it to the wedding?"

"We need to go back to the flat," Aaron stated.

"Urgh," Franklin rolled his eyes. "It's like a million tube stops from here. Let's at least stop at a Pret – my stomach is growling."

"Do what you want but I'm heading back." There was thunder in Aaron's voice.

"What's the rush?" Franklin demanded sourly. "Jasper got the car. Maybe he went for a long joyride. Maybe he's absconded with some girl."

"Or maybe he's lying in a hospital bed somewhere. Or worse – a ditch."

Grace whimpered at the bluntness of Aaron's words and turned away from them both.

"I'm just being realistic," he admitted to her back. "We need to go back to the flat and start calling all the hospitals along the route he'd take to get to the wedding. Police stations too."

"This is starting to feel like family work," Franklin objected. "Hospitals probably won't tell us shit because we're not next of kin."

"His entire family is busy watching his brother get married," Grace wiped at her eyes and coughed out the last of her sorrow. "It's up to us to find him. He's relying on us."

Aaron stared at them both. "Then let's not let him down."

*

An hour later and they were back at the flat. The sun was still shining but Grace ignored its gleaming presence as she sat on her bed, hunched over her rose gold laptop scouring any possible route home Jasper may have taken whilst shouting out relevant phone numbers to Franklin and Aaron who were taking it in turns to play caller.

Each time a number was a dead end Grace felt herself grow smaller. He'd left so little behind to tell them where he might have gone. He existed within his books and in them you could discover any number of meanings for his sudden disappearance.

"Another no," Franklin shouted from the main living area. "No one matching Jasper's description has come in. Hit me again."

Grace read the number for a hospital just north of London aloud. Jasper would have passed close by it as he merged onto the motorway. After a few minutes she heard Aaron's deep voice making yet another enquiry.

"Oh, hi. My friend went missing yesterday and I'm just checking local hospitals to ensure he wasn't in an accident or something."

A brief pause.

"Sure, yeah, his name is Jasper Edwards. He's around five foot five, blonde, Caucasian, blue eyes. Twenty-five years old. He would have been driving a blue Fiat 500."

A longer pause.

Grace was already looking up the next number they'd have to call.

"Okay, I'll wait."

Abandoning her laptop, she hurried to her doorway to stare at Aaron who was holding his phone firmly to his ear. No other hospital had asked him to wait. They'd all politely informed him that no one matching that description had come in. Franklin looked up from the sofa and caught her eye, mouthing the words 'don't worry.' But a knot was already forming in Grace's stomach. Her organs were twisting together, clenching tightly and shortening her breath.

How can a second sometimes feel like an eternity? Grace dug her fingernails into the palms of her hands, not caring if she drew blood. Time had stretched out to the point of snapping when she'd anxiously stabbed at the number nine three times back in the little flat she'd once called home. Her mother was still clutching a lifeless Peter and wailing like a banshee and so Grace had stolen into the kitchen and used the curled wire of the wall mounted phone to pull the handset free. She cushioned its crash to the tiled floor with her pudgy child hands and then nervously tapped in three numbers. The phone rang once. Twice. Then a brisk voice answered.

"999 what's your emergency?"

Grace placed her lips close to the mouthpiece and had to whisper for fear of her mother hearing. "My brother. I think he's dead."

The call handler asked her to stay on the line and so Grace did. She waited for several minutes which weighed on her young heart like several lifetimes. She was braced for her mother to find her, to snatch the phone from her grasp but instead she kept cradling Peter, kept sobbing. Heavy fists pounded on the front door. They didn't wait for an answer. The door came crashing in and strangers filled up the flat like water from a broken dam.

In the endless space that had followed the initial call the handler had asked Grace questions which she'd nervously responded to in strained whispers.

"Where are you?"

"Where is your brother?"

"Where is your mother?"

"How old are you?"

And most crucially;

"What happened?"

So many bodies had swarmed the little flat, making it feel even smaller. She had told the call handler the truth. But what if she shouldn't have? What if she should have heeded her mother's advice and just kept lying?

"I'm still here," Aaron stood and paced away from the sofa, his phone still firmly attached to his ear. "Right… uh huh. Okay."

Franklin and Grace exchanged panicked glances.

"It might be nothing," he told her, a tremor running through his voice.

"And it might be something." Grace hugged her arms against her chest like a shield, preparing for the inevitable blows that were about to come.

"Yes, absolutely," Aaron was nodding as he talked with the hospital. "A few hours. No, that's fine. Thanks for your help." He ended the call and released a long sigh.

"Well?" Franklin snapped from the sofa. "Spill! You're keeping us in suspense here."

"There was an accident," Aaron commenced flatly. "Last night on a motorway just north of London. A pile up. There were some injuries. A blue Fiat was involved. They've got someone in who matches Jasper's description."

"Right, well," Franklin stood up. "He's okay then. His phone must have just been bust up in the accident. We can call his brother and tell him that everything is—"

"We need to go to the hospital and ID Jasper."

Grace staggered towards the sofa and dropped against it.

"What?" Franklin's eyes shone with tears. "What the fuck are you saying, Aaron?"

"He's in a coma." Aaron looked at the counter tops in the kitchen, at his feet, anywhere except the desperate eyes of his flatmates.

"A *coma*?" Franklin choked on the word.

"That's why they've been unable to ID him," Aaron continued. "And yeah, his phone was smashed up in the crash so they couldn't use that. He had no documents on him. They were about to run the plates on the Fiat to find out who he is but I said we could come in and ID him. Let's hold off calling Jackson until we do. No point upsetting him on his wedding day until we know with complete certainty that it's Jasper."

"Yeah," Franklin agreed absently. Then, as his thoughts began to gather together he spoke with more conviction. "Yeah, I mean, yes. Let's go there, let's see if it's Jasper and then we can proceed from there."

Grace couldn't move off the sofa. Hospitals scared her. Terrified her. The last time she was in one her legs had shook so badly she couldn't walk. Every white coat, every blue set of scrubs reminded her of that awful night. When she saw them she was back sitting on a bed answering awful questions while the stench of piss and bleach sank into her skin.

"Are you up for this?" Aaron's hand was on her shoulder, his green eyes close and wide with concern. He didn't know everything about her past but he knew enough to be able to connect some of the dots.

"For Jasper I am," she dusted away her painful memories with a flick of her wrist and stood up. She needed to be strong. Her friend needed her. She could mourn the death of her childhood later.

"Let's go," Franklin was already heading out through the door. "Although we definitely need a sandwich stop on the way. I'm bloody starving."

*

Machines beeped and whined as though communicating with one another in a language indecipherable to human ears.

Grace stared at the pale figure in the hospital bed. At Jasper. Despite the plastic tube down his throat, the swelling on his cheeks and the blackening of his eyes she knew it was him. They all did the second they walked into the HDU. His arms rested at his sides, each heavily bandaged, and his eyes were closed and he looked almost… peaceful. But any serenity was ruined by the relentless shriek of the machines. As the trio huddled at the base of his bed several nurses made their way back and forth from Jasper's side, adjusting his IV drips, checking his temperature. Keeping him alive.

"What happened?" Franklin asked the kind faced brunette nurse who had met them at reception.

"He was involved in a multi-car pileup," she stated, her voice soft with sympathy. "The police reports indicate that your friend seemed to lose control of his car which made him break through the central reservation at speed. It's possible that there was a vehicle malfunction but you'd need to speak to the police more about that."

"And Jasper?" Grace tenderly stroked the thin sheet that covered him, wondering what awful wounds were concealed beneath it. "Will he be okay? Will he wake up?"

"He's suffered serious injuries," the nurse cleared her throat and looked nervous. "Really, we need to speak to family members."

"His brother is just finishing off getting married." Aaron stated. "I'm just working myself up to make the call that will ruin their special day."

"Make the call," the nurse urged. "Your friend's situation is… precarious. He's lost a lot of blood and may need a kidney transplant so—"

"Check us," Franklin was already pulling up the sleeve of his jumper. "Check each of us. Bloody, kidney, whatever, Jasper can have what he needs if we're compatible."

Aaron and Grace nodded in agreement.

"Fine," the nurse smiled appreciatively at them. "Let's get you all checked out. But first," her tired eyes settled on Aaron, "make that call. His family need to know what's happened to him."

10

No one spoke. Back at the flat the trio rested with unease, looking like the last few survivors from a brutal ship wreck, with hollowed eyes and haunted expressions. Grace was beside Franklin on the sofa. He was hunched forward, hands clenched between his knees. He hadn't even bothered to take off his long coat when they'd walked through the front door some forty minutes earlier.

It had been a long day. At the hospital they had drank down polystyrene cups of weak tea and then waited to pass on the grim baton of worry to Jasper's parents. They arrived an hour after receiving the call from Aaron with confetti still in their hair. It was their turn to linger at their son's bedside and wonder if, or when, he'd open his eyes again.

"Anyone want a tea, coffee or something?" Aaron was pacing the short distance of the kitchenette, unable to keep still. Grace craned her neck to look over at him.

"Sure. Franks?"

Franklin shook his head and said nothing. Which was strange since he always said something. He'd been oddly quiet the entire train ride home, keeping one eye on the darkened landscape beyond the window.

"His parents are there now," Grace pressed a hand against Franklin's back and leaned in to him, "they'll stay with him and the doctors, they are hopeful that—"

"I did this."

Grace stiffened in shock, drawing away from her friend. There was so much fire in his voice that she was singed by her close proximity to him. "What, Franks, no. It was an accident. The car seems to have malfunctioned, there was nothing anyone could—"

"I did this."

"Franks, listen to her," Aaron ordered sternly, driving the exhaustion out of his voice and replacing it with conviction. "She's right. The car did this. Not you. Stop making yourself a martyr over it."

"I did this," Franklin jumped to his feet and stared down both of his flatmates, eyes wide. "I told that fucking *thug* that it was Jasper, that he had the money."

"The two incidents," Grace stood at Franklin's side and soothingly rubbed his back, "they're not connected, Franks. There's no way. What happened to Jasper was just a fluke accident."

"Do you really think that?" The fire in his voice was still there and now it was burning behind his eyes too. "Do you honestly, hand on your heart, believe that the two events are in *no way* connected? Because you saw 'thug loving' at the door, Grace. You heard him. He wasn't messing about. The guy *threatened* us and I gave him Jasper's name. And now Jasper is in a fucking *coma*! I did this!"

"Franks, calm down." Aaron's words were gunshots, loud and piercing. Franklin had thrown up his arms during his lament and now they fell lamely to his sides. "This was a fluke accident. That's it. I feel terrible for Jasper but we just need to hope that he can make it through this. Okay?"

"He was pretty menacing," Grace stated quietly.

Aaron stared at her. "Who?"

"The man who came to the door."

With a grunt of annoyance, he turned his back on her and flicked on the kettle.

"Aaron, you didn't see him," she continued earnestly. "He was huge and... and threatening. And he'd somehow found us here. He could have easily found Jasper, followed him. Caused him to veer off the road. Even tinkered with the car before Jasper even got in it."

"That's one hell of a reach," Aaron didn't turn to look at her.

"Is it?" Franklin leapt on board her train of thought. "Grace is right, he could have got at the car. The thug traced the money here; he could have traced Jasper to his brother's house. It wouldn't exactly require rocket science to do so. Maybe the intended target was Jackson, not Jasper, to send a message to Jasper, to get him to give the money back."

"Will you two listen to yourselves?" Aaron raged. "You're talking like this is the plot for some thriller. And it's not. This is our lives. No one deliberately hurt Jasper so stop thinking that they did."

"You didn't see him," Grace said slowly. "He scared me." She looked at Franklin. "He scared us both."

"Then you should have woken me up so that I could have planted one right between his eyes and given the prick something to think about."

"Maybe I'm wrong," Franklin was approaching the kitchenette, creeping with the grace of a gazelle circling a lion, aware that he was on uneasy footing. "Maybe it was all just some fluke. Maybe Jasper's accident was purely the product of extreme bad luck. But, just humour me here, Aaron," he drummed his long fingers against the countertop. "What if I'm right? What if my dumb words did this? What if the thug wants more than just his twenty grand back, what if he wants revenge?"

Grace expected fireworks. She expected Aaron to fly into a verbal rage about what an idiot Franklin was, about how there was absolutely no way Jasper's accident was linked to the thug who had darkened their doorway. But instead he was quiet, head bowed in contemplation. When he finally looked up his eyes found Grace and his lips set in a hard, determined line.

"On the very slim chance that you are right I don't want to risk anyone else getting hurt."

"Okay," Franklin wilted against the countertop, weak with relief. They were all drained from their long day. There was only so much fight left in them. "So, what now? What do we do?"

"We go to the police." Grace wasn't sure where the words even came from that floated out of her mouth. Last time the police had shown up they'd kicked down doors and torn down walls. They'd changed everything. But fear had made her seek their intervention. And now, once again, fear was guiding her.

"'kay," Aaron nodded. "First thing tomorrow we all go to the police station. But right now, we all need to get some much needed sleep."

*

Grace's bed was a turbulent sea which forced her to toss and turn. No matter where she lay she didn't find comfort or respite from the chaotic torment of her mind. She couldn't stop thinking about Jasper, couldn't stop seeing his pale face so peaceful yet so broken. She'd give anything to see his blue eyes again, to hear the brittle sharpness of his nervous laugh. A kinder soul she'd never met. Unless she counted—

Peter wouldn't invade her thoughts. Not tonight. Grace bundled herself up in her sheets and rolled onto her side, pulling her knees up to her chest. Her hateful mantra began to play in her mind like an unwanted melody as she hung on the precipice of sleep;

You're not good enough. You need to go home. You need to give up.

Just as her eyes were sliding shut she thought she heard the coarse caw of a nearby crow. But lost in the darkness of a dreamless sleep she didn't care.

*

"We can't tell them about the money." This was Aaron's advice as they huddled together and hurried down the busy street. Even though it was Sunday morning it was busy out. Markets were springing up and store holders were braving the frost to lay out their wares for the day. Grace inhaled the greasy fumes of a burger van firing up the grill for the first time and her stomach ached with longing. A quick sandwich at a tube station had been the last thing she'd eaten. Consuming food had slid down her list of priorities since discovering Jasper in hospital, but now that her insides were churning like curdled milk she regretted that decision.

"We have to tell them about the money," Franklin contradicted.

"No, we can't." Aaron was resolute. "I'm not about to walk into a police station and implicate myself in a crime."

"Then what are we going to say?" Grace wondered, her attention drawn to another food vendor, this one offering chunky chips laden with salt and vinegar. She had to concentrate to keep moving forwards instead of diverting off towards the food.

"That our friend was in a road accident and we suspect foul play. Ask them to look into it."

"Maybe if we add 'pretty please with sugar on top' they'll drop everything and do it right away," Franklin suggested with a sarcastic pout.

"Don't be a dick, Franks."

Franklin continued, undeterred. "Because the police are always *so* helpful. If I've learnt anything from watching hours of *The Killing* with Jasper it's that—"

"We've no other choice," Aaron interrupted. "We go to them with some of what we know and hope it's enough. If someone did this to Jasper then they need to pay."

"We're going to sound crazy," Grace fretted as her stomach released a deep, ominous growl.

"Well, we are crazy," Franklin grinned. "Who cares who knows it? We're doing this for Jasper."

"I should call the hospital," Grace's hand drifted towards her pocket where her phone was stored. "Just check in on J and see how he's doing."

"Police first." Aaron stopped walking and looked up at the stone building which boasted a blue sign. They'd arrived.

*

In less than thirty minutes they were back on the street having failed to even bypass the acne ridden officer on reception.

"Are you reporting a crime?" he'd enquired in a nasally voice.

"Yes," Aaron stated. Then after a moment's hesitation, "I mean, maybe. We're not sure."

"Well, has a crime been committed, yes or no?"

"Don't you understand the word maybe?" Franklin hissed, shoving Aaron aside so that he could occupy most of the space in front of the little enquiry window behind which the officer sat. "We need you guys to determine if it's a crime or not."

"If you've seen a crime being committed fill out a witness form," the officer slid a piece of paper through his window, revealing chewed nails upon fat hands.

"We've not *seen* anything," Franklin groaned. "We weren't there. But we think something is afoot. Hence our presence here on this fine Sunday morning."

"Afoot?" The officer arched an eyebrow. "Sherlock Holmes doesn't work here you know. We conduct serious police business. Maybe you should take your theories elsewhere."

Ultimately, Grace had to wrestle Franklin and Aaron back through the main front doors before they all risked being thrown out. They were getting nowhere with the officer on reception who was clearly in no mind to act upon their theory.

"That was a bloody waste of time," Franklin kicked at the flagstones covering the street. The morning was grey. Looking up it seemed that the pewter shades of the police station had seeped into the clouds. Rain was coming. Or maybe snow. It was so cold that either could come hurtling down from the sky at any given moment.

"I need food," Aaron was making for a small café. A quaint chalkboard outside boasted that they did a full English breakfast for just over five pounds. Grace almost wilted with desire. At the counter Aaron almost made the mistake of ordering four breakfasts. So often the flatmates ate out together as a troupe.

That had been one of the stranger elements of dating Aaron; the exclusion of the others. On the rare occasions when they went out on a date Grace found herself looking beyond him, for the other two faces who were usually with them. Over the years the flatmates had become a family.

"I could murder this," Franklin declared when his meal arrived. With a wince he shook his head. "Sorry, poor choice of words."

Grace couldn't eat her breakfast fast enough. She cut open an egg fried to perfection and let its yellow innards blend in with the baked beans, sausages and bacon. She ate until her plate was clean and then washed it down with a cup of overly sweet tea. It was heavenly. And Jasper would have loved it. Though he'd have just had beans on toast since he was vegetarian, he'd have relished the camaraderie of them all being out and about so early on a cold Sunday morning.

"So, what now?" Franklin asked, as he dabbed a napkin against his chin which was mottled with bean juice and egg.

"Fuck knows," Aaron stared at his empty plate. "We tried speaking to the police and that got us nowhere."

"We could try talking to someone else," Grace suggested.

"Who?" Aaron demanded hotly. "A priest? The FBI? Batman? Who, Grace? Who exactly is going to help us?"

"I was just trying to be helpful," she filled her voice with equal heat. She'd been certain that the police would help, that they'd swoop in and take control of the situation like they had before. They'd looked at the little girl standing shyly in the corner of the flat, her floral dress soaked with her own urine and they'd promised her that everything was going to be okay. That she was safe.

"I'm going to head back to the hospital," Franklin flexed his hands before pulling on his gloves. "See how Jasper's parents are, if there's anything I can do to help."

"This isn't your fault," Aaron told him sincerely. "You didn't cause his accident, Franks."

"I'm acting out of charity, not guilt," Franklin confirmed, but Grace wasn't convinced. He was still quiet, a watered down version of his usual self.

"I'll come too," Grace got up and grabbed her coat off the back of her chair. "I'll feel better for checking in on him and seeing how his parents are holding up."

"So I'm to go back to the flat alone?" Aaron's chair squeaked against the linoleum floor as he hurried onto his feet. Grace looked at him and spied the fear he was trying to conceal behind his eyes. It gathered in the creases, in the barely audible tremor in his voice. Aaron was a book she'd read many times and though she failed to understand it completely she knew the signs, the patterns of behaviour. He was scared to go back to the flat and that meant that there was credence to Franklin's concerns. Should she be afraid too? Would the thug at the door try and put her in a coma next?

"You can go hang out with your friend, Jack," Franklin clasped Aaron's thick shoulder as he drifted by, heading for the door to the café and the grey street beyond.

"I won't be drinking."

"Why break a Sunday ritual?"

"I won't be drinking," Aaron was speaking solely to Grace since Franklin had already slipped outside. She wanted to believe him but the statement had grown thin over time. "I won't," he insisted with fervour. "I'll gather together all the stuff I can return to get our money back and I'll be practising with the band this afternoon, we've got a show tomorrow."

Grace knew she should be following Franklin but she found herself lingering at Aaron's side. It felt like a lifetime ago when they'd spent their Sundays in the dusty depths of old book and record stores, each searching for a rare gem.

"It's going to be alright." He stroked her cheek with such tenderness that Grace had a fleeting glimpse of what heaven must feel like. When Aaron was at his best he was home, she could curl up in his strong arms and finally feel the sense of safety she'd spent a lifetime searching for. But at his worst he was as temperamental as a tempest and it was exhausting to always be seeking a port in a storm.

"I have to go," she stepped away from him. "Jasper needs me."

11

Grace had never liked Mondays. She understood the sentiment to the old pop song which lamented melodically about wanting to blow the first day of the week away. The drizzle that accompanied most autumnal Monday mornings always seemed to fall with an extra amount of drudgery. People walked slower towards the tube, their steps leaden with regret.

"Normal," Franklin had kept whispering the word to her on the train ride back from the hospital after their latest visit. "We need to act normal, like nothing is wrong. If we don't we'll lose our heads."

Jasper was still dead to the world. The only sounds that came from his bed were made by the assortment of machines locked around him like robotic guards. His mother had been at the hospital and she seemed frail, so paper thin. She embraced Grace like a long lost daughter when she saw her.

"We just want him back," she'd whispered through pale lips. "Our precious boy, we just want him back."

There was no shortage of love in the hospital room. Even Jasper's brother had delayed his Icelandic honeymoon to stay at home. The family took it in turns to keep a vigil at the bedside and Grace and Franklin were trying to do their part too.

But as Grace stood on the train on the long journey back, getting rocked from side to side by the relentless motion, she felt a twist of jealously churn within her and take root. Jasper was loved by his family. Adored even. The thought of losing him had left them bereft. If the tables were turned, if it were Grace in that hospital bed closed off to the world, who would linger at her side? Franklin? Sure. Along with the rest of her flatmates. Her mother? No. She couldn't even come to her daughter's aid if she wanted to. Grace swallowed down the sour bile of her resentment. It wasn't Jasper's fault that he had a loving family, he deserved as much. But Grace couldn't escape the damaging thought that she too deserved to be loved so unconditionally, but years ago fate had dealt her a much crueller hand.

*

Franklin was pulling on a leather jacket. With his hair slicked back he looked as though he'd slipped back into the fifties overnight.

"Audition?" Grace asked as she left her bedroom, dance gear holdall slung across her back. She was on a mission to reclaim some of her money. The giddy moments of the spending spree already felt like a lifetime ago. After her splurge in the Apple store she took her meagre remaining amount and booked several weeks' worth of studio time. She was either going to dance her way to excellence or pirouette away her plethora of problems. But now she needed the studio to return her money.

Time was not on their side. She saw her fears gathered in the corners of Franklin's eyes in lines which seemed to have appeared overnight.

"Yep," He ran his hands against the sides of his bouffant hair. "Is this too much?" His voice lacked its usual resonance of mirth.

"What's the role?"

"Danny in Grease."

Grace looked her friend over. "I'd say it's just enough."

Franklin clapped his hands together in delight. "Awesome. This part is going to be mine. I just know it. Then I'll hopefully make some bloody money. Always about money." He clocked her dance bag. "Your plans for today?"

"Well, we're not needed at the hospital so I'm heading to the studio to try and reclaim some of the money I put down on rehearsal space."

"Good plan."

"Aaron about?" Grace slid a sideways glance towards the closed bedroom door near to her own.

"Nope. Didn't surface last night. Band practice must have run through until the early hours."

"Hmm." There was a time when Grace would have believed such a statement, would have clung to it. In truth, she envisioned Aaron slumped in a darkened corner of a bar somewhere nursing a Jack Daniels on the rocks. He'd sip at it until he felt numb. Aaron had never been good at dealing with feelings, good or bad.

"Don't sweat him," Franklin placed his hands on her shoulders and smiled brightly. "Don't sweat a damn thing, kid. We're going to grab this Monday by the balls and make it our bitch. By Friday we'll have recouped twenty big ones and everything will be *fine*."

"Franks—"

"We'll get all our money back, pay off thug face and Jasper will wake up within the hour. Come Friday we'll return to our usual impoverished equilibrium."

"I hope you're right."

"Until then," he applied pressure with his hands. "Act like everything is peachy fuckin' keen. You got it?"

"I think someone is in danger of straying into method actor territory," Grace offered him a watery smile as she slid out of his grip and made for the front door.

"Peachy fuckin' keen," he shouted after her.

*

The studio had been a dead end.

"Cash transactions are non-refundable," the peroxide blonde at reception told Grace pityingly. "Did you not read the fine print? We can reschedule your booked studio time or—"

"No." It was a couple of hundred pounds. Grace was going to have to find it another way. At least she could still return her laptop and phone, those alone would come to a decent enough amount. "It's fine, really. Thanks."

The lure to dance was strong. Grace knew she should be heading back to the flat, boxing up her new gadgets and taking them into town but she was at the studio, bag in hand. Perhaps she'd always intended to pirouette herself into oblivion, until her problems became just as blurred and distant as the world around her.

Accepting that her studio time was hers indefinitely, Grace went to change. As she pulled on her leg warmers and wound the ribbon of her pink satin shoes around her ankle something changed. She felt her stress slipping away. Soon there would be just the music and her movements.

As a child she'd learnt to escape into dance. When she spun and leapt people didn't see the broken little girl with the tragic past, they just saw the dancer. Grace hooked her old model iPod up to the stereo system and inhaled deeply as serene classical music began to fill the large studio. She swept across the wooden floor, first in long, elegant strides and then en pointe.

The tempo of the music increased and, becoming more empowered, Grace copied the rising intensity in her movements. She pivoted, jumped, became a whirling dervish across the floor, never putting a foot out of place.

"You're a natural," her first dance teacher had told her in her brisk Russian accent. "Small, yes, but elegant, too. And you have good centre of gravity, this will serve you well. Dancers, they cannot fall."

Grace's height however, served to hold her back as she grew older. At school she was never picked for the lead roles in key dances, her tutors opting for taller, more lithe girls for the crucial solos and pair duos. But Grace was doggedly persistent. She was going to be a great dancer, she had to be, else what was it all for? The years dancing, spinning, twirling, feeding on the thunder of applause. It had all been a means to an end, a way to escape. And now she was escaping again.

An hour passed like a minute and when a polite knock echoed on the far door Grace was panting, her leotard and tights soaked through with sweat. She clicked off the music, gathered her things and left the studio.

It was still raining. The dark clouds made the city streets appear as if they were awash with ash. Shadows swelled in every alley. Grace tugged up the hood of her coat, bowed her head against the elements and hurried to the tube station.

She loved the smell of burnt rubber deep in the bowels of the tube system. She'd stand against the yellow line and eagerly wait for the rush of warm air as the train arrived. It was a sensation she'd forever associate with freedom. During her first few weeks in London she'd become obsessed with the tube. After buying an Oyster card which granted multiple journeys for just four pounds a day, Grace began exploring the city. Every day she'd pick a different colour tube line to ride. She'd get off at various stops and explore the sights above, taking them all in with wide eyed wonder. Back then the city felt as infinite as her dreams.

Now the smell of rubber and the rush of wind were familiar sensations but the magic was still there, it still called to the part of Grace that kept clinging to her dreams, even when she could feel them slipping through her fingers.

It was busy on the tube but not busy enough for Grace to fail to notice the heavyset man at the end of her carriage who kept glancing at her. His attention immediately put her on edge. On the tube it is an unwritten rule to keep to yourself, to actively avoid making eye contact with anyone. Yet here was a man dressed all in black with closely shaven hair who kept looking in her direction. His wool coat was dappled with rain drops. Had he followed her from the studio?

Paranoia was a beast that had to be fed. As Grace reached her stop and hurried towards the platform she briefly glanced back and saw the man in black departing. Her heart began to creep up towards her throat. Was he following her? Surely not. It had to just be a coincidence. But there was something about him, something about his gait, his stare. He was hardened, just like the thug at the door had been.

On the escalator Grace hurried up the right hand side which was something she never did. She always stood patiently to the left but not today. As she neared the top she threw a glance back down the tunnel and saw the man in black ascending, his cool blue eyes locked onto her as he, too, strode up the right hand side.

Grace powered towards the exit, Oyster card in hand. She was shaking as she swiped and hurried out to street level. Rain slapped against her cheeks, fresh and welcoming. Wiping her eyes, Grace took a second to catch her breath and then she was hurrying down the street in the direction of her flat. Snatching a look behind, she saw the man in black moving in her wake. She felt like she was in some wretched horror movie. While her movements were frantic and rushed his were calm and collected, yet he was still managing to gain on her.

Questions darted through her mind like a frightened flock of birds –

Who was he?
What did he want?
Was this about the money? About Jasper?

There had been something wrong with the car Jasper had been driving, something which had caused him to careen across the central reservation into oncoming traffic. He could have died.

He might still.

Fear filled Grace's mouth with a metallic taste. Her feral instincts were kicking in. She wanted to sprint back to the flat, to bolt the door behind her and then call Franklin and Aaron. But in the flat she'd be alone. As she wove along the busy street Grace mentally jumped ahead, picturing the scene where she was holed up in her flat like a scared little piggy while the wolf at her door blew it down. And the man in black could tear it down if he so wished. He had bulged beneath his wool coat and more than that, doors in their ramshackle building had been broken down before. Mainly a few down at the infamous 3B where the supposed brothel was run, but the frightening fact was that it happened and the police never came. The door was kicked in, wood splintered and no sirens squealed outside, no uniformed officers came running up the communal staircase. Their building had a tarnished reputation which meant that the authorities gave it a wide berth. If she went back to the flat alone she'd be a sitting duck.

Grace crossed the street at the next set of traffic lights, taking a diversion. Once on the far side she turned and saw the man in black waiting to cross. Now she was certain that he was following her. She started to run. Her legs carried her down several more streets and into a bar that sat empty and quiet. Gasping, she hurried towards the back and found Aaron there with his band mates, head bowed in contemplation as he adjusted the strings on his guitar.

"Woah, Grace, you okay?" the drummer, Jimmy, noticed her first. He stopped spinning his sticks in his hands to glance over his kit at her.

"I…" she looked at Aaron. He glanced up and saw the fear plastered across her face.

"Shit, Grace," he abandoned his guitar and jumped to his feet. "Are you okay? What happened?

Is this about Jasper? Did the hospital call?" He led her away from his band, towards an empty booth. Grace looked towards the door she'd just run in through. There was no sinister figure stepping over the threshold. The man in black was gone. Cradling her head in her hands she groaned.

"I thought… I thought someone was following me."

"What?" Aaron reached for her hands. He was warm to the touch.

"I was on the tube and there was this… this creepy guy and I felt like he was following me." Her words failed to give credence to the fear she'd felt. In the moment there had been complete certainty. Each time his blue eyes locked onto hers she knew that the man was shadowing her, that whichever way she turned he would follow. But now in the dimly lit bar she just sounded like a little girl who had been spooked.

"Look, Grace, I know things are tense right now but—"

"He *was* following me," Grace insisted, blinking back tears. "I know he was."

And more than that, she knew that he had dark intentions. There was a look someone got in their eyes when they were about to do something awful, something truly inhuman. It was a look Grace would never be able to forget. She couldn't close her eyes because she risked being confronted with it again, on her mother's face.

"Okay, well, you're pretty shaken up. I should take you home."

"Don't leave me there alone." Grace didn't like it that her fear was making her weak. But the locks on the front door could only withstand so many kicks. "Franks is out at an audition and I'm not sure when he'll be back, I just—"

"I won't," Aaron stroked his thumb across the back of her hand. "You did the right thing by coming here instead of going back to the flat. It's not safe to be there alone right now."

"So, you don't think I'm crazy?"

Where had the man in black even gone? Was he leaning up against the wall outside just waiting for her to re-emerge onto the street or had he moved on, deterred from his intentions for the time being?

"I don't think you're crazy," Aaron confirmed softly. "I think we'll all rest a lot easier once we've paid that bloody money back and once Jasper wakes up."

"You reckon he'll wake up?"

"I hope he does," Aaron cleared his throat as he released Grace from his touch and slid back out of the booth. "And right now, hope is all we've got."

12

"Someone was *following* you?" Franklin was still dressed as though he'd walked right out of the fifties, but the scowl he'd been wearing since he walked through the front door told Grace that his audition hadn't gone well.

"I was really sure of it, yeah. This creepy guy dressed in black." Cradling her hands together she bowed her head and tried to breathe against the iron fist of fear that had settled between her lungs.

"Shit," Franklin looked to Aaron. "Did you see anything?"

"I saw Grace looking like she'd seen a ghost. That was enough."

Closing her eyes Grace thought of Jasper lying listlessly in hospital. Had the thug who'd made the house call put him there? Or was there a whole network of malicious individuals who were willing to do anything to get their twenty thousand pounds back? In a city like London it was easy to stalk someone, to blend in with the masses as bodies swept along the streets like fish swimming upstream.

"I don't want us living in fear like this." Aaron stood between the kitchenette and the front door as though he were standing guard and was too afraid to leave his post to come and join Franklin and Grace on the sofa.

"Then we need to do something," Franklin slapped his hands against his knees. "First we need to get the bloody money and pay it back. Then hopefully he'll call off his thug squad, Jasper will wake up and everything will be peachy—"

"Don't say keen," Grace muttered. Franklin's buoyant personality was normally more than enough to lift her up from the depths of a sour mood but not this time. She couldn't stop shivering even though their archaic heating system was turned up as high as it could go. She still felt the presence of the stranger at her heels, was certain that she'd turn round and see him standing where her shadow should be, wearing a sinister grin.

"Franks is right," Aaron took a single step forward, tentatively approaching the living area. "It's about the money. Whether Grace was followed or not, this paranoia is going to eat us alive if we don't do something. We get the cash, pay off the guy, that leaves us one less thing to worry about."

Franklin was on his feet. "Right," he dusted himself down. "Then let me go and bid adieu to all my beautiful possessions. At least we get to spend one last night together."

"You too," Aaron nodded his head in the direction of Grace's bedroom door. "Get all your

Apple stuff together because tomorrow you say goodbye to it."

"Yeah, of course."

Grace had never been materialistic. She couldn't be. But the things that she had acquired over time; her dance shoes, her box of memories, they became precious to her. Irreplaceable. Her bedroom closed behind her with a soft click. The gentle glow of her fairy lights made her room feel tranquil, safe. But the feelings were fleeting as Grace reached for her rose gold laptop and phone, placing them in the centre of her bed and then rummaging beneath it for their packaging. They were the nicest things she'd ever owned. She considered this as she ran her fingers over her closed laptop, savouring its smooth surface. If her mother were there she'd sharply state that they were ill gotten gains, things which Grace hadn't legitimately earned and the truth of it left a sour taste in Grace's mouth. Hastily she pushed the laptop back into its white box, the same with her phone.

"One day," she told herself. One day she'd own these luxury items again only she'd have bought them on her terms, with money she'd rightfully earned.

*

"Store credit only."

The three words spoken by the shop clerk sent shock waves racing through Grace. She stood on the other side of the immaculate white desk and clenched her fists at her side in an effort to stay calm.

"No," she fought to keep her voice level. "I bought these only the other day. Now I need to return them for a *full refund.*" Grace said the last part slowly, wanting the bespectacled assistant to understand the gravity of the situation. He raised his shoulders within his logo polo shirt in a nonchalant way and offered her a sympathetic smile.

"Store policy, I'm afraid. Returns on cash transactions are store credit only."

"But…" Grace looked down at her receipt, at her neat stack of technological purchases that were patiently resting beside the cash register. The terms were there on the slip of white paper she was holding, clearly written in black type but she'd hoped it was wrong, hoped there would be some way of appeasing the store to make an exception for her.

I'm in danger. I need this money back now.

Would she sound crazy if she revealed the truth? Would the assistant call the police and force her to leave sans devices, sans store credit, worse off than when she first walked in? Her palms grew sweaty as she fretted over her options. She could either take her purchases home or take the store credit. Neither was going to help her make the twenty grand they all needed. Perhaps she could take the laptop home and sell it on eBay, make a loss? But transactions like that required time which was something she was lacking, along with money.

"I'll keep them, thanks," she shoved the items back into the canvas tote bag she'd brought with her as her cheeks began to burn. Could the assistant see her desperation? Did she reek of it?

"Well, if you change your mind just come back with the receipt and we'll sort out your store credit." He was trying so hard to be helpful. To be kind. But he couldn't give Grace what she needed. She hurried out of the store and got caught in a brisk wind. It tangled up in her hair, dusted a discarded plastic bag past her feet. It was a crisp Tuesday morning; the kind of morning Grace would usually have savoured. She normally relished the bite in the air that came with the promise of snow. The previous year there had been heavy snowfall in late February. It had coated the city in several inches of pure white perfection. Franklin had burst into her room at just past five in the morning to tell her. The sun still hadn't risen when the flatmates burst out onto the street, disheartened to see that their steps wouldn't be the first to make impressions on the newly fallen snow. But it didn't matter. They trudged their way to the nearest park and built snowmen and made snow angels until their hands were numb. Grace had laughed so hard that day. As had Aaron. She couldn't remember the last time she'd heard him laugh like that.

"Tell me you had better luck than me," Franklin almost collided with her in the street, still in possession of all the designer shopping bags he'd left with that morning.

"Evidently not," she looked at his bags and then raised up her own.

"They give you the store credit bull crap too?"

"Uh huh."

"Since when were cash purchases non-refundable? God!" Franklin kicked at the kerb in frustration, grimacing.

"So, you kept all your stuff?" Grace tried to peer into his bags.

"What could I do?" Franklin raged. "Be like, hey Mr Thug, I know you wanted your twenty big ones back but how about some Ted Baker vouchers instead? I think that would have gone down like a lead balloon, don't you?"

"We're screwed."

Franklin nodded sadly. "Yep, we're screwed."

"I couldn't even get them to refund me at the dance studio," Grace recalled with a sigh.

"Any chance thug lovin' would want some size eleven loafers? They're barely worn," Franklin offered with a luke warm grin.

"Let's hope Aaron had more luck than us."

"Indeed," Franklin laced an arm round her shoulders and drew her in close, protecting her from the bared teeth of the winter wind. "Let's head home, together. Until we sort all this mess out none of us are going anywhere on our own."

"I meant to ask," Grace ventured carefully, "about the audition yesterday. How did it go?"

Franklin gave a dry laugh. "It went about as well as our little returns expedition. But thanks for asking." He hugged her tight.

"We're not having much luck at the moment, are we?"

"No," Franklin agreed sadly. "We're not."

*

Jasper's mother's voice was shaky on the phone. Hollow. She uneasily rasped out each word as though she were speaking from a script she was struggling to commit to memory.

"He's still not awake. He's the same as he was; stable but still in a coma."

Grace leaned forward as she sat on the edge of her bed, her new iPhone pressed against her ear. Using it felt like an insult to Jasper but what else could she do? It was all set up, her data transferred over and it was non-refundable. She might as well use it. But its surface no longer felt smooth and sleek in her hands; it felt oily. Unstable. Clearing her throat she tried to comfort Jasper's troubled mother.

"He's stable, that's a good thing. I can come and sit with him for a while tomorrow if you like?"

She heard a sharp intake of breath on the other end of the line. "Could you..." Jasper's mother sounded uneasy.

Grace's shoulders sank lower as she feared that she was about to be confronted with a worried mother's rage. What was the usually genially mannered woman about to say?

Could you give that bloody money back before someone else ends up in hospital? You did this, you put my son here!

Did she know?

"Could you read to him?"

Blinking, Grace straightened, certain she must have misheard the request.

"You know all his favourite books," Jasper's mother continued, "could you bring some with you tomorrow and read to him? The doctors have said he should be able to hear us and—"

"Of course." Grace was already mentally taking an inventory of the books stacked up beside the television which belonged to Jasper. She knew his favourites, the ones he loved to lose himself in time and again.

"Thank you," the tremor had returned to Jasper's mother's voice. "Thank you so much."

Grace said her goodbyes and hung up. She was staring at her phone when someone knocked on her bedroom door. When she failed to respond the door handle twisted down and Aaron came in. He wore his concern between his eyes in a thick furrow which seemed to have taken up permanent residence amongst his strong features.

"That about Jasper?" he pointed at her phone.

"Yeah, he's… the same."

"You didn't return it then?" Slowly he joined her on the edge of the bed. She could smell the cologne that covered him only now there was no musky undertone, no stale stench of alcohol and darkened bars that he was trying to conceal.

"They offered store credit," Grace turned her phone over in her hands. "I guess I'll have to eBay it or something."

Aaron delved into his pocket and produced a stack of twenty pound notes. "Guess I shop in places with more relaxed polices." He handed the money to Grace.

"They refunded your guitar?"

"Uh huh."

"Wow," she thumbed through the notes and felt her shoulders begin to fall, weighted down with sadness. Aaron had been so excited about his new guitar. It was something that was definitely going to aid him in the future, not just a frivolous purchase. And now it was gone and yet Grace still had her pink hued devices and Franklin still had his flashy designer clothes.

"So, we've got some of it back at least."

"Yeah." Grace wanted to sound upbeat, positive. But the amount she held in her hands was a long way off the total they had to find.

"We'll figure this out," Aaron's hand closed over hers. "Some way, somehow, we'll find that money."

"We've all got a pair of healthy kidneys, we could auction them off on the black market," Grace quipped. The furrow in Aaron's forehead remained deep.

"Hmm."

"Jeeze, I'm joking," she dug him in the ribs. "We're not about to start harvesting our organs, it hasn't come to that."

"Jasper's lying in a coma," Aaron got up and ran his hands down his face. Exhaustion clung to him. Grace wondered when he'd last slept. "Things have already escalated to a point where they are completely out of hand." He moved away from the bed but Grace threaded her fingers through his and drew him back to her side.

"When did you last sleep?" she wondered softly.

"I don't know," he looked down at his chest in dismay.

"If you want you can sleep in here, make sure you get a good night's rest."

Aaron cleared his throat and looked into her eyes. "I don't... I mean... things are complicated enough right now as they are."

"I said you could *sleep* in here," Grace clarified with a surprised smile. "And I meant sleep. I'm just looking out for you, that's all."

"But it's my job to look after you."

"I'm a modern woman, this whole looking after thing swings both ways."

"Okay then... yeah," Aaron twisted to look back at the sofa pillows pressed against the headboard. "I've always slept better in here. It's... peaceful. But are you sure it's okay?"

Grace wanted to ease all of the creases out of his face, to see him smile. "It's fine, trust me."

"Can I sleep in here tonight?" Franklin burst in wearing a pair of crimson satin pyjamas. His every step was accompanied by the gentle whisper of luxurious fabric. "I mean, I don't want to impose or anything," he was already climbing atop the bed and nuzzling down on the far side.

"What's wrong with your bed?" Aaron asked gruffly.

Franklin opened his mouth wide and yawned sleepily. "I just don't want to be alone. You get that, don't you?"

With a grunt Aaron kicked off his shoes and positioned himself on the opposite side of the bed from Franklin, leaving a narrow crevice between them for Grace. She eyed it with a smile.

Ten minutes later she was in her flannel pyjamas, hair tied back and teeth brushed. Both Franklin and Aaron were breathing deeply, already asleep. Grace nestled herself in between her flatmates, grateful for the steady rise and fall of their chests. She felt comforted on both sides. Lying on her back she looked up at her cracked ceiling and understood why Franklin didn't want to be alone. She wondered if in whatever darkness Jasper was in he felt alone or if he could hear the steady stream of voices that trickled around him? Did their words bring him comfort, remind him that there was someone there? That he was safe?

The question of safety stung. Grace was wedged between two of her best friends in the whole world but was she safe? As she drifted on the edge of sleep she thought of Peter, how they used to steal into one another's beds and hold each other tight as fear shook through their little bones. She'd promised to keep him safe and she'd failed and now Jasper was lying in a hospital bed unable to wake up. Tears rolled down Grace's cheeks as she kept staring at the ceiling, kept tracing the cracks along it until her eyes closed and the darkness claimed her.

13

"Are you awake?"

Peter's voice was thin, like an elastic band stretched too far, about to snap.

"Grace?"

He sounded so close in the darkness. She could feel his presence at her side, his delicate collection of bones curled up against her. "I can't sleep."

Grace exhaled slowly, deliberately. "You need to sleep."

"I can't. I'm scared."

"Peter—"

A door creaked open with a menacing whine and Grace's entire body turned to ice. She felt Peter tense and a whimper escape from his lips. "Is that her?"

"Peter—"

"I took the money from the side. The five pounds. I thought we could use it to—"

Turning quickly Grace clasped her hand against her brother's mouth, promptly silencing him. "She'll know it's gone," she whispered anxiously. "She knows everything."

Grace waited. She listened for another creak, for the sigh of a floorboard conceding to pressure. But everywhere was silent and the darkness was stifling. It felt too thick, as though the room were filled with oil. Where was the crack of moonlight that usually slid in beneath her curtains? She'd use that silvery light to guide her eyes, to help her see the monsters that stalked their little flat after dark.

"I'm scared." Peter mumbled the words against her palm. She understood his fear, felt its icy grip against her own heart. The seconds dragged out as she strained to hear something, anything, over the deafening silence of the endless night. "I took the money for the bus fare," Peter had wrestled free of her grip and was talking fast but keeping his voice low. "You and me, we can leave, together. We can—" He moved so suddenly, so swiftly, that Grace was screaming in shock before he'd fully left the bed. She sat up, mouth wide as she made a piercing sound.

Something had grabbed Peter by the ankles and hauled him out of her bed, had sucked him deep into the darkness.

The screams didn't stop. Grace shook as she cried out, willing the dark to recede. She could see nothing and Peter wasn't calling to her, wasn't squealing. Had he been forever silenced?

"Peter!"

"Grace?" There were hands on her shoulders but they didn't belong to her elfin brother. Drawing in heaving breaths Grace looked around, saw the soft string of lights festooned around her headboard and the frantic faces of both Franklin and Aaron staring at her, each with a hand on her shoulders as she sat up between them, soaked in her own sweat.

"I..." she looked down at herself. Where had Peter gone? What had taken him from her bed? Had she been having a nightmare or reliving a painful memory? She didn't know.

"Grace, you were calling out for your brother," Aaron explained.

"Scared the shit out of me," Franklin added. "I was fast asleep and then you were screaming flat out sat up in bed, it was like something out of the Exorcist."

She felt Aaron punch Franklin behind her back.

"I'm just saying," Franklin continued, "that it was creepy, that's all."

"She was having a nightmare."

"I..." Grace raised her hands and stared at them. She should have held on tighter to Peter, should have kept him quiet, should have—

"I'm getting up," the weight on the bed was disturbed as Aaron climbed out, stretching his arms up over his head.

"It's six in the morning," Franklin sounded genuinely disgusted.

"Got a busy day ahead." Aaron stalked out of the room leaving Franklin staring at Grace with a look of bemusement.

"Your nightmares must be some serious shit."

"Uh huh."

"You know, if you ever want to talk about anything," he pulled her in for a swift embrace. "I'm here for you, Grace, night terrors and all."

"Thanks." She could feel her pyjamas sticking to her. If Aaron wasn't already standing beneath the warm thrust of the shower she'd have hurried out to the bathroom, keen to wash off the remnants of her nightmare. "We should get up," with a sigh she hauled herself out of bed.

"It's six in the morning," Franklin repeated, eyebrows raised.

"Fine, go back to sleep."

He flopped dramatically against the pillows and tossed from side to side. "Dammit," with a grand sigh he sat up again and glared at her. "This bed is tainted now. I'm going to have to get up. Damn you all."

*

It was still dark when Aaron strode through the flat dressed in his thickest coat, a battered guitar case strapped to his back.

"Hey," Grace twisted on the sofa to look at him, her hair still damp from the shower she'd just taken. "Where are you off to so early? It's not even eight."

Aaron tapped the guitar case. "Going to hit the streets and do some busking, see what cash I can muster up." Grace eyed the case, already knowing what was inside. It was a beat up acoustic guitar which Aaron had been given for his sixteenth birthday. The only value it held was sentimental and she knew how it'd pain him to be reduced to playing it again. She gave him a smile which she hoped was more encouraging than pitying.

"That sounds like a good plan. Good luck."

"I'll be back late." Aaron directed his stare at Franklin who was beside Grace on the sofa, nursing a mug of tea and openly ignoring their discussion to focus on the television. "I advise you to try and be more proactive too."

"Who?" Franklin's eyes widened in astonishment. "Me?"

"So far you're the only one who hasn't been able to recoup any of the cash he spent."

"Uh," Franklin pointed a long finger squarely at Grace. "She's in the same boat as me, Banjo Joe."

"She didn't bring the briefcase here. Pull your weight." Aaron stormed out through the door before Franklin could respond.

"Jeeze," settling back against the sofa cushions Franklin looked at the television and gingerly sipped at his tea. "Some people can be so touchy."

*

A frost glazed all of the cars that sat outside the hospital. Grace noticed their ethereal sheen as she hurried towards the main entrance, hands pushed deep into her coat pockets. The temperature had dropped a few degrees. Snow was beginning to feel like less of a threat and more of a promise. It was a relief to reach the manufactured warmth of the reception area even if it did carry the lingering odour of stale urine and disinfectant curdled together like a most unpleasant perfume.

Jasper remained in HDU. The web of wires around him had not receded. Grace nervously clutched her tote bag of books to her side as she approached his bed.

"So you've got the morning shift," a tall nurse commented as she nodded at the vacant plastic chair at Jasper's bedside. "Good thing too, his poor parents are wrung out. I keep telling them to go home and sleep, eat."

"Yeah, I said I'd sit with him today." Grace nervously positioned herself in the chair and reached into her bag. She'd brought with her three books which Franklin had helped her select.

"This," he'd passed her *The Lord of the Rings* first, "he adores this. Did you know he can speak Elfish?"

"I… didn't."

"And this…" he passed her a modern detective novel with a bold coloured cover. "He was half way through this."

"Ooh," Grace plucked a book from the bottom of Jasper's stack. It was more dog-eared than the rest of the novels with a severely rippled spine which made it difficult to read the title. Turning it over she looked at the cover.

"*Peter Pan*," Franklin nodded in her direction. "Yeah, he loves that one. Caught him sat in here watching the Disney movie once."

"Right, okay," Grace pushed the last of the books into her tote bag. "I'm all set up to go and read to him for a few hours."

"You sure you don't want me to come?" Franklin stared at her like a sad puppy who didn't want to be left home alone.

"I think you need to stay here and try to find some more auditions or something. You saw how Aaron was when he left, he's getting mad at you, let's not make it worse."

"But…" Franklin's gaze strayed over to the front door.

"Don't answer the door to anyone," Grace told him sternly. "And if you don't want to be here go and sit in the Starbucks down the street. Pauline works there, she won't mind if you make a flat white last all day."

"You're right," Franklin agreed sadly.

The machines around Jasper beeped incessantly as though desperately trying to relay some coded message. Grace turned to the first page of the book she was holding.

"Hey," she leant as close to the bed as she dared. Jasper was frozen against his pillows, swollen eyes shut. His skin was like wax and Grace struggled to lock eyes with the tube protruding out of his mouth which was breathing for him. It kept his chest rising and falling, his heart beating. "It's me, Grace. I came to read to you for a bit."

Could he hear her voice? Would it bring him some comfort? Or was every word like a flung dagger? Did he blame her for putting him in this bed? Did he blame them all?

"This is one of your favourites," she pulled in a shaky breath, fighting to keep her voice level, contained. "Shall we start?"

Jasper was silent but the machines beeped in response. After pausing to clear her throat Grace began.

"*All children grow up. All except one.*"

*

Franklin met her at the station. She was relieved to see his long outline leaning up against a wall as she approached the surface of the street.

"How did it go?" he immediately fell in step with her.

"No idea. I read him about half of Peter Pan."

For half a street they just walked, letting themselves get swept along with the flow of people. The afternoon had turned grey and the biting cold had not abated. Commuters were swaddled in thick hats and scarfs, burrowing beneath their various layers to try and stay warm. Despite her own thick coat, Grace felt exposed to the cold. It scratched against her nose, her cheeks, and stung her eyes.

"It's freezing out here," Franklin rubbed his gloved hands together. "You should be grateful that I braved the cold to come and be your escort."

"Consider me indebted."

"You're about to consider yourself impressed."

Grace tilted her head in his direction, interest piqued.

"I made two hundred quid today."

"You did?" her surprise fogged before her.

"Uh huh." Franklin started to move faster, his steps infused with new found urgency.

"How?" Grace hurried alongside him.

"You'll see."

He brought her back to the flat, unlocked the front door and eagerly shoved her inside.

"So," clapping his hands together, Franklin took centre stage in their modest living quarters. "When you left this morning I was all uneasy and, let's be honest, scared. But I knew that I needed to make some cash and fast. Aaron was out busking and though it pains me to admit it, no one is going to discover my acting brilliance in the next few days. So, in the interest of being pro-active I went next door."

"You did what?" Grace dropped her bag of books. They landed at her feet with a dense thud.

"Oh no, I didn't do *that*," Franklin waved his hands at her. "I merely asked them for some entrepreneurial advice. They suggested I do some camming."

Grace stared at him blankly.

"Surely you're not *that* sheltered," Franklin huffed at her and strode towards her room. He returned a few seconds later with her laptop. Grace felt sick. "Here," he opened the computer up and turned the screen to face her. It was a still image of Franklin in his Calvin Klein boxers staring suggestively into the camera.

"Franks," Grace clambered to grab her laptop. "What did you do?"

"I did some camming." He made it sound so natural, so normal. "Remove that stick from up your ass, Grace." Franklin cocked his head at her. "Or actually, in the interest of camming, maybe not."

"Franks!"

"Everyone is doing it," he gingerly drew the laptop back towards himself to explain. "See," he tapped the screen. "I strut around in my finery, people join the chat room and make... suggestions, and I get paid."

"Suggestions?"

"Let's just say that I had to bin that cucumber in the fridge."

"Jesus, Franks!"

"Don't be such a prude, Grace. I made money. Cold, hard cash. Money that can go towards our twenty grand pot. Did you make any money today?"

"I..." Grace looked down at the tote bag of books. "No, I was with Jasper. You know that."

"Girls camming make more than guys do," Franklin eyed her with a calculating, level look. "You're pretty, petite, with an innocent look. I reckon you'd do great camming."

"Franks!"

"Just think about it – all you need to do is to strip down in front of your laptop, spank your ass a few times, maybe get the twins out and bam, some horny guy you never need to meet has just given you twenty quid."

"And you used my laptop to do this?" Grace finally reclaimed her computer and snapped it shut.

"Yes," Franklin told her stridently. "The laptop *you* bought with the *stolen* money. I figured that since we can't return it, we might as well use it as an asset."

"Fine," with a sigh Grace handed the laptop back to him. "Are you doing any more camming tonight?"

Franklin pursed his lips and shrugged. "Maybe. I have to admit it was really quite fun. Made me feel rather sexy."

"Well, maybe you can give me an hour with the laptop before you use it again."

"Ooh," Franklin's eyes lit up. "So, you are considering camming? Let me style you, Grace, please. I can make you more diva than demure which is what camming needs."

"I'm not using it for that," Grace blushed as she slid the device beneath her arm and made for her bedroom. "I'm going to apply for any dance job going."

"Right… okay."

She didn't need to turn round to know that Franklin was deflated by her decision.

"I mean, we wouldn't have to tell Aaron about it," his voice was coaxing, like a serpent trying to lure its prey into a false sense of security. "It could be our little secret. And think of the money we could make. We could—"

"I'm going job hunting," Grace entered her room and firmly closed the door behind her. When Aaron came back from his day busking he was likely to have made at least some money. And now that Franklin had discovered camming he looked set to have a source of income. That just left Grace. For too long she hadn't been contributing to the flat and now she needed to make money more than ever. With a sigh she logged into the website she used to search for dance jobs in London. The time for being picky had passed. She'd need to apply for them all.

14

"We're still massively short."

When Grace came out of her bedroom Aaron was stooped over the kitchen counter feverishly counting piles of coins and stacks of notes. His jawline was darkened by emerging stubble and there were dense shadows beneath his eyes.

"Hey."

He flinched when he saw her.

"Oh, hey." There was gravel in his voice. "Did I wake you? Sorry."

"No," Grace smiled thinly at him. Dressed in her pyjamas with her hair madly gathered about her head she probably did look as though she'd been sleeping. But as she lay in bed she just tossed and turned, unable to escape from her net of frantic thoughts and find peace. "I was already up, it's fine."

"Already up?" Franklin's head popped up from the sofa. He was draped in his favourite kimono and his cheek was creased from the cushions he'd been wedged against. "I don't even recognise us anymore," with a groan he stood up, reaching towards the ceiling to twist the knots out of his joints. "I remember when we used to be more nocturnal, none of this up at dawn crap."

"Some of us haven't slept," Aaron stated roughly.

"Well, you could have told me," Franklin flapped his arms around in anger, his silk sleeves billowing out like wings. "I was forced to cat nap on the bloody sofa and let me tell you – that shit isn't comfortable. I feel like I've woken up with the bones of an eighty year old."

"Jasper never complained." Grace said the words sadly, feeling her chest tighten as she released them.

"I know," Franklin hung his head shamefully. "But bloody hell, our living situation is insane. Two bedrooms for four people. We're taking cosy to a whole new level."

"We always intended to figure it out properly," Aaron resumed counting his coins. "We just never got the chance."

"That what you made yesterday?" Grace drifted over to the counter top and peered at the array of wealth spread on it. Even without making the effort to count it all she could see that it was a paltry amount.

Aaron winced as he nodded. "Yep. Slow day. Got a few fivers, pound coins. Some prick kept trying to give me copies of *The Metro*." He ceased counting to slap his hands against the smooth surface. "We're still so bloody short though. Between this and my money from the guitar we're at around seven grand. That's way off what we need."

"I have a contribution to make," Franklin glided over to them. "Put me down for two hundred, chief. And if I push myself today I might be able to come in at around the five hundred mark."

"Doing what?"

Franklin became mildly flustered. "You know… using my substantial charms."

"You mean whoring?" Aaron's nostrils flared. "Franks, don't be going there. I know we need the money but—"

"Camming. I'm camming. You know, on a webcam. Please, as if you don't know. You're a hot blooded male. I bet you've spent money in the past asking some busty blonde to take her g-string off for you."

A growl gathered in Aaron's throat.

"Or maybe not," Franklin hastily added. "But, despite what you may think, camming is safe and can be highly profitable."

"Two hundred?"

"Two hundred big ones," Franklin beamed. "I'm raking it in."

"It's Wednesday," Aaron drummed his fingers against the counter top. "Even if you cammed yourself to death between now and Friday we're not going to hit twenty grand."

"Actually," pressing a finger to his lips Franklin pivoted to stare at Grace. "Pretty girls can make big money camming. Especially if they do a host of firsts."

Aaron shoved him hard in the shoulder. "You can stop that train of thought right now. Grace isn't getting undressed for anyone."

"With the right guidance and styling she could make a grand in a day. I just know it and—"

"I said no. She's not taking her clothes off for anyone, got it?"

"I can speak for myself," Grace raised her chin and met Aaron's heated gaze. As much as she liked him coming to her rescue, so fervently defending her honour, she couldn't help but wonder where these chivalrous tendencies had been when she needed them? The Aaron she'd dated had been distant and at times negligent of her feelings. He couldn't suddenly pretend to have any sort of claim over her body. Grace shifted her gaze from Aaron to Franklin. "I'm honestly not sure I'm up to camming, Franks. I lack your natural confidence. But I'm going to make some money today. Some way, somehow, I'll do it." Emboldened by her own words she returned to her room.

*

Time felt stilted in her bedroom. 9 a.m. arrived reluctantly and with it a host of rejection emails from all the dance jobs she'd applied for the previous night. With a grimace she permanently banished them from her inbox.

Money.

The desire for it was haunting her every thought, every breath. Money was something Grace had never truly had, a luxury that seemed to be reserved for others. At dance school she'd been given a government issued stipend which worked as pocket money for minors in her situation. She saved what she could of it, but dancing was a drain on assets. She needed a new pair of pointe shoes every month, same for tights. The only way to become a professional dancer was to have a steady stream of income from being a part of an established company or going on tour with a show and such an opportunity was the holy grail she was still chasing.

Ducking beneath her bed she reached for her shoe box of memories, her comfort blanket. Popping the lid Grace let the familiar smell of old photographs and faded dreams drift up to her.

"You have poise. You are as your name suggests," her first dance teacher, Madame Ouellette, had told her. "If you push yourself you'll go far in this business. But you'll need to push, even those with natural talent have to push."

For so long Grace had felt like a salmon swimming upstream, desperately jostling for space with all the other fish. At each audition she looked around at a dozen or so faces just like her own; tired and hungry. And each dancer sat in their chairs with a perfect turn out, with arms elegantly resting in their laps, hair tidied back in a perfect bun. When Grace showed her CV, even with her prestigious training she was just another dancer from a good school. There was nothing to set her apart from the others. At least nothing she was willing to share.

Delving deeper into her shoe box, beneath a stack of old photographs Grace found a quartet of tickets she'd stored away for safekeeping. She gave a small gasp of surprise as she drew them out and fanned through them. Four tickets for a May showing of *Swan Lake* at the Royal Opera House. She'd bought them the previous October when they first went on sale, eager to treat her flatmates to a night at the theatre. Back then she'd naively believed that she was just one audition away from her night job and so had keenly dipped into her savings for the precious tickets. And now…

She sighed as she looked at the printed details; row and seat numbers, time of performance. Grace had giddily allowed herself to fantasise about a night out with her flatmates, a night when they'd walk around Covent Garden with their heads held high. She'd show them the beauty of dance and maybe even Aaron would let it in, would begin to understand why she loved it so much.

"Grace," Franklin entered her room without knocking, red faced. He positioned himself beside her on the bed and she could see that beneath his kimono he was sweating. "I'm all warmed up and ready to cam," he looked at her laptop which was open in the middle of the bed. "So, if you don't mind?"

"Sure."

"What are you looking at?" He leant forward to peer at the tickets in her hands. "Royal Opera House, fancy."

"I bought these last year," she tapped the stack of tickets against her palm. "I meant to surprise you guys."

Franklin gently took the tickets into his own possession and scrutinised them more thoroughly. "Lower circle, evening performance of *Swan Lake* by the Royal Ballet. *Very* nice, Grace. I for one would have relished such a night of elegant culture."

"Yeah, well," with a sigh, Grace reclaimed the tickets. "They need to go, need to be sold on. So far I've made absolutely no money for you guys and that has to change."

"Come camming, join the dark side."

"Not sure camming is for me. I'd rather just sell these."

"Really?" Franklin cocked his head at her. "Because you love to dance as much as I love to perform. It's in our blood. You sure you want to sell those?"

Grace looked down at the tickets and thought of Jasper. "Yeah, I'm sure."

*

It was easier to sell the tickets than Grace would have liked. A part of her was naively hoping that she'd meet a dead end but on her phone she found a website where you could swiftly sell on unwanted show tickets. A buyer had snapped up her quartet in under an hour. Feeling oddly dejected Grace stared at the phone in her hand, wondering if that should be the next thing to be auctioned off. Franklin had managed to make her laptop an asset to them. He was currently in the bedroom he shared with Aaron entertaining strangers.

Now all that was left for Grace to do was to post out her tickets to their new owner. Money would reach her account by the end of the week.

End of the week.

It was already Wednesday; the days were falling away like dominoes. If Friday arrived and they were still short on money, what then? Would Grace or Franklin be joining Jasper in hospital? Shuddering at the thought, Grace got up. She needed to go out, to the post office. Pushing open her bedroom door she found the flat eerily still. The curtains were drawn and the lights were off, letting shadows swell throughout the room. Boldly stepping forwards Grace flicked on the main light. Aaron had gone. All that remained of him was the stack of change he'd made the previous day on the counter. Was he busking again? He hadn't knocked on her door to say goodbye. To check that she was okay…

Resenting how much his absence irked her, Grace headed for the bathroom. She needed to shower, to wash off the remnants of her sleepless night and prepare for the new day. She could hear Franklin's voice within his bedroom.

"Oh, you are naughty."

He sounded so assured. And so cheeky. And most importantly, like he was having fun. Grace just couldn't imagine doing that. The only time she wasn't shy was when she danced, then she was able to hide behind the movements, to let each sweeping step say what she never could.

It felt good to stand underneath the shower, to have the hot water sliding down her back. Grace stayed in its warm embrace until her skin turned pink and numb, only then did she begrudgingly climb out and wrap herself in a towel.

"There you are."

Franklin cornered her the second she stepped out of the bathroom.

"This whole camming malarkey is more exhausting than I'd anticipated. I literally can't go again, at least not for a few hours." Pausing to theatrically sweep a hand across his sweat soaked forehead Franklin stared at her, his gaze full of eagerness. "So, what are your plans for today?"

Grace understood his impulse to not want to be alone. "I'm just going to dry my hair and then head out to the post office down the street."

"Then I shall join you," Franklin grandiosely declared.

"Got something to post?"

"No. But I figure neither of us should be walking these mean streets alone."

"You figure right. Give me twenty minutes."

*

It was closer to an hour later when Grace left the flat arm in arm with Franklin. He'd chosen to shower while she dried her hair and smelt strongly of lemongrass and lime. She drunk him in as they journeyed down the stairwell that was the spine of their building and then stepped outside.

Rain.

It dampened the street and gathered in drains. Only…

Grace tentatively stepped beyond the main entrance to their building. The rain drops were hard, icy. It was sleet.

"Ooh," Franklin shivered within his wool coat. "Bloody cold today. You sure you need to go to the post office. We could just head back into the flat and spend the morning with Tina. We're long overdue a Netflix binge."

"It wouldn't seem right without Jasper." Grace sighed and embraced the cold. "Besides, I need to post my tickets."

"You sell them okay then?"

"Yep, someone snapped them right up."

"Wouldn't it be great if that someone was the thug from our doorstep and this Friday he'll return with Aaron's guitar, your tickets and my… I don't know… dignity, and tell us all that it was some deranged prank of his, like in those cheesy Hollywood movies. Jasper will wake up and we'll all go out for a Sunday roast together like some strange dysfunctional family."

"That'd be more functional than my actual family."

"Mine too," Franklin laughed as he walked in step with her. "My dad doesn't even talk to me directly any more, he talks through my Mum. Like, 'Martha, tell our former son he's not welcome here at Christmas.' If I wasn't so emotionally gutted by the man I'd find it hilarious."

"Sounds…" Grace tried to find the right words. In truth it sounded preferable to the treatment she received from her own mother but she couldn't say that. "Sounds harsh."

"Indeed. No one hates you more than family, right?"

"Right."

They were at the post office. Grace's tickets were in an envelope in her bag they just needed to be stamped and weighed. She asked Franklin to go to the counter with them. She couldn't escape the feeling that she'd started to auction off parts of her soul. They were just tickets to a show but they'd represented unity and the former hope she'd once held in her own heart. Now they were going to belong to someone else, someone who would sit in her seats and soak in the beauty of the dance.

When Franklin returned to her and handed her the proof of postage receipt Grace wondered what part of herself she was going to have to sell off next.

"So, you'll soon be a hundred and twenty pounds up," Franklin sounded chipper, encouraging. Grace clung to his side, hoping his enthusiasm would spread across to her.

"We're still a long way off twenty grand."

"But we'll get there," Franklin gave her a quick squeeze. "We have to."

15

"She's going to have to go." Aaron declared hotly.

"No," Franklin leapt up from the sofa and went to the television's side, protectively draping his arms across it. "Absolutely not. We can't sell *Tina*."

"Franks, we have to."

"No!" Franklin tenderly stroked the sleek machine. "She's my lifeline, Aaron. Do you understand? She's *my* music. Without her I'd well and truly lose my shit."

"Well, without the money she could potentially bring in we're all set to lose a lot more than just our shit."

Grace tried to detach herself from the argument. It had been raging since Aaron came home exhausted and defeated just after nine. He'd emptied out the contents of his guitar case on the floor. An ocean of change had spilled out but people hadn't been generous despite the volume. There were a lot of coppers and only slithers of silver. Franklin had baulked at the inclusion of several packaged condoms and a half eaten sandwich.

"People are animals," he'd stated as he fished out the food from the change. "I mean seriously, who gives away a decent sandwich like this?"

"Eat it if you're so desperate," Aaron had snarled. Grace could sense the foulness of his mood infecting the entire flat. Now, an hour later, everyone's moods had descended to their lowest ebb and Tina was about to bear the brunt of it.

"She's going," Aaron stated forcefully. "I've got a guy who will pay us four hundred for her. Cash."

"Four hundred?" Franklin's mouth gaped open in shock. "She's worth ten times that. A hundred times that. Nay, she's priceless!"

"It's a good offer. He's coming by first thing to pick her up."

"No!"

"Franks, this isn't up for discussion!"

"Aaron is right," Grace felt forced to leave the side lines. "We really do need the money, Franks."

Dejected, Franklin let his arms fall to his side, no longer shielding his beloved Tina. "I know we do," he gazed sorrowfully at the vacant black screen of his beloved. "I was just hoping it wouldn't come to this." With a sigh he joined Grace on the sofa. Aaron was standing in the nearest corner, seemingly too tense to sit down.

"Even with this four hundred we're still short," he cracked his knuckles.

"Well, I've got the money from my tickets coming in."

"And camming," Franklin rubbed at his eyes, looking tired. "I can do some more camming. That's fine."

"Short of a miracle that still won't bring us to twenty grand." Aaron stared at his friends, his gaze penetrating. "You sure neither of you can go to your family for help? A loan at least?"

Grace leaned back against the sofa, trying to ease away from Aaron's enquiry. Franklin instantly responded. "Can you?" he pointed an accusatory finger up at his flatmate. "Because you know my situation, my old man doesn't even talk to me anymore, I fail to exist to him, remember? If I call him up and ask for money he'll tell me I've got the wrong number."

"And your mum?" Aaron pressed.

"She's too weak to rebel," Franklin shook his head in agitation. "Always has been. When my dad decided to cut me off she allowed him to sever both parents in one swift blow. Her only MO these days it to keep the peace. She won't help me."

"What if it means keeping you in London? Keeping you from moving back home?"

"I'd sooner live on the streets then go back there."

"Fine," Aaron cracked his knuckles one final time and focused solely on Grace. "Look, I know you don't talk about your family situation but—"

"You've got brothers," Grace told him heatedly. "Ask them for a loan. The only thing stopping you, Aaron, is your pride."

Her words had inflicted a wound. She saw the pain swell in Aaron's green eyes. "Is… is that what you think?"

"You don't want them to think that you've failed, I get it. But Aaron, we're desperate."

"I *know* we're desperate, Grace," there was anger in his voice. Too much. "That's why I'm asking you to step up too. Why can't you ask your mum for help? Your dad? There has to be something they can give you."

Shame and desperation gathered in Grace's lungs and made her feel like she was drowning. Struggling for breath she looked over at Aaron and realised she was crying. Focusing on his blurred image in the corner she took a ragged breath and reminded herself to stay calm, that it was okay, that no one knew the truth. "My mum has nothing. Truly, nothing. And my dad…" she looked down at her hands, afraid she'd already said too much.

"Grace, it's okay," Franklin was rubbing circles against her back with his hand. "You don't need to explain." He locked eyes with Aaron. "None of us do. What drew us together is that we're a collection of broken souls from shitty homes. No need to start forcing open old wounds now, no matter how desperate we are."

"Jasper could have gone to his brother," Aaron ran his hands across his head, looking tormented.

"Yes," Franklin agreed. "But Jasper can't do much of anything at the moment, can he?"

"I know that we need to find the money," Grace stood up, legs shaky. "And we will. We just need to figure a way out of this." She made for her room, keen to breathe in its vanilla laced air. Closing the door behind her she leant against it and stared at her string of fairy lights until the tears stopped and her chest ceased heaving.

*

"Who's coming tonight, to see you dance?" Francesca Collins asked, her black hair pulled back in a severe bun making her face seem plumper than usual.

It was a question Grace had been fielding for years. She continued lacing up her pointe shoes and tried to sound nonchalant. "No one tonight. My dad is working away again."

She'd sold a story to her peers at the dance academy, one that didn't involve her mother. Or Peter. In it she was an only child of a successful airline pilot. Her fantasy father was off flying the world while his little girl danced. But still the questions would come, her fellow dancers seeming to have a thirst for the truth.

"But what about your mum, won't she come?"

"Which airline does he work for?"

"Why have we never seen your dad?"

And, perhaps most pointedly, "Why don't you go home for the holidays, Grace? Why do you stay in the dorms?"

That was when her loneliness bred like mice in an abandoned house, during the weeks when everyone else got to go home. Grace would sit in her tiny room and wish herself Merry Christmas and Happy New Year. The school did what it could; teachers would take her in to their homes for dinner, buy her gifts of new textbooks. They knew the truth, had read it in her file. And Grace knew it was only a matter of time until the curiosity of girls like Francesca got too much and they broke into the HR office and unearthed Grace's file and all the ugly truths it contained.

How would they look at her if they knew? Would they still dance with her? Would she be shunned? Grace saw the pity and fear in her teacher's eyes and hated it. She wanted to be a ballerina, nothing more, completely detached from her dark history. Why wasn't that possible?

*

A succession of sharp knocks echoed against her door. Grace stirred from where she'd been lying face down on her bed. She wiped away the last of her tears and sat up.

"Come in."

Aaron pushed the door open but remained stiffly upon the threshold, his features locked in an apologetic stance. "Hey."

"Hey." There was anger in Grace's heart but she knew it shouldn't be directed at Aaron. He was just trying to help them all, trying to pay off a terrible debt. "Come in," she urged again, patting the space on the bed beside her.

"I…" Aaron took a single step and then hesitated. "Look," he hung his head. "If I said too much in there earlier, went too far."

"Really, it's fine."

"No, it's not." With great effort he lifted his head to stare squarely at her. "I know that you have family issues and I pressed and I shouldn't have and—"

"Aaron, I get it. You're desperate. We all are. Trust me, if I could go to my mum and ask for anything, anything at all, I would have done it. But the woman quite literally has nothing."

"Okay, I get it." He finally accepted her offer to sit down, carefully closing the door behind him as he came in. "It's just..." he stroked his chin and avoided her gaze. "The way you keep it all inside, it's not healthy."

"I know."

"Is it drugs?" Aaron tentatively looked at her out of the corner of his eye. "Is she an addict? Is that what you don't want people to know?"

"Honestly?"

"Honestly."

Grace shuddered out a sigh. "I wish it were that. Really, I do. If she were an addict people could understand."

"Grace," his hands were suddenly upon hers, grasping them tightly. "I would understand *anything*. There's nothing you could tell me that would change how I feel about—" with a wince he cut himself off, the crevice between his eyebrows returning.

With a sad smile Grace freed her hands from his hold. Already he'd changed the way he felt about her, they both had. There was a time when they'd shared a bed, planned to share a life. Only even then Grace didn't dare let him in, didn't dare let him learn the whole truth, every painful morsel of it.

"I'm scared for us," Aaron admitted, voice cracking.

"For... *us*?"

"If we don't find that money by the end of the week who knows what the dick who came to our door might do? Jasper's car just… just malfunctioned, made it impossible for him to steer. How could that happen? Is it a tragic fluke or did someone mess with it, knowing that he was going drive it? Every time I try to sleep these questions swirl in my mind and…" pressing his fingertips against his temple he groaned. "I wish Franklin had never found that damn briefcase."

"You and me both."

"I mean, he's trying to make things right," Aaron turned his head towards the wall. "He's in there, on my bed, where I sleep, gyrating on the webcam for strangers. It makes money though, good money."

"Look," Grace pushed her hands against the soft fabric of her duvet.

Money. It was always coming back to money. If she did some camming, forced herself to be brave, to put herself out there then she could contribute much more than she already was.

"Franks keeps saying that I should do it. That I could make a lot of money and he's probably right, so—"

"I'd face the judgement of my father before I let you do that."

"Aaron," Grace sighed his name. "You don't own me, you never did. If I want to show my body then it's my choice."

"That's just it," there was a fierce light in Aaron's eyes when he looked at her. "You think I'm being protective, jealous even. I'm not. I don't want you to do it because I know that *you* don't want to do it. You're shy, Grace. The only time you come alive is when you dance. Taking your clothes off online isn't dancing, it's not the same. I'm worried that you'd do it and lose some of your innocence."

"I'm not innocent."

It was a mistake people commonly made. With her petite frame, doe eyes, dark hair and pale skin Grace was often assumed to be sweet, naïve, coddled. Her features were soft, welcoming. She was the sort of girl old ladies approached in a supermarket when they couldn't find the tinned peas. She lacked the fierce confidence she saw in the other girls she danced with.

Peter had been the same – all softness, no sharp lines. Strangers would comment that he had a smile which could curdle milk, which Grace always assumed must be a good thing. He was gentle, kind, inquisitive. If he were still in the world he'd help her now in her time of need, the only person who couldn't judge her for her past because it was his too. A shared horror story.

"I get that you absolutely, positively can't go to your mum," Aaron continued. "But then what do we do? Where do we find the money?"

"We get creative," Franklin burst in, clad in his kimono and sweating. He laughed as he panted and pointed at his friends. "I've got some ideas for making money quick. They're crazy, but they might work. I just need to know, are you with me?"

*

No one ever came to watch Grace dance. Eventually she had to plead with her tutors to stop leaving a seat aside for her because it made her heart ache too much to peer out from behind the velvet curtains backstage and notice the abandoned seat amongst the sea of beaming faces.

"But it's customary to leave a seat for each student's family member," Mrs Simmons, the head, had told her curtly. "I know your situation is... unique, Grace, but it's tradition."

"Well, I'm asking you to break with tradition." Grace was fourteen going on forty. She'd seen and heard too much in her short life. She needed the music, the dance, to banish away the demons that gnawed at her every conscious thought. "No, I'm pleading with you," she corrected herself. "Because no one is coming to see me perform, ever. Give the chair to someone who will show up."

"But Grace," the lines in Mrs Simmons' wrinkled face had puckered as she frowned at her young ward.

"You might find someone to come and see you dance."

"I won't. I have no family, Mrs Simmons. You've read my file, please don't make me elaborate."

"No," the old woman leaned back in her chair and something creaked. "I won't make you do that, Grace. I'll give the seat up, if that is your wish?"

"It is."

"But things will change, know that. You might feel alone now but that won't always be the case. We all have our place in the world, you will find yours."

"I've already found it," Grace remarked. "Out on stage."

*

"Define crazy," Aaron urged, his voice bristling with caution.

"I'm in," Grace blurted out before Franklin could elaborate. "Whatever it is you need, I'm with you, I'm in."

16

Thursday morning. It arrived like a punch in the gut. It was almost Friday, almost the deadline.

Grace rubbed her eyes, the action more of a reflex than a necessity. There was no sleep to push away, she'd spent most of the night staring wide eyed into the darkness. The smell of fresh coffee greeted her as she entered the main living area. Aaron was on the sofa, head bowed over his acoustic guitar as he carefully tightened the strings.

"Franks has already headed out," he said without looking up.

"He has?"

The day was still achingly early, the sun having yet to break across the horizon. Grace wandered towards the kitchenette. She had a plan for the day ahead although it felt more like a compulsion. Perhaps it was the ever present threat of danger which clung to her back or the talk of family, but she intended to do something she hadn't done in many years. She was going to visit her mother.

"He was muttering and flapping his hands about, going on about some plan and how we both need to be here for seven when he gets back."

"Seven," Grace nodded. "Got it."

"What are your plans for the day?" Aaron strummed against his freshly adjusted strings and a single, rich note vibrated through the flat.

"Job hunting."

Why lie? The question pricked like a needle at the base of the neck. She assured herself that she had to lie, because if Aaron knew the truth of where she was going he'd insist on coming along and she couldn't have that.

"Ah, okay." Several more notes joined the lingering echo of the first. "Good luck with that."

The money for the ballet tickets had yet to go into Grace's account. It had been the second thing she'd checked on her phone when she'd got it, the first being the times she could go and see her mother. Thinking about the money, how much of it they were still lacking, made Grace feel like she was drowning in despair. When the knock came at the door the following night it was becoming increasingly unlikely that they'd be able to return the twenty thousand pounds they'd spent. What then?

"We'll figure something out."

Grace had been so lost in thought that she hadn't seen Aaron abandon the sofa and come over to her. He wrapped an arm against her shoulders and as she turned to look at him she felt the tightness in her jaw, every muscle in her body was overly clenched. She was afraid.

"I know it's tomorrow," he held her against his chest and Grace breathed him in, hoping his scent could perform its old magic. Just his presence used to be enough to lift her out of a dark mood. But things changed. Aaron started to become the source of her unhappiness rather than a solution to it. Life could be cruel that way.

With a swift sideways step Grace escaped from him, unable to fall into old habits, especially considering what lay ahead for her that day.

"We'll get through this," Aaron stared at her, forcing a smile. "Come hell or high water we'll find that damn money."

"Yeah."

"And Jasper... he'll..." he clearly wanted to say that he'd be fine but he couldn't. None of them could. Each day that Jasper didn't wake up felt like a day where he was getting dragged closer to death, moving further out of their reach.

"Make lots of money today," Grace went onto her tiptoes to give Aaron a brisk kiss on the cheek. She saw the skin reddening beneath her soft touch and smiled slightly to herself.

"You too," he replied as his fingertips strayed to his cheek and he watched her return to her bedroom.

*

"Sign in here," the stocky receptionist was sliding a clipboard towards Grace. "Print your name, arrival time and then sign."

Grace looked at the clipboard, at the biro in her hand. She'd made it this far. Throughout her entire train journey she'd felt numb. Three changes on the tube had taken her out of London, through green fields stiffened with frost. Now she was standing in a stark reception area, the air smelt overly sterile and the plastic chairs that were gathered around a coffee table were the saddest shade of grey.

"Miss?" The receptionist frowned at her from the other side of the desk, the Plexiglas partition she hid behind doing nothing to hide the disdain etched into her face.

"Sorry, right," Grace hastily filled in her details and pushed the clipboard back through the mailing slot to the woman.

"Wait a few minutes," she was told. "Then someone will be along to take you through."

Grace took a pew on the nearest grey chair and began to wait. Glancing over the out of date magazines fanned out on the coffee table she tried to assess how long it had been since her last visit. Three years? More?

It had been raining during her last visit. She remembered that. Grace deliberately didn't bother with an umbrella, wanting her mother to see the raindrops that clung to her, that had soaked her clothes and hair. Not that her mother noticed anything. She never did.

A door opened with a hiss and a tall silver haired man in a pin stripe suit strode through the reception paying no attention to Grace but nodding briefly at the stocky woman behind the glass. She curled her red lips up in greeting and then once he was out of sight her face promptly fell into its regular sour stare.

The seconds stretched by and Grace yearned to leave. All she'd done was sign her name. She'd made no commitment to stay, no promise. There was nothing holding her in the grey chair except her own will. She looked back towards the main doors and the car park she'd walked across as a cold wind snapped at her. Closing her eyes she mentally plotted the route back to the train station. If she left now she could be home by lunch, with no one any the wiser. She could just head back and—

Another hiss and an orderly was standing in a nearby doorway, his body angled towards the grey seating area. "Grace?"

"Oh, hi," she nervously got to her feet and smoothed her hands down the front of her coat.

"Do you want to follow me?" The orderly had a kind face and seemed vaguely familiar. Grace grabbed her bag and started following him along a corridor, their quick steps bouncing off the tiled floor. "We've not seen you here for some time," he turned briefly to look at her, flashing a smile. "It will do your mother the world of good to see you."

Grace wanted to laugh. She wanted her laughter to replace the echo of her steps, for it to bounce off the walls and come back to her. The likelihood of her mother being pleased to see her was less than slim to none. The orderly's words set in like a rot, spreading through her, and by the time they reached the end of the long corridor Grace wanted to go back. She'd made a mistake coming there. Fear had made her weak, she'd reverted to being a stupid girl just wanting to see her mother and she was more than that now, she'd been more than that for such a long time.

"Here we are." The orderly paused at the door and turned to assess Grace. She knew this door well, had stood before it many times before. On occasion, especially when she was younger, this was the point at which she'd turn back, unable to deal with what lay beyond it.

Grace was fourteen the first time she saw her mother in the institution. Her social worker had joined her and together they'd stood at this same door and peered through the glass. Grace's mother had been sat in a large open room, surrounded by people all wearing the same hospital gowns. Her mother was looking towards a window, sunlight warming her face. For a moment, Grace felt reassured that she could walk through the door, that everything would be okay. Then her mother started screaming, pulling against the restraints on her wrists that bound her to her chair and Grace felt the serenity of the corridor, the institute, falling away. Beyond the door chaos reigned. Turning, Grace ran back towards the reception area as her social worker shouted after her but she didn't turn round, she'd already seen enough.

"I know this is hard," the orderly's hand was frozen on the door handle, not going further until Grace had approved him to do so. "You coming here today is really brave. Your mother has been making progress and I'm sure that seeing you will—"

"Okay." Grace cut him off. She had never been comfortable with the way that the doctors and orderlies talked about her mother, in soft tones like she was delicate, like sharp words could damage her. But then they hadn't seen the side of her mother that Grace had, the inner monster that lurked beneath her skin. Had they seen that they'd never be able to speak of her with any soft inflection in their voices. "Let's just get this over with."

The orderly opened the door and Grace was granted access to what was commonly known as the 'day room.' A place where patients could sit on sofas, play board games, read pre-approved books and meet visitors as and when they had them. The far wall was floor to ceiling glass offering a scenic vista across the grand gardens which stretched away from the main building. In the summer the gardens were a rainbow of colour as a variety of flowers bloomed but the grounds, like everything else, were currently held in winter's grip. A barren, icy wasteland was all that was revealed beyond the windows, bordered by neat little footpaths and the occasional stone bench.

"She's just there," the orderly pointed to a cream leather sofa on which sat a frail woman in a hospital nightgown and a fluffy blue robe. Her head was bowed as she studied her hands in her lap, the hair gathered in a bun at the base of her neck wispy and greying.

"She looks so…" Grace wasn't sure which word she was looking for. Old? Frail? Unassuming? There was nothing to fear in the weak woman sat on the sofa. Yet Grace sensed the monster. It was the reason her feet remained locked in place, refusing to propel her forwards.

"It's alright, she's had her meds this morning, she's pretty sedated."

"Okay," Grace took in a lungful of sterile air and forced herself to move.

"I'll be right over here," the orderly pointed to a nearby group of patients who were playing draughts together.

Grace walked right over to the cream sofa and lingered awkwardly beside it, looking down at her mother. "Hey," she heard the tightness in her own voice, the fear. "It's um... me. Mum, it's Grace."

Slowly the gown clad woman raised her head. Pale blue eyes were sat amid shadows and thick lines, lines which Grace remembered being forged with each episode, each slap, each shriek.

"Who?" the woman parted her thin lips and spoke. There was a rasp to her voice but it was unmistakably her mother's. Grace swallowed and reminded herself that the woman was in a mental institution, on medication, completely unable to hurt her any more.

"Grace, Mum, your daughter. Jeeze, how doped up are you in this place?"

"No," her mother shook her head stubbornly, her thin eyebrows gathering together as they set in a firm line. "Where is Peter?"

"Shit," Grace whispered the expletive through clenched teeth. "So, we're playing that game again are we? You still trying to pretend that you're bat shit, that you can't remember what happened to your own son."

"Peter," her mother's eyes widened, "where is my son, my beautiful boy? Why does he not come to see me?"

"I'm here," Grace clasped a hand to her chest. "Me, Grace. Your daughter, your only living child. Peter will never come and visit because he's dead, remember?"

"Oh, Peter, he must come." Her mother was growing agitated. Grace suppressed a scream.

"You know what? This act is getting seriously old now. You perform it every time I come. Everyone knows what you did, stop pretending and actually start trying to be a parent to the one kid you have left."

"Peter, where is Peter?"

What had Grace expected? That her mother would suddenly be lucid and embrace her with open arms? As always it was about mind games, even now when she remained behind lock and key. Her mum still had to play, still had to try and mess with her children, manipulate them.

"Peter is dead!" Grace was done with the façade. She'd come here in the vain hope of seeing the only family she had and she was regretting that decision in epic quantities. "He's dead, Mum. Don't pretend you've forgotten since you're the one who drowned him in the bath tub, remember?"

"Peter, Peter, my sweet boy, where is he?"

Grace allowed the rage within her to take control. "You discovered he'd stolen five pounds from your purse, you took him outside in the rain until he was soaked then brought him in and slapped him until he was red raw. All the time he and I were both screaming. Then you struck me so hard you made my nose bleed, knocked me out and then you went to run a bath. I came to, went looking for you and found you in the bathroom with Peter under the water, he'd already turned blue."

"Peter, Peter, he'll come, he'll come to see me."

"And to finish it all off you tried to blame me," Grace smeared away the tears that had slipped down her cheeks. "The police arrived and you sat on the floor holding Peter and howling like a goddamn dog. And then you pointed at me and said, 'it was her, she did it, all of it.' I remember that. I remember you trying to condemn me for all that you'd done."

"Peter, where is Peter?"

"I think we're done here," the orderly gripped Grace's shoulders and began drawing her back from the sofa, from her mother.

"He's dead because you killed him," Grace yelled as the vast room fell quiet around her. "I lost a brother and a mother that day. You fucking bitch. To think that I came here thinking you might actually *want* to see me. Might actually act like a bloody mother and care about my life, care about *me!*"

"Right, let's go." Grace let the orderly take her away, let him remove her from the room, from her mother who was now sobbing as though she were the one who'd been grievously wounded. She'd been seeking comfort and all she'd found was damnation.

*

"It's okay." The orderly told her for the third time as Grace sat in a side office sipping on a plastic cup of vending machine tea. "Visits like this are hard and it's easy to understand why you feel the way you do about your mother."

"It's the pretending," Grace sighed and looked down into her cup. "It's the pretending I can't stand. She's kept it up all these years."

"She tells the doctors she can't recall what happened to your brother that day."

"She's lying," Grace put down the cup as her mouth filled with bile. "She spent years getting good at it, convincing people that me and my brother had fallen, walked into a door. Any pain we felt was inflicted by her hand."

"In some cases people may truly have forgotten what happened to them," the orderly suggested. "The doctors feel that her memories about Peter and yourself are all suppressed."

"She's just lying to avoid prison." Grace had always known it. Her mother was crazy but not in the way that needed to be sectioned, more in the way of someone who needed to be put down because her crazy made her dangerous. She was fanatical about religion, about her own neurotic theories such as the rain being God's tears. And her mother was cruel. She'd regularly beaten her children senseless for doing something she viewed as abhorrent like wetting the bed or crying after a nightmare.

"Grace, do you want to speak to your mother's lead doctor? Might that help you find some closure over the situation?"

"I'm still classed as her next of kin, right?" Grace tipped her head towards the orderly.

"Right. Sole living relative, that's you."

"And because she's not of sound mind I can make suggestions about her care? Allow certain treatments?"

"Grace, I—"

"Slap a DNR on her file and revoke her daytime privileges, she needs to be kept in her room at all times."

"Look, Grace, I know you're angry but—"

"I'll sign whatever I have to just… just make her suffer," Grace held back most of her tears. "She took him from me. He was all that was good in the world."

"How about this?" the orderly returned her discarded cup of tea to her hands and crouched down to be on her level. "You walk away from her and forget about this place, your mother, and you go on living your life. Like it or not, she's mentally unwell, this is where she needs to be. She's getting the help she needs, you might not see it but she's making improvements."

"She killed my brother."

"It's tough but you need to be the bigger person. Try not to let this haunt you, try to live your life as best you can."

"I…" Grace's mind strayed to Jasper.

"Sometimes we all need family, I get that."

"No," Grace shook her head and got up. "I… I have a family. I just…" she felt light headed and hot. The walls of the small room were closing in, she needed to get out of there. "I need to go."

"You're welcome back here any time," the orderly assured her as he walked her back through to reception.

Grace was zipping up her coat and positioning her bag against her shoulder. "Don't worry," she told him confidently, "I won't be back. Ever."

17

It was snowing. Flakes drifted down from pewter clouds like confetti. Grace drifted along the streets of the city, wandering aimlessly. Each time a stranger slammed into her shoulder she mumbled an apology, always keeping her head down.

Visiting the institution housing her mother had been a mistake, she knew that now. Did she go there to find closure? Security? Instead she found the lament of a crazed woman forever refusing to accept responsibility for what she'd done.

Hours passed. Grace kept walking. She felt like a ghost, transient and unattached. The clouds overhead darkened, night was drawing in. The cold had penetrated her coat, frozen her fingers. She barely registered the dull pulsing in her pocket. In a trance she reached for her phone and answered the call.

"Hello?" Her voice didn't sound like her own. She sounded broken, defeated.

"Grace!" Franklin was shrill on the other end of the line. "Where are you?"

"Um…"

"It's seven, Grace. I told you to be back here by then so I want to see you walking through the front door in the next thirty minutes!"

"Um."

She didn't even know where she was. Grace looked up at the brilliant glare of a store front advertising designer ladies' shoes. The display was familiar. She took a breath, then another. Covent Garden. She was in Covent Garden. Grace had no idea how she'd ended up there but she knew that just a few more paces and she'd find the Royal Opera House and the eternally pirouetting ballerina in a bubble against the wall. Why had her legs brought her there? To torment her further after a brutal day?

"I'm heading back now," she told Franklin confidently.

"Where are you?" He sounded so concerned, almost like a brother. Grace wanted to weep. Clearing her throat, she forced her voice to remain level.

"Auditions. I've been at auditions."

"Ah, okay. Any joy?"

No. None.

"We'll see."

"Well, get back here soon, Grace. I'm worried about you." Franklin hung up and Grace looked down at her phone as she slowly withdrew it from her ear. She had a family, people who cared. And

Jasper was going to wake up, he had to wake up. Grace couldn't lose another brother.

*

"Finally!" Franklin declared, before Grace had even fully walked in through the door. She sprinkled fresh snow across the floor with each step as she shook off her coat. "You had us worried sick."

Aaron was on the sofa staring at the wall. Tina was gone.

"Sorry, I got held up with auditions." With a grunt Grace removed her boots and then went towards the kitchenette, in need of a hot drink to fight off the chilled numbness which was spreading through her bones.

"I said seven," Franklin rolled his eyes and joined her by the kettle. "My big plan, I thought you'd be uber keen to hear it."

"I am."

"You look terrible."

Grace flinched at the brutal honesty of the comment. She'd yet to check her reflection. Were her eyes raw from shedding too many tears, her cheeks blotchy from the bite of the cold and the pain of her despair?

"You look positively frozen," Franklin hurried away from the kitchenette and returned a few seconds later with his largest, fluffiest dressing gown which he draped around Grace's shoulders. "Wisp of a thing like you needs to wrap up before going out in the snow."

"It's snowing?" Despite walking around in it all afternoon it hadn't quite sunk in that it was snowing outside. "We'd usually go to the park."

"At midnight," Franklin noted with a small nod of agreement. "We'd take torches and try to be the first to make our footprints in the snow."

"We never were though," Aaron commented from the sofa. "There was always some drunk or a couple of cats who'd beat us to it."

"We tried though," Franklin's eyes shone with the memory. "The fun was in the trying."

The trio fell silent, the only sound filling the flat was the gurgle and hiss of the boiling kettle. Grace knew what the others were thinking, the reason for their sudden introspective contemplation. If Jasper were there, if they weren't living in fear of a reprisal over stolen money, they'd all be preparing to head out at midnight. By the time she'd got home the snow was falling thick and fast, there'd soon be a glorious covering over the city turning London into a winter wonderland.

"What's this big idea of yours then?" It was Aaron who broke the silence. Grace made them each a fresh mug of tea and then joined him on the sofa. He was sat completely upright on the edge of the seat, not settled back amongst the cushions. And he kept staring at the wall, at the glaringly vacant space where their beloved television had been.

"Well, now you're both here I suppose I can divulge," Franklin perched on the empty television stand. The piece of furniture looked so forlorn, so out of place now it was no longer able to perform its sole function.

"You sold Tina?" The words slid from Grace's mouth before she'd even had a chance to sip at her tea.

"Yeah," Aaron's response was flat. "We had to. Got four hundred for her."

Franklin extended a hand towards Grace and bowed his head. "Before you ask, no, I'm not yet at a point where I can talk about it."

"Oh, Franks, I—"

"But I'm not the only one who made sacrifices today on an epic scale," Franklin's head shot up and Grace felt her heart patter nervously in her chest, upping its beats per minute. Did he somehow know where she'd gone? Had he followed her? Had Aaron? Shame bubbled in her stomach, toxic and painful. She didn't want them to know the truth, didn't want them to fear that some of the darkness that was within her mother had been passed onto her. Because it hadn't, had it?

Peter was always so good, so pure. When Grace cried in the night he offered her his hand despite the consequences of being caught doing so. If her mother found them connected via their little hands between their twin beds she'd beat them both and maybe break a finger or two. School would be told it was an accident. They were always getting into accidents.

"So clumsy, my twins," their mother would share with her Hollywood smile, perfected and false yet no one saw through it. She always looked immaculately polished in her knee length dresses and beige mac. Her heeled shoes made every step clip, her curled hair gave her the demure elegance of a fifties housewife. When people saw Grace's mother they saw a single mum doing her best. They never questioned her, never showed concern over the marks on her little children. Not until the day when the police came and the truth bled out as Peter turned deathly cold.

Did she kill the wrong twin?

In her darkest moments this was the question that found Grace. If Peter was light then she must be dark. Had he lived and she died would he have made more of his life? Would he have fought harder than she had to truly punish their mother? Had he—

"I sold my guitar."

Aaron's confession slapped Grace back into the moment. She stared at him, stunned, as he kept his focus towards the wall.

"You... you what?"

"I sold my guitar." With a grunt he cracked his knuckles. "My acoustic one. I mean, busking wasn't proving all that fruitful and I got two fifty for her so—"

"You've had that *forever*," Grace blurted.

"Sacrifices, Grace," Franklin gazed at her sadly. "We're all having to make them if we hope to make the twenty grand."

A lump formed in Grace's throat making it impossible for her to keep drinking her tea. "But..." she looked down at her mug. The first time she'd met Aaron he'd been playing his guitar in a pub. Music was a part of him, a ribbon wrapped around his soul, without it he'd surely fall apart? "The band," she wished he'd turn to look at her, that he wouldn't be ashamed of the hurt she'd find in his eyes. "What about the band?"

"I'm still in the band. I'll borrow one of the other guy's guitars when we play a gig."

But it wouldn't be the same. Grace knew it wouldn't. That would be like dancing in someone else's shoes.

"Well, if my plan comes off okay you might be able to buy your beloved back," Franklin stood up. "And I promised Tina she'd return one day."

"What is this plan?" Grace asked.

"Come." Franklin was on his feet and hurrying towards his bedroom. Grace and Aaron followed. In the centre of the bed were two food trays and madly strewn around them were dozens of packets of paracetamol and several bags of sugar.

"Franks…" Aaron lingered uneasily in the doorway. "What the hell is this? This better not be the part where you try to get us all in on your suicide pact."

"No, no, no," Franklin fanned a dismissive hand through the air and dropped onto the edge of the bed, beaming proudly at his strange collection of items. "It took me *forever* to get all this stuff. Did you know you can only buy one box of pain killers at a time? I had to haul ass to every damn chemist and Boots within a five mile radius of here."

"So…" Grace approached the bed, brow furrowed. "What's it all for, Franks?"

"Drugs."

He said the word with such pride that for a second Grace thought she must have misheard him.

"What?" Aaron's growled response told her that she'd caught the word perfectly accurately. "Drugs? Are you out of your fucking mind, Franks?"

"Not drugs drugs," Franklin clarified with a grin. "Faux drugs. Pain meds and sugar to be precise," he leaned forward to tap the nearest box. "All we do is grind them up together using my Jamie Oliver flavour shaker and a pestle and mortar," he pouted in Aaron's direction, "and to think you said I'd never find a use for them." With a shudder he straightened and returned to his plan. "Anyway, we grind them up good so that they look like a *powder*," he was glancing up at his friends, waiting for them to catch up.

"You think you can pass this off as coke?" Aaron was still in the doorway, refusing to venture deeper into the room. "That's ridiculous, even for you, Franks."

"Ridiculous, no," Franklin shook his head. "Ingenious, yes. There's a rave happening tomorrow night in an abandoned warehouse, a real underground event. I say we go and offload some of our homemade powder and make some cold, hard cash in the process."

"That's illegal," Aaron objected. "Even though it's not really coke, passing it off as coke is illegal. Besides, people will notice."

Franklin rolled his eyes. "Please, they won't. They'll be so baked off the cocktail of whatever else they've taken that night they won't notice. And even if they do, we'll be like Batman, in and out. By the time anyone wises up we'll be long gone with their money."

"I don't like this."

"You said tomorrow," Grace glanced anxiously between the trays and boxes of pain killers. "But the guy is returning tomorrow night. That's too late."

"Actually, we were talking about this before you got back," Franklin glanced round her to stare at Aaron who was cracking his knuckles anew.

"I'm going to ask for an extension."

"*What?*" Grace felt dizzy. Surely Aaron wasn't suggesting that he was going to try and reason with the man who'd come to their door and *threatened* them? "Aaron, no, you can't do that!" "Do you have a better idea?" He roared the question at her and Grace genuinely wished that she did. But she didn't even have an idea to put forward, she'd spent her day wallowing in her torrid history, allowing the tide of past turmoil to pull her under. And for that she'd made no money and now Aaron was going to have to take an epic risk.

"You two go to the rave, offload as much of that fake powder as you can." Aaron was withdrawing from the doorway. Grace tried to lure him back with her gaze but he wasn't even looking at her. "I'll take care of the guy. If he wants his money he'll wait another week. He's got no choice."

A gasp squeezed out from behind the lump in her throat and Grace looked frantically at her other flatmate who was busying himself with stacking up all his boxes of pain killers. "Franks, he can't do this. He can't put himself in danger like this. What if—"

"What if our thuggish collector brings along a friend? Or two? I've already been over this with him and he's resolute, Grace. You know how he gets. He's going to give the guy what we already have and plead for an extension."

"And if that doesn't work?"

Franklin stopped stacking to press the heel of his left hand against his eyes. "Christ, Grace. I don't fucking know. I called Jasper's mum this afternoon and there's no change. *No change.* He needs to wake up soon else he risks all sorts of long term problems and—"

Grace saw tears glistening upon Franklin's cheeks. She hurried to his side and hooked her arms round his waist, leaning against him. "He's going to wake up."

"We don't know that."

"We do." Grace squeezed him tight. "We're going to keep thinking the best until we're faced with the worst, okay?"

"Okay?"

Franklin turned and fully embraced her. "I miss Tina," he mumbled into her hair.

"I know."

*

The rest of the evening was spent emptying tablets and grinding their contents together with spoonfuls of sugar. Grace doubted if the final article looked convincing enough even though she had no real world comparison to make. The only time she'd seen cocaine was on television.

"You're so sheltered," Franklin had chortled when she'd admitted this. "As long as it's a white powder we're good."

Even Aaron helped. They made a production line where one emptied tablets, one added sugar and another ground it all up. Then everything was deposited into clear sandwich bags.

"Is this really illegal?" Grace asked as she sealed up another bag of fake powder.

"Pretty sure it is," Aaron confirmed.

"Well, let's pretend it isn't," Franklin suggested. "We'll just feign ignorance if caught. It's not like in school we were told not to make fake drugs, we were just told not to take real ones. There's arguably a blurred line over the legality of it all. Besides, we won't get caught."

"How can you so sure?" Grace had to keep stopping to wipe the sweat from her palms. The thought of police intervention made her extremely nervous. If they were caught then someone would read her file, know about her past, maybe even jump to illogical conclusions. She envisioned herself in handcuffs with a smug faced officer stating that the apple doesn't fall far from the tree.

"It's an *underground rave*," Franklin stated slowly. "Figuratively at least. It means only certain people even know that it's happening."

"Certain people?" Aaron raised an eyebrow.

"Cool people."

"And you don't worry that someone will tip off the police?"

"They haven't before."

"So you've been to these raves before?" Grace wondered, pausing for another swift sweat removal against her jeans.

"Few times," Franklin gave a modest shrug.

"And you never thought to take us along?"

Franklin squirmed as she looked at him. "These raves, they can be… intense." He glanced to Aaron for support but got nothing. "I'll prep you before tomorrow, you'll be fine."

"You think I'm too sheltered to enjoy something like that?"

"Not sheltered, no," Franklin pursed his lips and gave his next choice of words ample consideration.

"More like, you're too sweet. These raves can be raucous, primal. People can behave… indecently."

"You think I'm sweet?"

"Grace, you're the sweetest," he stopped emptying his pile of pills into a bowl to playfully nudge her. "You're seriously one of the nicest people I know."

Grace clung to the comment and hoped it was true. It was exactly how she'd always felt about Peter.

18

"Ready?"

Franklin popped his head around her bedroom door but Grace was too busy casting a critical eye over her reflection to notice him. She stood in front of the full length mirror she'd found at a second hand market for a more than reasonable twenty pounds. Its gold flourishes had been tarnished by time but it was still easily the grandest item in her bedroom. Nervously tugging on the hem of her very short denim skirt she took in her overall appearance. Her legs were clad in pink neon fish net tights which she'd previously worn for a show, her stomach was exposed thanks to the tight fitting crop top she wore, another relic from a previous production.

The outfit had not been of her choosing, it had been Franklin's. An hour earlier he'd swept into her room and raided every drawer and cupboard until he found something he deemed satisfactory. Grace's hair was loose, falling in waves to her shoulders and her eyes were overly darkened with smoky makeup.

"I said are you ready?" Franklin came and joined her in front of the mirror. In his ripped jeans and fishnet vest top he looked lean and dangerous. Grace tugged once more on the worryingly short hem of her skirt.

"I… guess."

"One last thing," Franklin plucked a marker pen from his pocket and cupped Grace's chin, tilting her head up towards the ceiling light.

"Franks, what is this?"

"Neon highlighter. Don't worry, it's for faces and will wash off before you know it. But we…" he puckered his lips in concentration, "we need it. It's important we blend in tonight."

When he released her Grace nervously looked at her reflection. He'd drawn neon yellow stripes along her cheeks making her look like a warrior about to go to war with disco. It was a strong look, but also a strange one. Seeing herself dressed for a rave reminded Grace of the times she'd steal out of her dance academy to go to nightclubs with the other girls. They'd all wear too much makeup and heeled shoes with too steep a gradient, anything to make themselves look older than their seventeen years. She felt like that now, like she was putting on a costume in an attempt to be something she wasn't.

"You look perfect," Franklin commented as he slid the neon marker across his own cheeks. "We're totally going to nail things tonight."

"Hmmm." Grace's focus strayed to her bedroom door. Whilst she and Franklin were heading out

Aaron was staying in. He was going to face the man who'd show up demanding payback alone. The thought made her stomach dip as though she were plunging down the first drop on a rollercoaster. "Maybe we should leave it."

"What? No!"

"I don't like leaving him here alone."

"Grace, he insisted. And you know how pig headed he can be, it's pointless to argue with him."

"I know, but…" she couldn't risk crying, couldn't risk smearing the mountains of makeup on her face. She already felt the weight of it suffocating her skin. Grace normally left the flat wearing only a slick of lipstick and a hint of mascara. Heavy makeup had always been reserved for shows, when she'd be beneath the unforgiving stage lights and had no choice but to pile on concealer and foundation else risk appearing like a ghost to the audience.

"He'll be here when we get back," Franklin capped his marker and returned it to his pocket. His hands settled on Grace's shoulders. "Aaron is the toughest guy I've ever met, and believe me, I've had my fair share of macho types. He's going to give the guy all that we currently have and cut a deal. If the guy is that desperate for the money he'll accept, simple."

"But what if he hurts Aaron?" Grace could scarcely speak. Aaron wasn't the kind of guy to readily feel pain, he'd so often hide it beneath a grunt or a mask of indifference. But she'd seen him in more fragile moments, seen through the cracks in his manly façade and glimpsed the vulnerable soul within.

"Aaron will be fine."

"Franks—" Grace pushed out a sob as a cough. Jasper was already in a coma. What if they returned from the rave and Aaron was gone, only to show up several days later as a floating body in the Thames? "I can't lose him," she crumpled against Franklin's almost bare chest. "I just can't."

"I know Grace, me neither. But he's got to do this, we have no choice, we simply don't have the money. We've barely scraped ten grand together."

Aaron wasn't in the main living area when they left Grace's room.

"Where is he?" she instantly demanded, spinning around.

"He's probably holed up in his room," Franklin looked at the closed door just behind them. "I'd leave him be, Grace. He doesn't want to face us, not now."

"No," Grace stormed towards the door. "I need to see him before we leave."

"Grace—"

She didn't bother to knock, just burst straight in. It was dark inside. The curtains were open, allowing silver threads of moonlight to seep in. There was still thick snow on the ground which made the night feel brighter than it actually was. Aaron was at the window, head bowed as he looked down at the city.

"Hey," Grace hurried over to him. "Weren't you going to say goodbye before we left?"

Aaron turned, his expression as dark as the shadows which clung to the corners of his room but as he looked Grace over a slight smile tugged on the corners of his mouth. "Jesus, what do you look like?"

"It's all Franks."

"I can tell."

"He says that this outfit will help us blend in."

"Blend in where? The eighties?"

Grace laughed. It felt strange to laugh in the gloom of not just the room, but their situation; but it was also liberating, like releasing a caged bird. "Thanks. Now I don't feel the least bit paranoid about going out."

"Make sure you wrap up," Aaron looked down at her legs, at her short skirt, and then his gaze lifted to her bare midriff. "It's cold out. You risk catching your death in that, it's basically lingerie."

"It's not."

"It is." He turned away from her and scratched his fingers along his jawline. "Can't you put some jeans on or something?"

"You'd have to refer that question to Franks."

"So, he's bloody Gok Wan now is he?"

"Hasn't he always been our resident stylist?"

"I don't like this." Aaron dropped his hands to grip the window sill.

"I'll change as soon as I'm back."

"No, all of this. The rave. The guy. It feels… messy."

"That's because it is messy."

"I don't want you to get hurt out there."

Grace laced one of her hands over his. "I don't want you to get hurt in here."

"I'm strong."

"So am I."

"Grace—"

"Just promise me you'll be here when I get back."

Aaron hung his head.

"Please, promise me, I need to hear you say it."

He turned and embraced her, pulling her tight against his chest and then leaving a lingering kiss upon her forehead. "Fine. I'll be here when you get back, I promise."

*

Grace had never been to a rave before. She found the music played at such events too fast, too wild. People danced to it as a reaction, there was nothing co-ordinated about their movements and she found that disorientating and exhausting. But Franklin was a seasoned raver. He'd led them to the right tube station, staunchly marched through the snow towards the abandoned warehouse that was to be their destination for the evening.

Even tucked inside her thickest coat Grace was cold. Icy fingers pinched at the exposed parts of her legs and her feet went numb not long after they'd left the flat.

"Franks, I'm freezing," she complained through chattering teeth as they walked from their final station.

"We're almost there. Try walking faster to keep warm."

But the cold was the least of Grace's worries. Pushed down her crop top were dozens of bags of powdered pain medication and sugar, moulded around her own breasts to give her a heaving cleavage. There were more bags taped to the tops of her thighs, she felt their plastic caress with every step. If the police stopped her now and deemed her worthy of a pat down they'd find her quite literally stuffed with fake drugs and what then? Prison? A fine? She should have looked into the legality of it all before she left the flat but she'd been too afraid of what she might find.

"Okay," Franklin turned to look at her showing no signs of being penetrated by the cold. "Once we get inside we hand in our coats and then we split up, got it?"

The street was empty around them but Grace still feared being overheard. She nodded silently.

"And what do we say?"

"Franks—"

"We went over this. You pick a target and…"

"I pick someone whose pupils are already dilated, make sure they are sweating heavily and go and ask them if they'd like to make it a really great night."

"Careful on the delivery," Franklin warned, "make sure they know you're peddling drugs not yourself."

Grace swallowed, feeling the lump that was once again wedged firmly in her throat. She'd put on countless performances over the years but nothing like this. In the rave she needed to rely on her words, on her posture, not a series of pre-choreographed steps. "Are you sure I can do this?"

Franklin stepped forward through the snow, his heavy boots leaving deep, fresh prints. He gripped her shoulders and looked down into her hazel eyes. "You can do this, Grace. I know you can. Twenty a bag, got it?"

"Got it."

*

The rave was unlike anything Grace had ever seen. Suddenly, out of nowhere, the snow covered street they were walking along developed a heartbeat. Then they saw the flashing lights pouring out of the large abandoned building. Inside there were bodies, hundreds, maybe thousands of them, swirling together in time to the pounding music like shoals of fish. There was neon everywhere. Ravers gripped neon glow sticks, brandished them high above their heads like batons. Grace saw stripes on the faces of others like those on her own cheeks. After handing in her coat she approached the sea of bodies. Franklin reached out and gave her one last reassuring hug and then he was gone. The hour they'd allocated themselves to move their 'produce' had begun.

Despite the flashing lights and all the glow sticks it was still dark out on the dance floor. Grace had to squeeze up close to strangers to study their pupils, the sheen on their skin. Twenty minutes passed and all she'd done was nervously wander through the surging dancers and not make contact with anyone. Standing on her tiptoes she searched for Franklin but couldn't find him.

"Hey," a guy with ginger curls and pock marked skin grabbed her. "You should be dancing." He pressed himself against Grace and she could feel that he was sweating. She checked his eyes; they were glazed and wide. He was already high. This was it, the kind of target she'd been seeking.

Leaning in close to his ear Grace had to shout to be heard over the thump of the bass track currently playing. "You look like a guy who enjoys having a good time. Want to have a *really* good time?" She cringed at how much she sounded like a hooker but Franklin had assured her that ravers should understand what she was implying. The ginger guy stepped back from her, smile widening. He understood.

"What you got?"

"Coke." The lie was both bitter and dangerous upon her tongue, like trying to swallow a scorpion's tail.

"How much?"

"Twenty for eight."

She was reciting the line Franklin had fed her with little knowledge as to what it really meant.

"Okay, sounds good."

The ginger guy led her away from the dance floor, to a vacant corner in the warehouse and passed her a crisp twenty pound note as she plucked a bag of sugared pain medication from her bosom. He took his purchase and hastily shoved it into the back pocket of his green neon surf shorts.

"Thanks, darling." He kissed her cheek and then darted back to the dance floor.

After that first encounter people began to seek Grace out. She figured that the other revellers must be talking amongst themselves but she didn't question it too much. With each sale she feared she was dealing with an undercover officer, she waited for them to snatch at her wrists and coldly tell her that she was under arrest. But there was no snatching, only the exchange of cash. Soon Grace began to feel lighter, not just because she was unburdening herself of her illegal assets but because the hour was growing to a close and she'd done it, she'd made the money she'd set out to make.

Franklin was already waiting for her outside in the snow as Grace hurriedly pulled on her coat and left the warehouse.

"So," he gazed at her expectantly. "How did you fare?"

"Sold it. All of it."

"Ooh, my little prodigy," he hugged her tight sounded genuinely delighted. "I knew you could do it, Grace. Between us we must have made almost a grand."

"Yeah."

It was a lot of money, but still not enough.

Together they walked back towards the tube station.

"Has he called?" Grace asked as she looked down at her feet which were dusted with snow.

"Aaron?"

"Mm."

"No, nothing yet."

Grace was back on the rollercoaster. She imagined Aaron in the flat, bloodied and beaten.

"We should call him."

She expected an objection from Franklin, some comment about how they shouldn't be disturbing Aaron. Instead he agreed and began reaching for his phone. Perhaps he was as worried about their friend as she was. Franklin dialled and then pressed his phone against his ear.

It had started to snow again. It wasn't dense but gentle, like someone covering the world in icing sugar with a sieve. Grace looked at the flakes which gathered on the sleeves of her coat. For a moment they were perfect, pure, but then they swiftly melted against the fabric.

"It's ringing," Franklin glanced at her. Then his posture stiffened and he sped up. Grace hurried through the snow which was becoming slush at her feet as they reached the busier part of town which housed the station along with the more generic nightclubs.

"Franks—"

"Hey," Franklin raised a hand to silence her. "We're just heading back, it went well. How did things go your end?"

Grace waited. Waited for Franklin to hang up and frantically hammer a trio of nines into his phone. She should have called Aaron herself, but she knew that if he were hurt he wouldn't tell her the truth, he'd keep up his bravado with her until the end. At least with Franklin there was the hope for honesty.

"Really?" Franklin was nodding. "Oh, okay. Well, good then. We'll be back in about forty minutes." He hung up and took a deep breath.

"Well?" Grace was instantly at his side, tugging on his sleeve. "What did he say? Is he alright?"

"He bought us a week."

"He did?"

"But that costs us two grand."

"What?"

"The grand sum we owe thuggy delight now stands at twenty-two thousand, eight of which Aaron gave him tonight."

"Shit." So in asking for more time they'd managed to add to their sentence. Another two thousand pounds, more than they'd just made at the rave. Grace felt like she was sinking into the slush. It was all beginning to sound, and feel, so impossible.

"Grace, this is good," Franklin pulled her close and guided her towards the entrance to the tube station. "Aaron bought us time. Yes, it cost us, but we needed the time. We've got a week. We can still do this."

"And he's okay, they didn't hurt him?"

"He sounded fine on the phone."

"Another two grand," Grace squeezed her eyes closed in frustration. "That genuinely sucks."

"I know."

"I mean, we're struggling to find the twenty as it is."

"No one ever said that thugs are fair." Franklin placed her in front of him on the escalator and protectively kept his hands on her shoulders. "My idea to sell a kidney each is beginning to look pretty good."

"Franks, I don't think we're there yet."

"Aren't we?"

Grace said nothing as they descended lower into the bowels of the city.

19

Saturday brought more snow. The city sparkled with it. Grace pulled on her thickest tights to help deal with the cold and then stooped down to double check the contents of her dance bag. She had four auditions, lined up one after the other like a set of dominoes. If she could land one job, just one, her financial situation would be looking considerably less dire. Tossing her bag over her shoulder she left her bedroom.

"He still not up?" She glanced at Franklin who was slumped on the sofa, hands clasped around a steaming mug of coffee.

"What?" His voice was rough, sounding like his tongue had been replaced with sand paper overnight.

"Aaron," Grace looked towards the bedroom door that was still closed, which seemed to be that way far more than usual. She couldn't shake away the feeling that Aaron was avoiding her. He'd already gone to bed when they returned the previous night with strict instructions not to be disturbed. Was he hiding a black eye? Bloodied nose? "Is he still sleeping?"

"I guess so."

"I should go and see him." As she dropped her bag to the floor Franklin clicked his fingers at her impatiently.

"Mmm no, he's sleeping in. Remember?"

"What if he's hurt?"

"He's not. I checked."

"So he let you in there?"

"It's my bedroom too, you know," Franklin pouted. "I have a legitimate reason to venture in, all my fabulous clothes are in there."

"Well, why the hell can't I go in?"

She knew that Aaron was being ridiculous, letting his pride become a barrier yet again. Releasing a haughty sigh Grace marched for the closed door, extending her hand towards the handle with every intention of thrusting it open in a truly dramatic fashion.

"Woah there," Franklin grabbed her shoulder and pulled her back just as her fingertips grazed the handle. "I think he's avoiding you for a good reason."

"So, he is avoiding me then?"

"He…" Franklin tapped a finger against his chin, clearly struggling to think on his feet at such an early hour. "Fuck," he sighed and then wedged himself between Grace and the door. "He feels guilty, okay? I hope to God he is actually sleeping in there because if he hears me telling you this he'll be furious."

"Guilty? But he bought us more time."

"Yes," Franklin nodded but he was grimacing. "He did buy us time. He also got to meet 'thug loving' and two of his equally lovely friends apparently."

"What?" Grace felt her eyes widen fearfully.

"And well… they were far from charming. He said they were moderately reasonable, made some threats. Thing is," Franklin warily glanced at the door behind him, "he dismissed our fears over the guy initially. And now he feels guilty for doing so, feels guilty for having you face the chap without him being here. So, he's doing the manly thing and completely avoiding you rather than discussing his feelings."

It was such typically Aaron behaviour that Grace wanted to scream. Instead she ground her teeth together and then spun away from the door.

"So, he's being a big baby, great."

"Grace," Franklin hurried after her. "He's brooding. Let him brood."

"This is hardly a decent time to brood."

"Things between you guys are still… fragile. I don't know," Franklin pushed his hands through his hair, looking at a loss as to what to say next.

"Fine, whatever," Grace decided that she could be equally as churlish as Aaron.

"Where are you going today, anyway?" Franklin glanced back at her discarded dance bag.

"Oh, auditions."

"Oh?"

"Four. All over the damn city and right after one another. I'm going to run myself ragged getting to them."

"But if you land one it'll be worth it, right?"

"Right."

Grace smiled at Franklin, thankful that he understood the pressure of auditions, the agony and the ecstasy of following a dream.

"Well, knock 'em dead," Franklin gave her a nudge, smiling back at her. "Oh," with a wince he quickly regretted what he'd said. "Not dead, damn. I mean, break a leg. Or something."

"Thanks."

"The auditions," he was still stalking her steps as she went to retrieve her bag. "Tell me about them."

"You seem unusually interested."

"I'm unusually scared. Aaron's clammed up and won't tell me hardly anything about last night, just that we need to find another two grand. I used to feel safe in the city, like I belonged."

"And now?"

"Now I'm scared. So, distract me with the excitement of these auditions of yours."

"Okay." Grace nodded, understanding Franklin's fears. Just leaving the flat filled her with dread, especially doing so on her own, but she wasn't making any money staying in her room. She needed to get out there, needed to start earning. She'd pretty much sold off everything she had of any value. "First audition is for a night club."

"Hmm," Franklin frowned. "Maybe not totally you but pay might be half decent."

"Agreed. Second is for a music video."

"Well, that sounds juicy. Artist?"

"A rapper."

"Ooh," Franklin eyed her tentatively. "Can you twerk, Grace? Because I've a feeling they didn't teach you that in ballet school."

"Twerk? I… I don't know. Sure. Whatever. I can try."

"What's the third audition?"

"Fitness YouTube channel."

Franklin's eyes widened.

"What?"

"Nothing, nothing," he flapped his hands at her. "You're giving it the old college try, more power to you."

"And the last audition is to go on tour with some teen singer."

"Well," Franklin clicked his fingers. "That sounds right up your street."

"What? Why?"

"Because," he looked her up and down. "Grace, you're basically a diddy version of Snow White incarnate. You'd be perfect for some Disney brat's show."

"I think they might be… you know… post Disney now."

"So overly sexy and try hard?"

"Uh huh."

"Damn, that might scupper your chances."

"Thanks for the vote of confidence, Franks."

"Want me to come with you?" He was following her towards the front door.

"No, I'm good."

"You sure?" He was being uncharacteristically eager.

"I'm sure."

"But Grace, it's dangerous out there and—"

"Franks," she reached out and gripped his arm. "Today I need to be fast. Four auditions in four different boroughs of London. I simply cannot dawdle on the tube. I'll be one of those asses sprinting up the right hand side of all the escalators."

"Urgh," Franklin grimaced at her in exaggerated disgust. "In that case, yes, most definitely go alone. No one should ever be in *that* much of a rush. Right laners are just downright crazy."

"Yep, so leave me to my crazy and wish me luck."

Leaning forward he kissed her cheek. "Good luck, Grace. Sure you'll kill it." He winced as he withdrew. "Dammit, I really need to work on my vocabulary."

*

It proved to be a punishing day. When Grace arrived at her first audition she had to dance on a podium to pop music for twenty minutes in an empty club. She did her best to improvise what she hoped were sexy, alluring moves but the style was so beyond her realm of expertise that she really struggled. She didn't even recognise any of the songs she was dancing to.

Grace arrived for her next audition fifteen minutes late thanks to turning out of the tube station the wrong way and getting lost. The casting director scowled at her and scribbled something down as she frantically made her apologies. Despite the heaps of snow on the streets it seemed that everyone else had been able to make their way there on time. For this audition Grace did have to twerk, just as Franklin had predicted. As she stepped up for her slot she wished she'd asked him to show her how it was done that morning as she really didn't have a clue. She was used to extending her body into long, clean lines, executing perfect jumps and spinning relentlessly without moving an inch. It felt strange to move her body in a more jerky, sensual way. As Grace stepped away from the scrutinising panel helmed by the casting director she already knew she'd failed to land the job. But that was okay because it was two down, two to go.

After grabbing a sandwich and eating it on the tube she arrived at the third audition. By this time it had stopped snowing, but the sky remained dark and ominous. For the fitness video she had to follow the instructor at the front of the room, keeping up with all the movements as best she could. Grace lifted her knees, punched her fists into the air and high kicked for the next forty minutes. By the end of it her leotard was soaked through with sweat and she desperately drained her entire bottle of water that she'd brought along with her.

"We'll let you know," the man casting the video told her. Grace left, embracing the cold which felt blissful against her overheated body. But there was no time to dwell in the snow, she had to hurry to her fourth and final audition.

She'd known other dancers who branched away from classical styles like ballet to go on tour with singers and bands. She'd heard how gruelling the schedules could be but also how rewarding. If you got on a good tour you could literally travel the globe. Though Grace had never felt compelled to travel she had to admit that it had its allure. She'd get to see sights and cities that would be completely new to her. But first she'd need to nail this final audition.

It was by far her most gruelling appointment of the day. She was asked to freestyle, then to follow steps by an instructor. Then she was taught a quick routine, given twenty minutes to rehearse it with the other dancers auditioning and then had to perform it before a panel of judges. She started to feel like she was on some dance reality show.

"It's always like this for tours," a blonde with tight curls told her as they grabbed drinks and towelled off during a brief break. "The process can be brutal but it's rewarding."

"It's definitely brutal," Grace agreed. Her skin was on fire and her muscles were beginning to throb and ache.

"I hear that this isn't just for the European leg of her tour but for the whole thing," the blonde said with a dreamy look in her eye.

"Wow, really?"

"Uh huh," the blonde stretched out her legs and bowed her head over them. "I would love to land this job."

"Yeah, me too."

Going on tour would mean leaving London. Leaving Aaron. A barb of uncertainty pushed into her heart and Grace flinched. They were over, weren't they? So much had been said, so many doors closed. Yet still…

"Try and be more loose," the blonde glanced over at her.

"Loose?"

"You're classically trained, right?"

"Right."

"It shows."

*

With her fourth audition concluded Grace made for the tube station. Exhaustion was a lead weight against her back. She longed to flop onto her bed, to spread herself out into a star shape and remain that way until she fell asleep.

The snow which had been diamond white first thing had been dirtied by the city. It clumped in the streets as blackened slush. Grace hoped that more snow would fall to return the world to its previous pristine canvas but no more came. Instead pewter clouds began to drift away from London, allowing a watery winter sun to shine down upon the streets, the final death knell for the snow.

One good thing about Saturdays was that there wasn't the usual swell of foot traffic around rush hour. It was half four and Grace easily found a seat on her train and sat waiting patiently as it sped her through darkened tunnels towards her destination. She wondered if Aaron had surfaced from his room during her absence. She wanted to talk to him, to push through his stubborn pride and connect, even just as friends. Because they had been friends first and it looked as though they'd be friends last and Grace hadn't really processed how she felt about that.

Jasper had asked. He was always so quietly observant of the rest of them. Not long after the storm which had been Grace and Aaron's final argument he'd found her in her room. With a book tucked under his arm he'd given her a long, thoughtful look.

"Are you going to be okay?"

"Huh?" Grace looked up from her book and wiped away tears that she hoped he hadn't noticed.

"I heard about you and Aaron. Will you be okay?"

"I've survived worse." This was true.

"But," Jasper folded his legs and perched carefully upon the end of her bed. He always respected her boundaries more than the other guys, never bursting into her room without politely knocking first. "You two were in love. Do you really believe you can go back to being friends?"

"I honestly don't know."

"Because I don't want you to leave, Grace."

"I don't want to leave."

"But isn't it going to be hard for you to stay?"

Grace was about to start crying all over again when Jasper reached out and grabbed her hand. "I mean, your feelings will make it hard, that's all. Franks and me, we'll always be your friends, Grace. No matter what."

No matter what.

Would that hold up if they knew the truth about her? About her past? About her mother?

"Jasper—"

"I know what it feels like to have your heart break," he told her quietly, looking down at his lap.

"I didn't know that, Jasper. I'm sorry."

"In Japan, when something breaks, say a vase, they glue it back together and paint the cracks gold, to turn its flaw into something beautiful. That's how I perceive a broken heart."

"It's a nice way to look at it."

"I'm here, Grace. If you ever need to talk."

"Thanks, Jasper."

"And I'll always be here. No matter what happens."

*

The doors to the tube hissed as they drew open. Grace dragged herself off the train and followed the throng of travellers towards the exit. She was nearly home, nearly able to kick off her boots and throw herself against her bed.

Cold clawed at her as she came up from the station towards street level. Grace bowed her head against it and shuffled through the last of the snow. Then she saw something black move at the edge of her vision. Turning, she noticed a crow perched atop a street lamp, its glossy black eyes studying the street below. As she stared it opened its beak and released a single, shrill cry.

Grace gasped and staggered away from it. Crows still had the power to make her unnaturally uneasy. Finding her footing she spun round and sprinted the whole way back to the flat, ignoring the ache in her muscles. She just wanted to be away from the crow.

20

Sunday morning found Grace at the hospital, sat at Jasper's bedside. She'd thought about the crow at the station all through a long, sleepless night. Grace feared it was an omen, a sign that Jasper would soon be taken from her just as Peter had once been.

"I'm here," she carefully enveloped his hand in her own. "It's me, Grace." She hoped that he could hear her, that in whatever abyss he currently resided her voice might be a beacon, a way to find his way home.

"Oh, Grace, sweetheart." Despite the surprised lilt in her voice Jasper's mother still sounded woefully tired. She was stood in the doorway of what was now Jasper's own room. He'd been moved from the HDU some two days previously. His web of machines had followed him, still constantly beeping to one another as they presided over his bed. "I didn't know you'd be here today." The tired woman in the doorway wrung her dry hands together, working the last of the anti-bacterial gel she'd used on her arrival into her palms.

"I'm sorry, I just…" Grace looked at her sleeping friend. His expression was so peaceful but the tube that parted his lips, the bruises across his face that were turning from red to black told the violent truth about his situation. "I just wanted to see him."

"I understand." Jasper's mother drifted towards her son's bed, her movements directionless and uneven, like a leaf caught in a rough wind. The whites of her eyes were completely shot through with ruby flames and the shadows which hung in the crevices of her face had deepened to black holes. "We all feel like that."

A week. It had been over a week since the car Jasper was driving had malfunctioned and flung him into oncoming traffic. The investigation into the vehicle was ongoing but no one really cared about that, not while Jasper still dwelled in the no man's land of his coma.

"I so want him to wake up," Grace admitted tearfully. She kept thinking about the briefcase, the money, how she'd spent it so easily under Franklin's tutelage. But he wasn't to blame, not truly, she should have said no, refused to buy herself shiny new things. Grace was at fault; all of the flatmates were. Their hands were soiled by dirty money and blood.

"The doctors say it's all up to him now," Jasper's mother settled at her son's side, smiling wistfully at him as though he were a babe in arms though her sore eyes glistened with the promise of fresh tears. "They've done everything they can. He just needs to wake up on his own.

"And he will." Grace needed to be believe it just as much as the woman at her side. "Jasper's strong, he's going to get through this, he's going to wake up." Because if he didn't Grace wasn't sure she'd be able to live with herself.

*

"You should cam." Franklin stood over the stove, stirring a saucepan of gravy. The flat smelt of richly cooked meats and roasted potatoes. Grace couldn't remember the last time Franklin had prepared his famous Sunday dinner for them all. It usually followed a Saturday night he was keen to remove from his friend's memories, the gravy soaked meal becoming a peace offering.

"Huh?" Grace ruffled the towel she was holding through her hair. Fresh from the shower she wore her flannel pyjamas, keen to collapse into bed shortly in the hope that sleep would find her. Her joints had only just stopped aching after her gruelling day of auditions. The heat from the shower helped but she needed real, genuine rest, not a night spent worrying about what the presence of a single crow might mean.

"Camming," Franklin briefly ceased stirring his gravy to crouch down and check the contents of the oven. "I've been at it all day. It's good money."

"I don't know." The homely scent of a fresh meal drew Grace over to the small kitchenette.

"What's holding you back?"

"I just…" she ruffled her hair with more intensity. "I worry about who might be watching."

Resuming the stirring of his gravy Franklin arched an eyebrow at her.

"I mean," Grace let her towel settle across her shoulders. "Anyone could be watching and that kind of freaks me out. Because you wouldn't know. I could be in Tesco Express and the guy behind me in line might have seen my butt. That freaks me out."

"You're so demure, you know that?"

"I think it's called just being shy."

A door wheezed open and Aaron slumped into the main living area dressed in loose jeans and a tight fitting white t-shirt. He looked flushed from sleep. After massaging his hands against his eyes several times he noticed his friends and breathed in the rich meaty aroma radiating out of the kitchenette.

"Sunday dinner?" Aaron asked, crinkling his nose. Then, staring solely at Franklin, "what did you do?"

"W-what?" Franklin dropped the spoon he was holding and pressed his hands against his hips. "What did I *do?* How about, 'thanks for cooking us a wonderful meal, Franklin.' Or 'Franklin, you're so very kind.'"

"Franks, how have you fucked up this time? You found another case full of money you want us to all spend?"

"I am both hurt and appalled by the insinuation that I can't simply make you all dinner out of the goodness of my heart."

"To be fair, it'd be the first time," Grace stated quietly. "Normally your Sunday dinners serve as an apology on a plate."

"Christ," Franklin glowered at his flatmates. "What a bitter pair you are. I merely thought we could all use a bit of a pick me up. It's been a shite week to say the least. Yet my good Samaritan intentions are being torn apart, wonderful."

"Fine, Franks, you're a saint." With a grunt Aaron dropped down onto the sofa and Grace saw him reflexively reach for the television remote, only it wasn't there, Tina was gone.

"I appreciate the gesture," Grace gave Franklin's arm a squeeze and then cautiously left the kitchenette to approach the sofa. It was the first time she'd seen Aaron emerge from his room since Friday night. A number of questions settled on her tongue, each keen to be unburdened.

"I'm not talking about it." He seemed to sense her desire to interrogate him. Shifting on the sofa he leaned forward and reached for one of Jasper's books from a nearby pile.

"I want to know what he said."

"Grace—"

"You owe me an explanation, Aaron. We're all involved in this. You can't talk to Franks about it but not me."

"Look—"

"We're *killing* ourselves trying to get this money, taking risks which we never usually would. All because we fear the guy who came to our door." Lack of sleep had made Grace irritable and worse, honest. "Who the hell is he? Do we legitimately need to fear him like we do?"

"He threatened us, Gracey pants," Franklin called from his position by the stove. "Don't make me relive his horrid words just to jolt your flaky memory."

"My memory isn't flaky," Grace replied hotly. "I just…" she looked down at her hands which she'd twisted into a knot. "What if Jasper's accident isn't related to the money? What if this… this thug is just trying to shake us down. He saw us take the briefcase, why not report us to the police? Why not—"

"Stop being naïve." The coldness in Aaron's voice chilled her to her core. "I saw the guy. His mates. It's legit that we take their threats seriously."

"But how can we *know* that?"

"Are you going to tell her?" Franklin asked, as he hauled a sizzling joint of beef out of the oven and placed it on the side.

"Tell me what?" Grace unclasped her hands and stared at Aaron. She searched his face for signs of poorly concealed bruises, of fresh wounds, but found nothing but exhaustion stretched across his skin. He seemed to be sleeping more than ever, or at least he was locked up in his room most of the time yet whenever he emerged he was bleary eyed and lingering on the knife edge of exhaustion. They all were.

"Yesterday," Aaron sighed and leant forward, resting his elbows upon his knees. "While you were out dancing up a storm all over the city I went to see my Uncle Paulie."

"Your Uncle Paulie?"

"My dad's brother."

Grace tensed. Aaron rarely spoke about his family. She knew that his father disapproved of his artistic dreams, of his desire to live in London and regularly urged his son to be more grounded.

"I didn't know your dad had a brother," she picked at the bobbles in the fabric of her pyjamas, hating herself for sounding so needy. It's not like she told Aaron everything about her family, why should she have expected him to? Yet she had. Like a fool she'd constantly hoped that he'd open his heart up to her in its entirety even though she was never prepared to do the same herself.

"Mmm," Aaron hunched further forward. "My dad and him don't really speak. Paulie lives in London, never had a legit job."

"Ooh," Franklin hurried over, spatula in hand. "Tell me he's some rugged thug type, I'm picturing the taller, leaner Mitchell brother."

"None of his earnings are exactly legal," Aaron admitted flatly. "Hence why my family ostracise him. But me and Uncle Paulie, we always got along. So I sought him out and explained our... unique situation."

"You tattled?" Franklin brandished the spatula like a weapon, ready to slap Aaron across the face with it.

"I didn't *tattle*. I made legitimate enquiries. Because Grace is right, why fear someone based on just their words?"

"And?" Franklin slapped the spatula against the back of the sofa. "What did Uncle Paulie say?"

"Based on the description I gave where the money was stashed, he ID'd the guy."

"What did he say about him?" Grace felt a storm stirring in her stomach. Suddenly Franklin's roast dinner didn't smell quite so appealing.

"He said," with a strained sigh Aaron got up. He paced towards where Tina had been and then spun round to face his friends. "Paulie said the guy is dangerous. Really dangerous. He traffics drugs into the city amongst other things." His gaze drifted towards Grace. "Best thing we can do is pay the guy off before we risk pissing him off any more than we already have."

"So, your uncle thinks that 'thug loving' really could have hurt Jasper?" Franklin asked as his free hand fluttered up to rest on his neck.

"It's plausible. The guy has done far worse, at least, the guy 'thug loving' works for. And before you ask, no, I don't want to mention to Paulie what we owe. He'll only try and help us out."

"And what's so bad about that? We could use the help."

"He's kind of a favours for favours guy. I don't want that."

"Shit. I guess not."

"Shit indeed," Aaron pushed his hands into his jean pockets. "So, yeah," he nodded towards the kitchenette, "I think we're definitely in need of one of your apology dinners. And Grace," she steeled herself beneath his pained gaze, "we need to find the money, all of it. The threats are legit. And all of us," he looked between his flatmates, "if we went missing we'd just be a by line in some local paper. We wouldn't make the evening news, wouldn't have family desperately searching for us. We need to be careful."

Grace felt the heat of tears gathering behind her eyes. "I'd search for you," she looked at Aaron and then turned to face Franklin. "I'd search for both of you to the ends of the earth. You're more than friends to me, you're family."

"Right back at you, kid," Franklin pointed his spatula at her as he smiled and then turned towards the kitchenette.

Looking up at Aaron, Grace waited for an equally kind response, or at least some sign of sentiment. But his expression was flat. "Family?" he muttered as he withdrew from the sofa and marched towards his room. "So, we're family. I'm grouped in with Franks, great."

When Grace heard his bedroom door slam she knew better than to chase him down to talk things through, this wasn't the time.

*

Sunday night brought surprising contentment to the flat. When Grace headed to bed, stuffed full of rich meats and crispy potatoes, her body felt warm, relaxed. She curled up beneath her duvet and tried to ignore her fears over the thug at the door, over the legitimacy of his threats. She focused solely on how blissfully full she was, how the flat still smelt of roast dinners and normality.

The clouds, and any snow they still held, left overnight. Come the morning the sky was clear and bright, a brilliant shade of blue that stretched far across the city. Grace saw the glistening rays of the early morning sun finding their way through cracks in her curtains. Turning onto her side she released a soft sigh. There had been sleep, lots of it. She felt rejuvenated, powerful, ready to take on the world. And she hadn't even had her coffee yet.

Thirty minutes later she sat on her bed, coffee in hand, a half-eaten plate of toast at her side as she opened up her laptop. It was almost ten in the morning, the day was new, fresh, sun kissed and full of potential. If they needed money then money is what Grace would make. Opening up her emails she almost choked on the mouthful of buttery toast she was chewing. Four new messages were stacked in a neat row, all arriving within an hour of each other. The responses to her auditions. Grace drained the last of her coffee before opening the first message, needing the caffeine to bolster her confidence. It didn't make for decent reading.

A rejection, there on her laptop screen in neat type. She hadn't landed the first job. The casting director felt she was too 'classical' for their needs. After a swift delete Grace opened the next email, it basically read the same as the first. As did the third. A pit was opening up in her stomach as Grace clicked on her fourth and final email. She needed it to be positive, needed the money the job would bring. Growing impatient she scanned through the pleasantries;

Thank you so much for coming in and auditioning.

"Come on," Grace gritted her teeth. "Get to the point."

Unfortunately, at this time, we don't feel like you are best suited to our needs.

Four auditions. Four emails. Four rejections. Grace lurched forward, gasping for breath.

You're not good enough. You need to go home. You need to give up.

She'd failed. Four times over she'd failed. It was about more than just the money, it was about getting paid to do something she loved, it was about her dreams. A strangled gasp rattled out of her throat.

"Hey," Franklin sauntered in a few seconds later. "What's going on in here? It sounds like you're harbouring a startled goose." He looked between Grace and her laptop, saw her haunted expression.

"Shit," he joined her on the bed, leaning in close. "Is this about the auditions?"

Numbly she nodded.

"You didn't get them?"

"Nope. Not one." Her throat was suddenly raw, as though her toast had been coated with nails not creamy butter.

"Well, fuck them," Franklin slammed her laptop shut. "What do they know? Grace, I've seen you dance and you're beautiful, like an ethereal little pixie in pointe shoes. You're going to make it. Maybe not today, maybe not tomorrow, but one day."

"Money," Grace croaked. "We need the money."

If even Aaron was afraid of the man who'd come to their door it completely upped the ante of their situation. They needed money and they needed it fast.

"About that," Franklin stroked a strand of hair out of her eyes. "Tonight there is somewhere you and I should go."

Grace blinked at him, feeling doubtful. She didn't want to go anywhere, she only wanted to hide under her duvet. All of her previous optimistic energy had been drained by the succession of rejection emails she'd just read through.

"Trust me," Franklin urged. "I think I have the answer to all our money woes."

21

Grace pouted her lips and applied the red lipstick Franklin had given her as he shoved her into her bedroom.

"Trust me," he'd stated, hands pushing against her shoulders. "Where we're going, you'll want to be wearing this. The theme for the night is fabulous."

"I don't know, Franks."

"Put it on. Be ready in fifteen."

Beyond the thin walls of her room Grace could hear drawers being flung open with force in the flat's only other bedroom. Franklin was clearly lost in a maelstrom of shirts and tight jeans as he deliberated over what to wear. Once again he was the white rabbit leading Grace down some perilous black hole. Was she a fool to follow? Their night at the rave had proved fruitful, just not quite fruitful enough. Where were they headed this time? Another club? Was Franklin going to bound into her room with more bags of powder he wanted to pass off as drugs?

Skirting so close to the boundaries of the law was exhausting. When Grace wasn't worrying over Jasper she was fearing for her own future, her sanity. Since the discovery of the briefcase they'd all been trapped on a terrible treadmill where no matter how fast they ran they weren't allowed to get off.

"Another two grand," Grace muttered the additional debt owed as she checked her ruby lips and cast a discerning eye over her outfit; a black bodycon dress she'd found in a charity shop the previous winter and worn for New Year's Eve. The stroke of midnight had been accompanied by a kiss from Aaron. Things had been so different then.

"Coming in, ready or not." Franklin bounded into her room like an over excited puppy. His eyes were wide and elegantly framed by a flick of black liner. He looked beautiful and dangerous. "Ooh, Grace," he extended his hands towards her and nodded in admiration. "You look simply divine in that dress."

"Thanks."

"Et moi?" He spun around so that she could take in his leather trousers and loose fitting red silk shirt. Franklin could have been a vampire in some teen show, one set to break a dozen hearts. He smiled at her, his perfect cheekbones lifting as he did so.

"Franks, you are sexy personified."

It was true. He wore his clothes like a second skin, looking effortlessly comfortable in them. Not like Aaron who looked like he was about to suffocate whenever he had to wear a shirt.

"Thanks, my dear." Franklin winked at her.

"So, are you going to tell me where we're going?"

"Where's the fun in that?"

"Franks, I'm serious." Grace pulled on her thickest coat as she followed him into the main living area.

"Trust me," he repeated but Grace knew that trust went both ways.

"You could be taking me anywhere."

"True." Leaning down Franklin grabbed his faux fur leopard print coat which he'd strewn across the sofa. He spun around as he tucked himself within in. "I'm taking you *somewhere*. And where we're headed people make money. Lots of it."

"Franks…" Grace glanced towards the door that didn't belong to her bedroom. It was ajar which meant that Aaron wasn't inside.

"He's got a gig tonight."

"Oh." Grace blinked away any lingering disappointment. So what if Aaron didn't see her all dressed up? It didn't matter. She needed to focus on money, on Jasper. "He didn't mention having a gig." The words slipped out.

Franklin regarded her with a sympathetic stare. "When the dust settles from all this shit maybe you two can figure stuff out."

"There's nothing to figure out."

"Uh huh," rolling his eyes he linked arms with Grace and ushered her towards the front door.

"That's why you keep staring at his bedroom door like it's an oasis in the desert."

"I don't I—"

"Hush," Franklin pressed a finger against her lips, lightly enough so as not to disturb her carefully applied lipstick. "Tonight is not about boy drama. Understand? Tonight is about money. Lots of money."

*

Two stops on the train brought them to a part of London Grace was vaguely familiar with. The streets were lined with pubs and various clubs. She'd frequented a number of them to watch Aaron play gigs. People were already gathering outside doorways in clouds of smoke.

"Come on, nearly there," Franklin strode purposefully down the street, his arm locked against her own.

Grace breathed in the tobacco, the beer. Even though it was a Monday, life stirred in every bar. Hedonism was not deterred by the day of the week.

"And… we're here." Franklin stopped outside a club with blacked out windows and a suspiciously empty doorway that was currently blocked off by a red velvet rope. The outer walls were as black as the windows save for a neon green sign that shone out, boasting the venue's name; Menthol Tiger. Grace took a step back.

"No, Franks. Just no."

While the pubs were thick with revellers the clubs were still quiet. In an hour or two the scales would tip between them as last orders rolled around.

"Grace, trust me."

"No."

Menthol Tiger was a famous club, part of a chain owned by an eccentric billionaire. Even Grace was aware of the notoriety attached to it. The Tiger was an exclusive strip club. Hollywood actors had been seen in there, along with premiership footballers. There was no cloud of smoke fogging its entrance, no waft of stale beer leaking out through the doors.

"You don't want to cam," Franklin turned to look at her, his voice level, his tone logical as though he were explaining a simple fact of life to a child. "You don't like the idea that you don't know who is watching. Here," he gestured behind him to the neon sign and the red velvet rope, "you can see who sees you. And the money is good. Really good."

"Franks," Grace took another step backwards. "I'm a ballerina, not a stripper."

"Both are dancers," Franklin was reaching for her shoulders, trying to turn her squarely in the direction of the club. "I know the guy who hires the girls here, he owes me a favour. He says he can put you on midweek, when it's quiet. Grace, for a debut you could make two grand in one night. We could seriously use that kind of money."

"Two grand?" The added fee, a tenth of what they'd previously owed. It would go a long way to paying their debt. But Grace felt exposed in her bodycon dress, there was no way she could possibly get completely naked in front of a room full of strangers. She lacked the confidence, the sex appeal.

"I can't do this." Shaking Franklin off, she hurried back down the street. He followed her, refusing to let her slip out of his reach.

"You *can* do this."

"No," Grace threw the objection over her shoulder as she kept running.

"We need the money. I'm sorry, I can't think of another way to get it." She could tell that Franklin had given up the chase as his voice became smaller with every harried step she took. Grace was outside a pub, The Duke's Duchess. She could hear the tangle of chatter inside, smell the heady aroma of hops and liquor. Grace wanted to shed all her fears like an unwanted skin, to walk into the pub and be surrounded by friends, by laughter. To be just like everyone else out on Monday night, looking to have fun.

With a sigh she turned and looked back up the street. Franklin was a few steps beyond Menthol

Tiger, hands in his coat pockets, head angled steadily in her direction.

"Just come in and take a look," he shouted to her. "If you hate it, you hate it. But at least check it out."

You owe it to Jasper.

These were the convincing words she said to herself. If she wanted the money she was going to have to rely on herself to make it, she had no support system beyond the flat and her friends needed her.

"Okay," her steps clicked a brisk beat along the damp street as she returned to the front of the club. Snow had given way to a wetness that clung to every part of the city. If the temperature continued to drop that night the streets would soon glisten with ice. "I'll go in," she let Franklin link arms with her once again. "But just to take a look. I'm not promising anything. Got it?"

"Got it."

*

Grace had never been inside a strip club before. She'd seen them on television – all darkened corners and up lit stages upon which scantily clad girls draped themselves over silver poles. Grace anticipated a seediness which would clot the air and soil even the most lavish furnishings. After dropping off her coat she followed Franklin up a darkened stairwell which led to a door that opened out into the main club.

Menthol Tiger was spread out before her and Grace found herself blinking in surprise. It was dark, yes. Sumptuous velvet lined booths covered the outer walls and within the centre of the grand space were numerous circular stages, all complete with poles. From the ceiling hung a trio of glistening chandeliers and some gilded cages, which whilst currently empty, would clearly house erotic dancers on busier nights. Between some of the booths Grace noticed floor length curtains, blood red in colour.

"So, what do you think?" Franklin leaned in close to ask the question. The music in the club was loud but not deafening and the song playing had a sensual beat. It was the kind of song that you could just listen to and instantly feel sexy. Grace followed Franklin over to the bar, trying not to stare at some of the girls up on the circular stages as she passed them.

One thing all the dancers had in common was their beauty. They were all striking, and curvaceous, dressed in either lace or leather lingerie and grinding to the music as though the rhythm echoed the beating of their hearts. They were like water, fluid and mesmerising in their every movement.

"See," Franklin grabbed Grace's elbow and pulled her towards the bar. "Not as seedy as you thought, right?"

"Right," she replied slowly, peering over her shoulder to glance at the men gazing adoringly up at the dancers, most of whom wore suits as though they'd come straight from the office.

"Two tequilas," Franklin told the barmaid, "and is Stiles about?"

"I'll call him to come down," the barmaid was as beautiful as the dancers, blonde and buxom in her uniform. She batted her eyelashes at Franklin like flirting was second nature.

"This place isn't like what I thought it would be," Grace admitted. It was more sensual than seedy, she could see that. But she was still a minnow in a shark tank. "But I'm serious Franks, I can't do this. I mean," she gestured to the nearest dancer whose amber skin glowed beneath the twinkle of the chandelier as though she'd bathed in gold. "Look at these women, look how inherently sexy they are. They're up there just… owning it. I can't do that."

Grace didn't fear the stage, she was drawn to it. Given the right classical piece, the right choreography she could turn from shy wall flower to dazzling butterfly or elegant swan. She lost herself in the steps, in the drama. Up on the podiums at Menthol Tiger there was nothing to hide behind, nothing to get lost in. To dance there would render her utterly exposed.

"You don't even need to strip completely," Franklin told her. "You can keep on your best undies and just… entice."

"Franks—"

"Channel your inner Natalie Portman from *Closer*. We could get you a pink wig if that'd help?"

"I just—"

"I believe you can do this, Grace," he slid a shot of tequila across the bar to her. "You just need to believe that you can, too."

"Franklin!" A slim guy with a blonde beard dressed in a white shirt and dark trousers approached them. "To what do I owe the pleasure?" the men briefly embraced and then Franklin pointed at Grace.

"Stiles, meet my dear friend, Grace."

"Well, hello Grace," Stiles reached out and shook her hand. His skin was soft but his grip was firm. His blue eyes quickly scanned her entire body before he'd even released her hand from his.

Franklin leaned in with his request. "She's looking to work a few nights here, just this week."

"Is that so?"

Grace felt like she was on fire. Heat burned across her cheeks and her palms became horribly clammy. Discreetly she wiped them against her dress and glanced nervously at Franklin. "I don't know about—"

"Have you danced before?" Stiles cut her off, still staring at her.

"I…"

"Classical only," Franklin quickly responded. "She's a professionally trained ballerina."

"Oh?" Stiles eyes lit up with growing interest.

"This would be her debut as an erotic dancer," Franklin continued.

"Hm," Stiles stroked at his beard. "You look pure, very innocent. Some of our regulars would love that."

"Wouldn't they?" Franklin gushed, clasping Grace's shoulders like a proud parent. "I mean look at this face, like butter wouldn't melt. Put her in some classy lingerie and it'd be boner city in here."

Stiles cracked a dry laugh. "True. But I can't agree to let her dance just a few nights, especially when she's a novice. That's not how things are done around here."

"You owe me." Something changed in Franklin's tone, a darkness swiftly smoothed over his words turning them into a poisoned arrow which struck Stiles in a single blow. He laughed again but the sound was hollow now.

"Fine, that's how you want to call in your favour?"

"It's how I want to call in my favour," Franklin kept holding Grace's shoulders.

"I can offer her Tuesday, Wednesday, Thursday this week. No more."

"Which will be?" Franklin's grip on her shoulders tightened.

Stiles sighed. "Three flat."

"Three and a half."

"Franklin, she's an unknown, completely untried on the circuit. If she'd had a bit more experience then maybe, but—"

"Three and a half. Consider the add on hazard pay."

"What hazard? Our security here is top notch."

"This will be Grace's first time dancing for another's… pleasure. You only get one first time."

Grace swallowed nervously, feeling like she was somehow caught in the middle of something she didn't quite understand.

"Fuck, Franklin," Stiles sounded annoyed but he was extending his hand for both Grace and her chaperone to shake it. "Three nights, three and a half, done. But no more. Any tips she makes stay in house. She gets none of the perks the regular girls do."

"Understood."

"And you need to make her lose that Bambi act of hers. She needs to seem pure not fucking virginal."

"Under my tutelage she'll flourish. Might I suggest a pink wig?"

"Do whatever you want," Stiles grunted and looked to the barmaid, raising his hand to order a shot. "You always do anyway."

"Pleasure doing business with you."

Another grunt. "Whatever. Are you at least going to stay and drink with me awhile?"

"Alas, no," Franklin turned his mouth down in a dramatized sad smile. "We have a routine to perfect. But every night she's here I will be too. Should give you something to look forward to."

"Don't make me regret this, Franklin," Stiles warned as Grace was directed away from the bar.

"As if I would," Franklin called over his shoulder as he kept pushing his small friend back towards the door they'd previously come through. "Well," he turned to her when they were alone in the stairwell, a new song starting beyond the dark walls where the heart of the club resided. "I think that went pretty well."

"Franks, what the hell have you got me into?" Grace shivered even though the air around her was warm. She was desperate to bury herself in the dense layers of her coat.

"I just did you a favour, a huge one," he told her contritely. "You're about to make three and a half thousand pounds in three days which is pretty good going."

"Franks—"

"You can do this, Grace. I'll help you. Tomorrow night you'll get up on a podium and be just as sexy as all the other girls in there."

Grace couldn't respond, she was too busy trying not to be sick.

22

The cold wind felt like nails hammering into Grace's cheeks. Her teeth knocked together involuntarily as she walked with Franklin down the street towards the nearest tube station. Still she couldn't speak. Her only responses to her friend's questions were mutters. She knew that Franklin was asking too much of her, asking her to exhibit her own skin in a way she'd never done before.

"The girls in the club are just completely at ease, comfortable with themselves," he was saying as they stepped onto the first of many escalators. "You can be like that too, Grace."

Only she couldn't. For so many years Grace had felt like a lie wrapped in ribbon. She hid behind the rigid regime of the ballet world, let her toes speak on her behalf. But to get up on a podium in just her underwear she'd be more naked than she'd ever been and what if her truth was evident to all who gazed up at her? What if rather than seeing a lithe seductress they saw a terrified little girl on the brink of collapse as she watched her mother cradling her dead brother in her arms?

"We'll work on a routine. Something simple, yet sexy." Franklin talked the entire journey home, his words coming fast and fluid. The more he talked the more he used his hands, filling their empty train carriage with his thoughts and ideas. Grace zoned out. She watched the unmoving darkness beyond the windows of the train, listened to the echo of her teeth gnashing together as cold and shock rattled through her bones.

*

"Shall we start practising now? I'm feeling inspired." Franklin entered the flat as though it was an arena, disrobing his coat and extending his arms. But there were no cheering hoards to greet him, just silence. "Why don't we move the sofa back and—" he had his hands on the arm rest, ready to move the worn out piece of furniture when he finally looked at Grace, really looked at her. Instantly deflated, he abandoned the sofa and joined her where she still stood by the doorway, unable to move deeper into her home. "Oh, shit, Grace," he hugged her. Even his arms around her didn't lessen the cold that gnawed on her bones. "I know this must all feel overwhelming but I'll help you through it, I swear." He tightened his embrace. "Damn," Franklin released her but they remained tethered as his hands remained on her shoulders, "Grace, you're bloody freezing. Damn. Let me go and run you a nice warm bath, okay?"

Grace couldn't respond. It was like the cold had frozen her tongue.

Ten minutes later and Franklin was gently nudging her into the steam filled bathroom. She glanced down at the tub, full of fragranced bubbles. The air smelt of lemons as though in their little bathroom alone it was spring.

"Now you soak in there for a bit," Franklin ordered, helping her out of her coat. "It'll do you a world of good and stop you catching a chill."

The water looked so warm. So inviting. As the door closed behind her Grace slid out of her dress and underwear and dipped in a single toe. The hot caress of the bubbles against her skin was intoxicating. Grace climbed in, submerging her entire body up to her shoulders, letting her head rest against the end of the bath. The cold left her. There was only warmth and the sweet scent of fresh lemons.

*

Peter's skin was blue, his eyes wide beneath the water.

"That's it," Grace's mother was bent over the bath, hands firmly pressing down on the little boy's slender shoulders. "Let the water punish you, feel God's sorrow against your skin. This will teach you not to steal. Water purifies. Water punishes. All are punished."

From where she stood on the threadbare bathmat Grace stared at the grim scene before her. She wanted to scream but her head felt light and strange. Was she about to faint? Tentatively she stepped forward, praying she'd see some movement in her brother, some thrashing of his limbs. But there wasn't so much as a bubble drifting up from his parted lips, forever locked in a fearful scream.

"Peter?" She squeaked his name and willed him to respond, to turn in the water in her direction. Her face throbbed from where her mother had struck her. "Peter, are you sleeping?"

"Water, he belongs to the water now."

Grace shook with understanding. Her heart clenched with the terrible certainty that Peter had left her alone in this world. Turning she ran. Ran as fast as her little feet could carry her towards the kitchen and the phone which hung upon the wall. Perhaps there was a way to bring Peter back, if only a doctor could get to him and—

"You'll join him in hell, you wretch." Her mother's screams followed her like a plague but Grace refused to be infected by them. She pressed down on the nine button three times.

*

Grace opened her eyes. Everything looked murky, distorted. There was a great pressure against her chest as though a giant had decided to use her lungs as a chair. She gasped and water surged into her. It stifled her screams as she thrashed about. Grace kicked and flailed, watching the light shift against the surface of the water above her. Somehow she'd slid down to the bottom of the bath. Had she fallen asleep as the warmth overwhelmed her or had someone pushed her down?

Grace smacked at the smooth sides of the bath, tried to scream. Somehow she couldn't climb back up, couldn't get out. Everything sounded muffled, muted, even her own despair.

No, no, not like this.

She wasn't about to meet Peter's end. But she could feel her chest tightening as it was deprived of vital air. Then there were hands on her shoulders.

Suddenly Grace was screaming, the anguished sound filling the small bathroom. The hands moved to her back and began slapping hard against her skin.

"Breathe," someone ordered her. "Just breathe."

"Peter," she coughed and spluttered his name. "Peter!"

"Grace, just calm down and take deep breaths."

"I won't let you take me, not like you took him." She found the strength to turn round, certain she was about to face her mother. Aaron was there, soaked by her bathwater, with Franklin looking stricken in the doorway, towel in hand.

"You… you must have fallen asleep and slipped under the water," he explained softly, extending the towel to her.

"Grace, it's okay," Aaron found her shoulders again as she began to weep. Drenched and naked her secret was there for them both to see, there was no hiding any more.

*

"You don't have to tell us anything," Aaron reassured Grace as he handed her a mug of tea. She was on the sofa, swathed in her flannel pyjamas and Franklin's fluffiest bath robe. Her hair was still wet.

"Seriously, Grace," Franklin tapped her knee from where he was nestled beside her on the sofa. "We're just glad you're okay."

Aaron perched on the now vacant television unit and looked at Grace, unable to focus on anything else.

"I…" gently she raised a hand to let her fingertips graze against her neck. She could still taste lemons. "What happened back there—"

"It's over now, you're okay," Franklin kept his hand on her knee and squeezed. "You're safe."

"You did really freak out," Aaron's voice was husky, low. "You were screaming, you couldn't get yourself out of the bath."

"I…"

The water. It had been all around her, against her back, at her sides. She usually liked how getting soaked in water challenged her mother's insane ideas. But this time it felt like the water was trying to punish her, trying to hold her down.

All are punished.

She could lie. She could look her friends square in the eye and say she just fell asleep in the bath and panicked when she came to under the water. She could blame the stress of the evening, the cold outside. But the concern etched into their expressions told Grace that she finally owed her friends the truth, that she was done hiding the worst parts of herself from them.

"Okay…" she drew in a deep breath. "If I tell you why I freaked out do you promise not to disown me?"

Franklin crossed his heart and Aaron solemnly nodded. "I'd never disown you," he confirmed. "No matter what."

"The other day," Grace plucked at a loose thread in the towelling robe, needing her hands to find some sort of distraction from what her mouth was about to say. "I went to visit my mum. She's..." she took another long breath, her lungs still aching from all the water they'd taken in. "She's in an institution because years ago she was diagnosed as insane. And still is."

"I feel like my old man should be in an institution," Franklin jested, before being silenced by a hot look fired at him from Aaron.

"She's there because she's the reason my brother died."

There it was, the truth Grace was forever trying to shed but kept stubbornly growing back like a second skin. No matter where she went, what she did, she was the daughter of a murderer. A crazed one at that.

"What happened?" Franklin's voice was soft, careful, like raindrops on rose petals.

"My mum was fanatical. She was a devout Christian but she twisted things. Like, she believed that rain was God's tears and that you couldn't let it touch you. And she abused my brother and me," Grace's chin dropped against her chest. "She would beat us for doing something she deemed insolent and then tell our teachers that we fell. No one ever questioned her because she went to church every Sunday and wore dresses without a single crease in. She was well turned out, polished. But Christ, was she crazy."

The agony of her history sliced across Grace's skin which was still pink from her dramatic time in the bath. Peter was still gone, the truth lacked the power to bring him back.

"What did she do to your brother?" Aaron queried, leaning forward, his eyes locked on her with grave intensity. "Remember you don't have to tell us if you don't want to. I know this must be painful."

"He wanted us to get away," Grace raised her head and let her tears flow freely down her cheeks. "Peter wanted us to be somewhere safe. He stole some money from our mother, a paltry amount, thinking it'd be enough to buy us a bus ticket. We didn't care where we went, just as long as we got away from there. But she found out. Of course she did. She turned on Peter, I tried to stop her and she hit me. I blacked out and when I came to…"

She could almost feel the worn fibres of the damp bathmat beneath her feet. The memory was still so real, so powerful.

"Peter was in the bath," Grace gasped, handing her tea to Franklin so that she could bury her head in her hands. "My mum was holding him down by the shoulders. He was already dead."

No one spoke. The wind rattled along the wall accompanied by the slap of rain against the window.

"Shit," Franklin finally puffed out a breath he'd been holding. "Grace that's… that's beyond awful."

"She tried to blame me," Grace wiped at her eyes and sniffed heavily. "When the police arrived she said I'd done it, but they could see she was lying. I was immediately taken into care. I didn't see her again for years."

Aaron said nothing, just kept staring.

"Please," Grace looked between her friends, imploring them. "Please don't judge me. I'm not like her, I'm not crazy. I'd never hurt anyone I—"

Franklin fell against her, all weight and cologne. He squeezed her tight, pressing her to his chest. "I will never, ever, judge you for having a fucked up mother." As he made his declaration he kissed her forehead repeatedly. "You can always be honest with me, Gracey bear, I love you. If Jasper were here he'd say the same thing."

Jasper.

Grace's tears fell with renewed force. The second brother she risked losing. Jasper was hanging in the purgatory between life and death, so terribly close to being taken from her.

"He needs to wake up," she wept against Franklin's shoulder. "He needs to wake up." She wasn't sure who was speaking; the adult on the sofa or the little girl on the bathmat staring at her submerged brother. "Please, he needs to wake up. He can't leave me."

*

For the next thirty minutes Grace cried and Franklin held her. When she finally slid back from his embrace he still seemed reluctant to let go.

"Franks," she sniffed and forced a smile. "It's late, really late. We need to sleep."

"Pfft. Who needs sleep. More hugs." He reached for her but Grace stood up before she could be engulfed in another bear hug.

"Tomorrow is a big day," she told him. "We've a routine to rehearse."

"Oh, Grace," Franklin clambered to his feet and paled. "No, no. We can forget about that. You've been through so much and—"

She held a hand up to silence him. "I'm doing it for Jasper. For you and Aaron." Glancing around she saw that Aaron was nowhere to be seen. "I *can* do it," she told Franklin confidently. "With your help of course."

He gave her one last hug and then let her drift over to her bedroom. Grace was ready to sleep. The stress of the evening had drained her. Closing her door she looked over her twinkling fairy lights and tried to let their soft glow calm her.

"Hey."

Her bed was not empty. Aaron was resting against her pillows, book in hand. As she approached he marked his page and placed his current read by the side of the bed.

"Hey," Grace frowned as she positioned herself beside him. "What's this? You looking to sleep in here tonight?"

"You should have told me." His green eyes studied her like she was a pearl in a clam he'd just prised open.

"Look, Aaron—"

He cupped her chin with his warm hand and drew his face close to hers. "You should have told me. I'd never, ever have judged you, Grace. I'd have just been there for you."

"But…" Grace could still taste the salt of her tears mixed with the lemon of the bathwater. "I didn't want what she did hanging over me, to colour people's view of me."

"It would have made no difference to me. It *makes* no difference to me."

"Because we're friends?"

"Stop saying that we're friends."

"But—"

"I love you."

And then his lips found hers. Grace melted into the kiss, his embrace. She kissed him until there was no air left in her lungs and then she kissed him some more. With their bodies they made amends to each other in a way that words never could. When dawn came Grace was still in his arms, sleeping deeply.

23

When Grace awoke the bed was empty, the sheets beside her crumpled. Yawning, she sat up and looked for Aaron but he was already gone. For a fleeting moment she wondered if she'd dreamt their reunion but her lips still tingled from the pressure of his kiss. Smiling softly to herself she climbed out of bed and headed for the bathroom.

"I know that look," Franklin was buttering toast in the kitchenette when Grace entered the main living area.

"What... look?" she tried to twist her features into a less revealing expression.

"The look that says you got laid," Franklin deadpanned, eyebrows lifting.

"Franks—"

"No judgement here," he raised his hands in submission. "I merely urge you to channel all that lingering sexual energy into tonight's performance."

"Performance?" Grace wilted. The events of the previous night had almost, but not quite, erased her time at Menthol Tiger from her memory. Now there was just a dozen hours separating her from a date with a podium. "Shit." Her head thumped with the onset of a headache as reality caught up with her.

Wincing, Grace massaged her temple and made for the sofa. "I totally forgot."

"Well, I didn't," Franklin followed her over and passed her a plate of freshly buttered toast. "And once you're fed and watered I've a master class in seduction planned out for us."

"I…" Grace looked at her breakfast, felt her stomach churn. She couldn't do this, could she? Perform erotically? It was against everything she'd ever trained for, the opposite of every delicate, poised movement which she could perform from muscle memory alone.

"A ballerina is grace, is elegance," her teachers would say. And she *was* Grace. It was her destiny to be a dancer.

"I'm not built for the podium," she had one bite of toast and then placed her plate on the empty television unit.

"Grace, Grace, Grace," Franklin was in his kimono, hair slicked back, looking like a matinee idol from fifties Hollywood. "Do you ever think that it's in your best interest as a dancer to, you know, diversify?"

"No."

"As an actor I have to embrace every aspect of my craft. I have to be able to play the lover, the villain, the hero. Everything needs to be in my repertoire."

"That's acting, Franks, not dancing. Dancing is different."

"Is it?" Franklin challenged. "Because right now, Grace darling, you have one speed, and it's classic and slow. In the future, don't you think you'll do better at auditions if you dance something *other* than ballet?"

"Other than ballet?" But ballet was her life. When Peter died it became her surrogate family. Amongst the classic piano notes and the various plies she found comfort, stability. Ballet was home.

"Just humour me," Franklin urged, "give erotic dancing a try. Move beyond your comfort zone and think of it all as an exercise in diversifying, in honing your craft by expanding your horizons."

Grace had known other dancers branch away from ballet, take up tap and modern. But the greats, they remained purists to their pursuit.

You're not one of the greats.

The thought kicked Grace squarely in the ribs.

You're not good enough. You need to go home. You need to give up.

"Where's Aaron?" she desperately needed to change the subject of the conversation, move it away from herself.

"He headed out early." Franklin turned away from her as though hiding his expression.

"Why?"

When he leapt up from the sofa and swept across the room towards the kitchenette Grace hurriedly followed.

"Look, Grace," he turned to face her, one hand on his hip. "I'm not getting involved in your couple drama, okay?"

"What drama? I just asked where he was!"

Franklin sighed and looked weary. "And he asked me not to tell you." Clicking his fingers in frustration he turned away from her. "Shit, I've already said too much. I'm just no good at keeping secrets."

"Franks, where is he?"

"Christ," Franklin rolled his eyes and pushed up his ornate silk sleeves. "I'm telling you this because it will just get out anyway, stuff always does around here. *But*," he narrowed his eyes at her, "you did *not* hear it from me and you're forbidden from using information I'm about to impart to make a scene. Are we clear?"

"Crystal."

"He said he was going to see Paulie."

"His uncle?" Grace wasn't sure why the level of secrecy was needed when it was just a family visit.

"Mmm," Franklin pulled his lips into a firm line. "He said something about going to ask for help."

"Help?"

"He doesn't want you to dance."

The words were pressure against her skin, uninvited acupuncture. "What?"

"Don't you see," Franklin threw his arms up and shook his head. "He loves you. He never stopped loving you, the caveman within him just prevents him from expressing himself in productive ways. Now you're back on your pedestal, back as his delicate little Grace and he can't handle the thought of you dancing for money. Hence, he's gone to pay his gang lord uncle a little visit which, if you ask me, is a very bad idea."

"How's it a bad idea?"

"This is *our* debt, Grace. *We* need to pay it. Old Paulie might show kindness to Aaron but what about us? We're not family. A thug is a thug no matter the bloodline."

"But surely—"

"He'll want Aaron," Franklin laid it out. "He'll want his strong shouldered nephew to do work for him in return for his assistance, work of the less than legal variety. Work which would pull Aaron further and further away from his dream of making it as a musician. Is that what you want?"

"I... no. Of course not."

"He thinks you're this orchid he needs to carefully tend, that you can't expose yourself to the elements, that you're too fragile. Grace," Franklin's hands were now both on his hips, "excuse me for the real talk but you called the police on your own mother. That took some balls, girl. Then you carved out a life as a ballerina. You're so much braver, so much stronger, than you let on."

"I was always just surviving, Franks, there's nothing brave about that."

"And what are you doing now?" he demanded. "You're surviving. The money from Menthol Tiger would go a long way to getting us out of this hole we're currently in. It'd save Aaron from being indebted to his uncle. But," Franklin cocked his head to the side as his tone softened, "this will always be *your* decision. You tell me you want to dance tonight, we'll spend all day rehearsing. You tell me it's not for you, then I'll explain things to Stiles and we won't speak of it again."

Grace chewed her lip as she considered her options. She loved the thrill of performance, the way the thunderous applause of the audience shook her bones. But getting up on a podium in her best underwear wouldn't be like gliding across the stage to Tchaikovsky. No one would clap, they'd just leer. Is that what she wanted? But it was just three nights. She'd grown from a girl to a woman without the love of a mother, she could do this, couldn't she?

"I want to dance."

She knew that she had to save Aaron from himself, from the path he was beginning to venture down. His future was out on stage with his guitar, not lurking in back alleys. She would dance to set him free. To set them all free.

"You'd better be completely committed to this," Franklin warned, "because I'm going to push you here. *Fame costs*," he began, quoting from his favourite film, "*and right here is where you start paying in blood, sweat and tears.*"

*

Franklin made good his threat. When six o clock came round Grace had been rehearsing for four hours straight, stopping only to rehydrate. Aaron had yet to return to the flat.

"These work," Franklin had rooted through her underwear drawer and chosen a matching set of black lace French knickers and a balcony bra, items Grace had bought a year ago when her friendship with Aaron had first ventured into unknown territory. With her fancy lingerie hidden beneath a navy shirt dress Grace wolfed down a plate of cheese on toast and tried not to think about the night ahead, about the podium waiting for her in the darkened nightclub.

"You've got this," words of encouragement seemed to be on a permanent loop. Every time Franklin looked at her he said something reassuring.

"Just remember to keep your hips loose and let the music guide you."

There was no strict order of moves, not like a ballet routine Grace would have to commit to memory, dancing through each step even in her sleep until it was perfect. Franklin taught her a few key elements, like bending low and then flicking her head up, letting her hair fall against her shoulders. They were about to leave when he clapped his hands together excitedly and disappeared back into his bedroom.

"I almost forgot," he told her as he hurried back with a large box. "I knew I still had this somewhere and it'll be perfect for tonight, plus it'll help keep your anonymity." Franklin popped the lid and Grace peered into the box. It contained a soft pink wig styled in a blunt bob, just like the one Natalie Portman wore when she worked as a stripper in the film *Closer*. It was Jasper who'd introduced them all to the movie, citing it as one of his favourites because he loved that it all revolved around a writer.

"This is…" Grace pulled out the wig. "Really cool."

"Here, let me fix it in place," Franklin plucked a handful of hair grips from his pocket. A few minutes later and the wig was in place.

"Just let me check it out." They didn't have much time but Grace needed to see it. Dashing back to her bedroom she opened the door and approached her antique mirror. The woman looking back at her appeared exotic and beautiful, like a hummingbird. Her dark eye makeup was set off by the light hue of the pink wig. The bluntness of the bob highlighted the softness of her jawline. She was an innocent siren. Grace stared, wishing she could be the woman in the mirror, could embody all the characteristics you'd expect her to have.

"Okay, vanity time is over," Franklin was in the doorway sounding tense. "We've got a show to perform so time to move that pert little bum of yours."

*

Nothing had changed at Menthol Tiger. The music was still a heartbeat throbbing through the walls, darkened booths still housed suited men. Beautiful women owned their podiums, moving as though they didn't have a single insecure bone in their body.

But Grace was different. Her scalp itched beneath her wig but she didn't dare touch it. It provided her a way to hide in plain sight, she couldn't take it off. At coat check she and Franklin had to part ways.

"I'll be out there the whole time," he told her, sounding just like the protective fathers Grace would overhear with their children before a show. "If there's a problem just look for me, okay?"

"Okay."

Grace was shown through a door she hadn't gone through before, one which led to the dressing rooms for the performers. Or rather, dressing room. There was no single annex for the star, at the club everyone got ready together just like they were all part of the chorus. Grace was used to these communal changing areas, she used to thrive on the energy, the camaraderie as everyone carefully applied lipstick and fake lashes before squeezing into their costumes for the night.

However, there was little preparation required. Grace needed only to slip out of her dress and she was ready, Franklin had seen to that. He'd coated her skin in glittery body gel, framed her eyes with shades of pewter and black and applied thick lashes.

"I like the wig," a slim brunette was mounting her curled hair atop her head, peering into the single mirror which ran the length of the longest wall in the changing room.

"Oh, thanks," Grace nervously touched the ends of the pink hair with her fingertips. The fibres were blunt, lacking the softness of her natural hair.

"First time dancing here?" the brunette leant back from the mirror, adjusting the gold bra she was wearing.

"Yeah, does it show?"

"It shows." The gravity defying shoes the brunette was wearing clipped against the floor as she doubled back towards her bag. Bending low she scooped out a bottle of expensive vodka. "Here," she proffered it to Grace. "Take a swig."

"I—"

"It'll help. Trust me." She passed Grace the bottle and thrust her other hand forwards. "I'm Cleo, at least in here I am."

"I'm…" Grace hadn't had time to think of a stage name, hadn't known she'd need to. "Petra," she suddenly blurted. It was as close to Peter as she could get and she needed him in her thoughts, needed the memory of his reassuring presence. She sipped from the bottle of vodka and the liquor burned against the back of her throat.

"Have a good first night," Cleo smiled kindly at her. "And remember, you don't have to agree to go behind the curtain if you don't want to."

"Behind the curtain?"

"Christ, you are new, still wet behind the ears." Cleo had an accent that Grace couldn't quite place, there was a hint of something American, Bostonian perhaps, but she seemed to be going to great pains to hide it beneath a more British tone. "Sometimes a guy asks for a VIP dance, that means you go behind the velvet curtain into one of the club's private spaces. There you dance solely for your punter, maybe take off your pants and bra, you know, the usual."

"Right."

Cleo laughed heartily. "Maybe stick to the podium tonight, Petra," she slapped Grace on the shoulder. "You look genuinely terrified. Drink some more vodka to take the edge off."

It was Stiles who came to collect Grace from the changing room, who led her through the back corridors of the club before releasing her via a hidden door into the main area, facing a currently vacant podium.

"That's you," he prodded her in the back. "Now get up there and don't make me regret this, Grace."

"Petra," she quickly turned back to him. "In here, call me Petra, please."

"I don't care what the fuck you call yourself, just don't get me fired, okay?"

Grace was about to reply when the hidden door slammed shut and Stiles was gone. She was alone. Tentatively Grace approached the circular podium. The pole erected in its centre shone under the twinkling glow of the chandelier. She tottered up, reaching to it for support as she climbed onto the podium. Her overly high heeled shoes felt clunky on her feet. Grace deliberated for a second and then removed them, knowing she'd move with much more ease if her feet were bare.

A song was playing that she faintly recognised, something about a pony. She listened for the main beat, let her hips start to swing in time to it.

You're not good enough. You need to go home. You need to give up.

The vodka in her system wasn't enough, she was still under siege from her constant negative thoughts.

Aaron.

Jasper.

Franklin.

She was doing it for them. For her friends. Besides, in here she was no longer Grace, she was Petra. Pink haired Petra was sexually liberated, confident. Shutting out the rest of the club Grace focused on the podium, the pole, and the music. The strident beats and the sultry tones welcomed her like an old friend. In music and performance she'd always been able to hide, to find sanctuary and they weren't letting her down now.

24

"I want a private dance."

The music pounded in Grace's ears. She swayed against the pole, letting her hips flex in time to the beat.

"Hey." A man was sat near the base of her podium, eyes and stomach bulging. The buttons of his shirt straining against his rotund midriff. Sweat pooled beneath his arm pits, darkening the fabric of his suit jacket. "I said I want a private dance."

Grace sashayed to the other side of the podium, turning her back on the man. She tried to imagine she was somewhere else, wished the darkness of the club would envelope her like a cloak. But each podium was beneath a spotlight, exposing every inch of her glittering skin to the lecherous audience who were concealed in the shadows.

She pretended that the pulse within the music was not an incessant rhythm but the rush of waves running up to greet her as she stood on the shoreline, Peter's hand held in her own. The chandelier became a sun as the duo raced over to the rock pools to search for mermaids.

"VIP experience, let's go, now." The man was on his feet. He raised his voice and shattered the illusion

Grace had created for herself. She was now well and truly in the club breathing in the smell of stale liquor and the odious fumes from the man which wafted up to her.

"Look," she spun round to face him.

Just be polite, she told herself. This was the first of only three nights, she wasn't expected to go behind the velour curtains into the private booths, was she? That hadn't been part of the deal. She was just to dance out in the main club, out in plain sight.

"I'm sorry but I can't offer that... service." She gave the man the sweetest smile she could muster and then resumed dancing.

"I'm growing old here, sweetheart. Let's go." Balding and overweight the man was a soiled sandwich wrapped in expensive paper. His suit shone from more than just his sweat, it was clearly embroidered with luxurious fibres. But all his efforts were in vain. He was still balding, obese, with angry blue eyes that had sunk into the bulge of his plump face. Who was he in the light of day? A banker? A media mogul? Some guy who got lucky on the lottery?

"Like I said, I'm very sorry but—"

"You're not paid to talk, sweet tits," he scowled at her. "You're paid to shake that ass. Now get in the VIP area and give me a real show."

"I—" Grace's skin burned with indignation. A thousand insults surged up her throat, desperate to reach her tongue and be fired at the man like angry little arrows. But before she could speak a hand grabbed her wrist and tugged her back, away from the podium. "Hey," twisting round she saw Stiles. But he wasn't looking at her, he was looking at the large man in the designer suit.

"I'm so sorry, she's new. Cindy over there will join you in the VIP area, on the house."

The man rubbed his hands together, his fingers like overstuffed sausages, and slowly shifted himself over to the next podium where a tall redhead was dancing.

"Thank you," Grace sighed with relief as Stiles hauled her back through the door hidden in the wall panelling. Within the confines of the corridor the music sounded like she was hearing it from underwater, all the notes muffled.

"Christ," Stiles released her and pressed the tips of his fingers against his temple. "I should never have agreed to this. You're too naïve. What the hell was I thinking?"

"Did I not do okay?"

Stiles slammed one hand against the wall. "Mr Latchkey is one of our biggest tippers and a platinum member of the club."

"I didn't know."

"I can't afford to make him unhappy."

"He was asking for a VIP dance and—"

"You're done for the night," Stiles was shaking his head as he looked at her. "Next time someone asks you for the VIP experience direct them to another girl, okay? Never say no."

Next time.

The two words filled Grace with dread. She would have to dance on the podium again, have to feel the penetrating stare of strangers against every inch of her body again.

"Why are you even doing this?" Leaning against the wall Stiles folded his arms over his lean chest and stared at her. A naked light bulb buzzed and flickered overhead.

"For the money." Wasn't that obvious?

"Is Franklin in some sort of trouble? How did he even rope you into this?"

He found a briefcase.

Franklin was in trouble, and so was Grace. But she couldn't risk Stiles, or anyone else, knowing that. Beyond the flat it was becoming increasingly difficult to tell friend from foe.

"He's just in some debt. We both are."

"Sounds about right," Stiles rolled his eyes. "Champagne lifestyle on a lemonade budget, that's Franklin."

"So, yeah," Grace hugged her arms against herself, longing to put some clothes on. "We both need the money pretty bad."

"Fine." Stiles resumed walking back up the corridor and then stopped abruptly, spinning round to face Grace. "He tell you why I owe him?"

She shook her head.

"Huh," a soft smile pulled on Stiles' lips. "Maybe he's more trustworthy than I thought. Okay," he clicked his fingers towards the rest of the corridor, "go change and get the hell out of here. I'll see you again tomorrow night."

*

"You did great," Franklin met her at the coat check, wearing a broad smile. "Amazing even. Everything was going fine until Lord Lardarse began hassling you."

"He wanted a VIP dance," Grace explained as she pushed her arms into the sleeves of her coat, grateful to be hidden beneath several layers of clothing.

"Mmm, I bet."

"You really think I did okay?"

"Grace, you were..." they stepped outside and Franklin placed his arm around her shoulders, "you were elegant and alluring, everything you needed to be."

There was ice on the road, the streets. It glistened beneath the street lights. Some pubs had strewn grit outside their doorways to help revellers keep their footing as they hobbled by.

"Do you think it will snow again?" Grace craned her neck to look at the sky. There were no stars, their shine dimmed by the glare of the city. She missed being able to see them. At her dance school she'd gaze up at them from the window of her dorm room. They became glittering diamonds of hope, twinkling in the sky in the endless desire of being wished upon. But Grace didn't bother with wishes as the only one she'd ever want to make couldn't possibly come true.

I wish Peter were still here.

"I'm all for more snow," Franklin hugged her close as they wandered down the street together. "I've some heavy duty boots I really need to break in."

"Franks, how do you know Stiles?"

Beside her his pace slowed considerably. "Why, did he say something?"

"No. Nothing. I just wondered."

"Let's call him an old friend and leave it at that."

"Franks—"

"I'm not keeping secrets from you, Grace. At least not mine. Stiles has his own secrets and it's up to me as his friend to keep them."

*

Grace slept away most of the following morning. Bundled underneath her duvet she tried to forget how it felt to be almost naked in a vast room. But her dreams taunted her, reminded her of the flutters of adrenalin she felt up on the podium, how when her shyness subsided she actually felt sexy and confident.

When she sat up yawning and reached for her phone she saw that it was almost noon.

"Dammit." She needed to rehearse, to perfect what she did up on the podium. Pulling on a pair of joggers that had been strewn across her bedroom floor Grace hopped over to her door and used her elbow to pry it open. She spied the top of Franklin's head over the sofa. "Hey," she yelled over to him, "you could have woken me up."

"I decided to let sleeping beauty rest," he replied sagely.

"Humph." With her joggers on Grace scanned the clothes left haphazardly around her room for a jumper. She spotted a hoody emblazoned with her old dancing school's logo and hastily forced it down over her head. "We need to be practising," she told Franklin sternly as she headed for the kitchenette.

"You were fine last night, really," he told her between bites of toast. "Maybe throw in some more sweeps down and shake your arse as much as you can."

"Thanks for the constructive criticism."

"Grace," swallowing down the last of his brunch he leant against the back of the sofa and looked over at her. "This is Menthol Tiger, not the Royal Opera House. You just need to be sexy, that is your prerogative and once you're in your undergarments you're pretty much there."

"Yes, but…" Grace dropped a tea bag into an empty mug and exhaled. She was so accustomed to seeking perfection in her performance. On stage she hid behind her dancing, behind every meticulously rehearsed position and lift. At the club it was different. There was no strict routine, each dancer was allowed to pursue their own fluid interpretation of the music. And to what end? The night didn't end with applause. It ended with—

"Don't overthink it," Franklin urged. "Up on that podium overthinking is the enemy."

"You speaking from experience?" Grace teased.

"Perhaps."

"You really think we don't need to rehearse more today?"

"I think you need to rest," Franklin clicked his fingers at the kettle. "One for me please." He turned back to face the vacant television stand. "Rest and process. Nights at Menthol are long and we've two more to go."

"And Stiles is going to make good on the money he promised, right?"

"If you're asking if we can trust him then yes, we can." Grace might have imagined it but she thought she detected a hint of hostility in Franklin's voice. "He's going out on a limb for us, Grace, and this money, it's going to be a huge help."

"Did Aaron come back last night?"

"Mmm," Franklin waved an arm in the direction of the bedroom door that was still closed. "Think he's sleeping. I told him not to accept any offer his uncle made."

"And what did he say?"

"What do you think? He told me to get the hell out."

*

Grace didn't spend the afternoon resting as Franklin had suggested. She called Jasper's mother for an update.

"He's the same, stable but not awake. The doctors are positive that he should wake up soon but…" his mother's voice shattered into sobs before she could complete her sentence. Grace uttered her goodbye and well wishes before hanging up.

Twice she'd typed into Google the long term effects of a coma but failed to hit the enter button and call up any results. She needed to believe that Jasper was going to wake up and that when he did he'd be fine. He'd come back to the flat and chide the others for going through his book pile. Then he'd resume his position on the sofa and lose himself in his latest read.

The evening came around far too quickly. Grace resented its presence the moment the sun dipped low in the sky. As the streets darkened her heartbeat began to race. A new night meant another performance up on the podium.

"Be breezy," Franklin suggested when Grace queried him on how to deal with further Mr Latchkeys. "Breezy but seductive. Bat your eyelashes, squash your boobs together as you lean down to tell him that you'd *love* to give him a VIP dance but unfortunately you're new and aren't allowed to yet. Then gesture to the next podium."

"The VIP booths," they were on the tube and Grace's scalp was already itching beneath her pink wig. "How much goes on in there do you reckon?"

"You've seen *Closer*."

"I know but—"

"Grace, you're not going in so don't stress."

But all she could do was stress. Stress about dancing, about money, about Jasper, about Aaron and whatever deal he might have made with his uncle. With every breath a new, anxious thought was formed in Grace's mind.

You're not good enough. You need to go home. You need to give up.

Had it all been a mistake? Was she never destined to dance the way she did in her dreams, against a backdrop of classical music and applause?

"You're made of tough stuff, Grace," Franklin patted her knee just as they reached their stop and stood up to climb off the tube.

"You think?"

"I knew it when I met you," he continued as he swept ahead of her on the escalator. "You were so dainty and polite but there was a fire within you. No one keeps chasing a dream this long unless they're a warrior."

"Or a fool."

"Are we fools to want more?" Franklin was rising above her as the escalator carried them up out of the bowels of the city. "Wouldn't it be more foolish to accept what we have and never strive for more?"

"I guess."

"Stiles was one of the first people I met when I came to London," Franklin's expression became soft, reflective. "He was kind to me, Grace."

"Kindness is underrated."

"Do you resent me for bringing the case home?"

"What?"

Grace had been mentally preparing for the podium, for the sensation of the circulated air against her skin, for the pressure of hungry stares against her soul.

"The briefcase." Franklin's voice was flat as they left the escalator. "You hate me for bringing it home, right? You must do."

"Franks, I could never hate you."

"Because I hate myself for doing it," he quickly interjected. "I hate myself for always being so damn nosy."

"You weren't to know what was inside."

"True. I was quick to spend it though."

Grace looked down at her feet, unable to argue with what he'd said.

"You battled your demons in the bathtub," Franklin stepped closer to her. "And maybe they're not gone, not completely, but you're trying, you're fighting. I just let my demons consume me."

"Franks—" Grace lifted her chin and met his gaze.

"I tell myself that if I dress in the finest clothes, the most expensive shoes, then maybe I'll be good enough, maybe when I go home my dad won't just look straight through me." His eyes sparkled with unshed tears.

"Franks, you're a magpie," Grace squeezed his gloved hands. "You're drawn to beauty and I love that about you. You see it everywhere and you bring it into our little flat with all your elaborate purchases."

"But will I ever be good enough?"

"You're already good enough."

"Tonight you're dancing because of my mistake, because of what I did."

"We're in this together," Grace leant in and hugged him tight. "Our friendship is like a marriage; for better for worse."

"This is definitely worse."

"True," Grace kept hugging him. "But that means it can get better. Let's cling to that."

25

Two nights dancing were done. As Grace rolled into bed during the early hours of Thursday morning she longed for sleep to steal her away to a different kind of darkness than the one that filled Menthol Tiger. She wanted to dream, to venture beyond the flat, the city, her problems. Instead her sleep was deep and devoid of thought. When Grace awoke after nine, tentative threads of sunlight were streaking in beneath her curtains and casting patterns on the floor.

"Urgh," remaining on her back she massaged her temples. She ached but not in the way she did after a ballet performance. Her throat felt thick and clotted, her skin sticky beneath the sheets as she hadn't showered off the glittery gel that Franklin insisted on coating her in.

Beyond her room the flat seemed quiet. Grace tugged on some joggers and a jumper and cracked open her door. She could hear the steady rhythm of Franklin's breath as he slept on the sofa. Tip toeing towards the kitchenette Grace looked at the kettle and hesitated. To turn it on would be to fill the silence with bubbling bursts of sound. Franklin would surely wake and Aaron—

Grace twisted in the direction of his still closed bedroom door. He had not visited her again. Each time she returned from the club he'd already locked himself away, either already asleep or just pretending to be. Both scenarios hurt.

"No," Grace withdrew her hand from the switch for the kettle. The yearning to escape from the flat was still pressing against her, still demanding to be acknowledged. Dancing at Menthol Tiger didn't make her feel free and liberated in the way dancing usually did. On the podium it was impossible for her to hide behind her movements. The city, its sounds, its dense collection of souls, was hammering into her. Grace knew she had to get away for a moment of respite, needed to find some peace, some solitude. And there was only one place where she'd find that.

*

An hour later she was on the train nursing a cardboard cup of vanilla laced coffee. As she'd crept out of the flat she'd been careful not to disturb Franklin. Once she was on the tube she fired off a text explaining that she was going out but would be back later for her final night at the Tiger. Not that she relished returning but she was bound by a promise, by a need.

But for the day, at least she was now free. Bundled in her thickest jumper and a faded green parka she felt warm and blissfully covered up. She'd even shoved a black woollen knitted cap down over her ears to stave off winter's bite and also for extra coverage. Grace would have wrapped herself up in her duvet if she thought she'd be able to weave her way along the streets in it. Her curves, her skin, were hidden away out of sight.

The train had pulled away from the city. Bleak skyscrapers became empty fields. Grace sipped on her sweet coffee and hoped that her instincts were right, that this visit was needed. Because the last time she'd followed her gut and gone to see her mother things had not turned out as planned. Everyone at the institute was fooled, believing her mother had repressed all the terrible things she'd done. Only Grace saw through the act.

With a judder and a hiss the train came to a halt. She'd reached her destination. Grace followed the handful of other passengers who climbed off. They didn't race towards the exit like the commuters in London did, instead they ambled along the platform. Grace joined them in their slow rhythm as she climbed the steps out of the station and entered the little town she'd once known so well.

Chistone was a small place, not quite a village but arguably not quite a town. It boasted one single supermarket, two post offices and three churches. But there was no cinema and prior to the supermarket, barely any shops. Thankfully for Chistone, it bordered a larger town with many more amenities so the residents didn't miss out too much. It was the place where Grace had attended infant and briefly, junior school. She and Peter would admire the ducks on the pond as they walked past the little church nearest their home.

The block of flats where they lived were considered a boil on the porcelain skin that was Chistone. Erected in the seventies no one wanted them and locals regularly campaigned for them to be torn down. But the off white building was saved by technology. When mobile phones took off signal towers were placed on top of the flats, towers which brought in considerable revenue for the little town. So, the flats stayed.

As Grace walked through the town she refused to turn in the direction of the stone colossus where she'd once lived. She couldn't bear to look up at the dingy windows and remember what had happened on the sixth floor. She kept her head straight and increased her pace to brisk. There was still snow in Chistone. It was clumped against the side of the road, clustered at the base of street lights.

Turning a corner, the buildings thinned and the pavement stretched up into a steep incline which led up to a small church. The cold began to nip at Grace as she reached the church. It stood silent now but she remembered hearing its bells toll on a Saturday morning as a blushing bride stepped out through the main doors amid a blizzard of rice and confetti.

"One day," Peter would say as he watched her dreamily. "One day I'll get married." He was more inclined to flights of fancy than Grace was. She'd scrunch her nose up at him and stick out her tongue.

"Euw, married, who'd want to do that?"

Now the church was still, there were no hymns being sung that morning, no ringing of the bells. Grace followed the small path that bordered the church round to the modest cemetery. Headstones poked up from the ground like granite tree stumps. Some had been neglected over time and begun to sag back into the earth, listing at a dramatic tilt. Others were adorned with fresh flowers; roses, carnations, lilies. Generations had been laid to rest behind the little church. Grace shuddered as she walked by the large tree whose long branches reached out towards her brother's grave. She searched its stripped mass for the sheen of black feathers but no crows were gathered in the graveyard. Grace was alone.

Peter's grave did not stand up like many of the others around it. He had a flat headstone, pressed firmly into the ground bearing his name and two dates – one of which he shared with Grace.

Crouching down she pressed a gloved hand against the stone, wanting to feel its cold caress seep into her body.

"Hi, it's me," she whispered. There weren't even any leaves to rustle in response. The churchyard felt as cold and stark as a mortuary. "I just... I wanted to see you." Grace used her other hand to mop at the tears which had begun to slide down her cheeks. "I miss you."

She had no flower to lay against her brother's name. She should have stopped in the city to buy one, even a single rose. Instead his grave was going to remain bare, seemingly forgotten. Sometimes Grace wondered if anyone else came by to remember her brother. The few school friends he'd had would have grown up, moved on. As adults did they ever stop to think of the tragedy that befell the slender dark haired boy when they were young?

Grace knew that her mother didn't visit the grave, she wasn't allowed. The doctors at the institute feared it might hinder her recovery.

Recovery.

It was hard not to scoff at the word, even when knelt in a graveyard. Grace knew there was no cure for a blackened soul. Her mother had always been wicked, twisted into something inhuman by her broken mind.

"Sometimes I wonder who you'd be now," she blinked through her tears as she peered at the flat gravestone.

A doctor.

A lawyer.

A musician.

Peter could have been anything he set his mind to. But Grace figured that his innate kindness would have led him into a profession that helped others. So perhaps he'd now be a doctor, a vet. And what would he think of his sister dancing on a podium in her underwear to make money? Grace hung her head and coughed against a sob.

A ballerina. She was supposed to be a ballerina.

"Dream big, dream bright." Those were the words Peter would utter as they both lingered on the cusp of sleep.

"I will," Grace patted his grave one last time and then stood up. "I'll keep dreaming, I won't stop."

Snowflakes began to softly fall from a clouded sky. Grace tugged up the collar of her coat, knowing it was time to return to the city before the weather set in.

*

"You've been gone for hours." Franklin was upon her the moment she walked through the front door. "I've been worried sick, Grace."

"I texted you, I told you I was going out."

"Yes, but you didn't say *where*." Franklin threw his arms up in the air, then tutted and threw them around Grace and hugged her tight. "I even had to wake the beast."

"Aaron?" Turning, she looked for him, thought she'd find him sat on the sofa, staring blankly at where Tina used to be or perhaps he'd be smiling in her direction, his eyes bright with what now burned between them.

"Oh, his lordship is showering," Franklin frowned. "Apparently I'm a selfish idiot who should respect a man when he's sleeping. I say, whatever." He released Grace and stormed deeper into the flat. "I was worried, I needed to vent to someone."

"He doesn't like being vented to."

"Well, I know that *now*. Anyway," Franklin marched towards the kitchenette and tapped the countertop. "You hungry? I'm making pizza."

"Making?"

"Fine, heating from frozen. Still pizza. You want some?"

"Yeah, I'm starving." Grace hadn't eaten all day. On the journey home she'd felt too twisted up with old emotions to be able to face food. But now she was back in the warmth of the flat her stomach growled, reminding her that she needed to pay attention to it every now and then.

Franklin heard the grumble, his gaze dropping to her core. "Ooh, sounds it. So, where the hell were you today?"

"I went to see my brother."

There was no need to elaborate, not now Franklin knew the truth about her past. He nodded solemnly and then set about preparing a trio of pizzas. "I assume he'll want one too," he muttered as he loaded up the oven.

"Any word about Jasper?" Grace had crossed her fingers for a large portion of the train ride home, hoping against hope that her friend would wake up.

Within the kitchenette Franklin straightened and shook his head sadly. "No change today I'm afraid."

"Shit." Throwing off her coat Grace dropped onto the sofa and began kicking off her boots.

"Oh, Aaron wants to come along with us tonight."

"What?" Grace turned round so fast she felt dizzy. "He wants to come to Menthol Tiger?"

"Uh huh."

"He can't!"

"I told him you wouldn't want him there."

Her face was in flames at the thought of Aaron being there, stuffed inside a booth within the shadows looking up at her, watching her.

"Franks, he can't go."

"He's insisting," Franklin raised his hands defensively. "And you know how stubborn he can be. Don't make me get between you two on this."

Grace sighed, having no idea why Aaron would want to accompany them to the club.

"I…" as the flat filled with the smell of melted cheese and pepperoni Franklin appeared at Grace's side, looking sheepish.

"What?"

"I might have told him about Mr VIP."

"Franks—"

"So, he's just being protective. That's a good thing, right?"

Grace sighed again with added drama. Having Aaron at the club would only complicate things. After all, was he there acting as her friend or her—

"I can't deal with all this right now." She pushed herself off the sofa and made for her bedroom.

"Wait!" Franklin dashed after her, seeming to want to reach her door first.

"Franks, what the hell?"

"There's something in there."

With a start Grace released the door handle from her grasp. "Like what?"

"A surprise."

"Oh, Franks, what have you done to my room!" with a grunt she barged open the door expecting to find the contents of her friends' wardrobe adorning every available surface. Instead everything was how she'd left it, even her fairy lights were still on. The bed was made, several items of her own clothes were clumped in piles on the floor. Then she saw them. Four long slips of white card neatly aligned atop her duvet. Even from the doorway she knew what they were – tickets.

"Oh, my God," she hurried to them, keen to hold them in her grasp. Grace read the printed text upon them. Four tickets for a staging of Giselle at the Royal Opera House for the twentieth of February. That was just over a month away. "Franks," Grace rifled through them, unable to find the right words. "I… just…"

"Without sounding like a broken record I had a friend who owed me a favour," Franklin placed a hand on her shoulder as he remained just behind her. "I know how much you wanted us all to have a night out at the ballet and well, now we can."

"Four tickets," Grace kept counting them over and over. Four seats in the stalls. "One for each of us."

"Because he's going to wake up," Franklin's hand clenched against her shoulder. "I have to believe that he will. He's stable and—"

"You're right, he's going to wake up," Grace put down the tickets and rested her hand atop of Franklin's. "We're going to pay off that damned thug, Jasper will wake up and everything will go back to normal."

Franklin leant down and kissed the top of her head. "You're due a happy ending, Grace. And I, for one, am desperate to see you get one."

"Huh, yeah." She felt her blood begin to run cold as shards of ice gathered in her veins. She was back in the cold of the cemetery, back kneeling at Peter's grave. Where was his happy ending? His story finished in the shallow depths of a bathtub, at his mother's hand. He didn't get a wedding day, a chance to beam as the bells tolled. All he got was a modest grave devoid of flowers.

Turning, Grace pressed herself against Franklin's chest to try and stifle her sobs. If Peter didn't get a happy ending then why should she?

"Hey, come on now," he rubbed her back in a soothing way and held her close. "This will work out, Grace. Come February we'll all be watching Giselle totter across the stage at the Royal Opera House. It will be exquisite."

"And if we can't all make it?" she withdrew from him slightly and noticed a tear sliding down his cheek.

"Don't think like that," Franklin ordered. "We can't afford to think like that. It's all going to work out in the end, you'll see."

"You sound like Mrs Potts," Grace said with a brittle laugh.

"And she was right, wasn't she?"

"She was also an enchanted tea pot."

"Regardless," Franklin pressed her back against his chest. "I'm trying to think positive. You should too."

"But what if we don't deserve a happy ending?"

"Pah, I don't know four more deserving souls."

"Then you don't know many people."

"Grace, darling, I know everyone. We're making the money, Jasper is stable, let's stay on the bright side of this. Let's at least pretend that a month from now we'll all get dressed up and have a night at the theatre."

"Okay," Grace agreed. "I'll pretend, for now."

26

Grace stared at her laptop screen. All of her eBay auctions had ended and she'd successfully sold off her MacBook along with a few select items of clothing. She'd made just over two thousand pounds.

"So you're really selling it?" Franklin was beside her on the sofa, wrapped in his beloved kimono. He nodded at her laptop.

"It's sold." With a sigh she closed the device. "I'm keeping the phone but that's it."

"Seems... reasonable."

"And your items which we put up for sale, they've sold too."

Franklin grimaced. "Damn. There was a part of me that was hoping no one else had such exceptional taste and wouldn't bid on them."

"I know."

"But, I guess, needs must."

"Uh huh." Grace ran her hands over the smooth exterior of her MacBook. It was the most expensive thing she'd ever owned and now it was going to be packaged and sent to someone else. "We've done everything we could think of," she drummed her nails against the rose gold finish. "Is it enough?"

"Aaron is our resident Scrooge McDuck, he's been keeping tabs on all our finances."

"Okay," Grace twisted to peer over the back of the sofa. Aaron's bedroom door was shut tight. "Is he still coming tonight?"

"I assume so."

"Great," she could taste the bile in her voice. Having Aaron at the club would be a terrible idea, all of her senses were screaming at her to keep him away.

"It won't be so bad," Franklin patted her knee and then stood up. "I think he's just trying to be supportive."

"Mmm."

There was a whisper of silk and then Grace was alone. She contemplatively glanced around the small flat. So many little changes had altered the feel of the room. Tina was gone, already rehomed and soon the last of their luxury items would follow. One by one they were losing all their portals to the outside world. She knew that if Jasper were there he'd object, tell them how important it was to nourish all their senses, that a healthy home needed music, film and literature. Aaron no longer had his guitar, Franklin had been forced to part with his beloved television, soon their only escape from reality would exist within the stack of books that belonged to Jasper.

*

It was busy in the post office. Grace waited in line, her boxed items held in her arms as Franklin lingered at her side with a pile of his own, impatiently tapping his foot. His boot kept a manic rhythm against the linoleum floor which thankfully no one seemed to be annoyed by.

"We're here too much lately," he told Grace without lowering his voice.

"We've had a lot of things to sell."

Slowly they shuffled their way up the queue. Outside a dark sky held dominion over the city. Even though it was almost noon it felt closer to midnight. Ebony clouds gathered above skyscrapers, swollen with an icy rain which according to reliable forecasts was due to commence falling any minute.

No more snow. The Met Office had seemed certain in its declaration. The days were marginally warmer and about to get considerably wetter.

"Urgh," Franklin nodded towards the windows of the post office which overlooked the busy street beyond. "I hope we're done here before it starts to rain. This coat isn't waterproof."

Rain.

Grace closed her eyes and imagined how it would feel to be caressed by its icy sharpness, to feel it soaking through her hair, finding her scalp and chilling her bones. She knew that her mother would have abandoned her chores at the post office to hurry home.

"We cannot let it touch us," she used to tell her young children as she dragged them along behind her by their slim wrists. "It is God's sorrow; we can't be touched by it, not even a drop."

Something poked her in the back. "Daydream later," Franklin hissed in her ear, "first let's get this crappy job over and done with."

They'd reached the front of the queue. Grace had all her items franked and weighed before parting with them. Her laptop had been released from her possession and would soon be en route to its new owner.

Rain was already falling from the sky as they emerged from the warmth of the post office. Each drop was long and fell with rigid force, like a watery arrow. Franklin turned up his collar and began hurrying along the street. Grace dawdled behind him, feeling raindrops pound against her coat, her hood.

"Listen, its gunfire." Peter would sometimes wake her in the night when rain was fiercely lashing against their bedroom window.

"What?" Grace would rub the sleep from her eyes and sit up to look at her brother who was already on his knees beside the window sill, peering between the drawn curtains.

"Gunfire," he'd beckon her over. "Listen."

"No," by the time she knelt beside him the fog of fatigue had all but lifted. Her senses were keen, sharp. She'd been forced to teach herself to wake up quickly, their mother was always unforgiving if they were sloth like in their morning routine. "It's rain, not gunfire," Grace knowingly corrected her brother.

In the darkness she'd just make out his indifferent shrug. "Same difference. Both are dangerous."

"Really? Are we doing this?" Franklin had eased his frantic pace and fell in step with her. "Do you really need to *dawdle* in the rain, Grace?"

She breathed in the damp air and nodded. "I do. I find it liberating."

"Fine, then we'll endure a natural shower together. Can't say I understand it," he linked arms with her, "but hey, who am I to judge?"

*

Everything was soaked. Grace tossed off her coat and it landed on the floor in a puddle of its own creation. Her shoes squelched and her hood had failed to save her hair from the onslaught of the rain.

"Christ," Aaron was stirring a Pot Noodle in the kitchenette. "You two swim in the river while you were out or something?"

"We merely *savoured* the rain," Franklin was already ramming his coat over the nearest radiator, fawning over its sodden fabric as though it were a wounded lamb.

"Well, make sure you dry off properly else you'll catch your death. It's cold out." He sucked down a forkful of noodles and kept watching his friends warily.

Grace felt the hook of his words cut through her.

Catch your death.

Was death something that could be caught?

"Oh, damn," Aaron tapped his fingers to his temple. "Shitty choice of words." His gaze settled solely on Grace. "I didn't mean anything I just—"

"It's fine," she moved away from him, needing the solitude of her bedroom. Already she was reaching into her drenched handbag for her phone which was thankfully bone dry. She called up the now familiar number for Jasper's mother and waited out the preceding four long rings.

"Grace, hi."

Within her room Grace firmly closed her door behind her, pulled off her damp socks and flopped down onto her bed, her phone pressed tightly against her ear.

"Hi, how's he doing today?"

"The same, there's no change." She could hear the exhaustion, the pain, which flowed through Jasper's mother as freely as her own blood. How many hours had she spent at her son's bedside? Did she wake up every day filled with the hope that he'd soon open his eyes or was that hope beginning to fade away?

"I was hoping to come by and see him on Saturday."

Saturday. Two days away. One day after their extended deadline. Would Grace even be able to see him them? If the thug at the door was yet again denied his money which threat would he enact first?

Grace's eyes squeezed closed as she recalled how it felt waking up in the bath tub, splashing desperately beneath the surface as scented bubbles seeped into her lungs. She didn't want to drown, didn't want the thug to drag her out to the river and shove stones in her pocket so that she drifted down to its bottom where Peter was waiting for her, extending a blue hand to help guide her into the depths.

"Saturday would be fine." Grace heard the way Jasper's mother tried to lift her tone and appreciated the gesture.

"Great, I'll bring some more of his books."

"Thank you. He'd... he'll like that."

"It's no problem," Grace hauled herself into an upright position. "And if anything changes please keep me posted, okay?"

"Of course, dear."

Jasper's mother hung up and Grace hunched forward. Really she needed to dry her hair, she could already feel her forehead becoming clammy and pinched with the threat of an imminent headache. Beyond the thin walls of her room she could hear the angry hiss of the shower which Franklin had already commandeered.

Falling back against her pillows Grace lay there until her breathing slowed and her eyes closed. Her bed became a calm lake on which she was serenely floating, untethered and free, letting the ripples in the water guide her.

*

"Last… night," Franklin forced her wig into place and then stepped back. "Tell me you're so attached to this you'll keep wearing it once you're no longer a tigress?"

"But then I'd be lying," Grace turned and glanced at her reflection. Yet again she was adorned with a pink bob and darkened eyes, clad in a tight fitting dress and heels that were almost too high to walk in.

"Okay, we're running a bit late," Franklin helped her into her coat. "But this is it, one final shimmy and then we're quids in."

It felt good to think that this was the last time she'd need to dance at the club, that she was so close to the valuable sum of money they so desperately needed. She followed Franklin out of her bedroom and any positive feelings she'd had quickly evaporated. Aaron was stood by the sofa in his worn out leather jacket, hands thrust deep into the pockets of his Levi's jeans. He was freshly shaved, a slick of gel dragged through his hair. When she walked in he cleared his throat and nodded in the direction of the front door.

"I guess we should get going."

"Why are you even coming?" Grace marched straight up to him. "Franks and I have handled ourselves these last two nights, we don't need your help."

"Okay, alright," Franklin grabbed her hands and began pulling her back, "we don't have time for a lover's quarrel right now. We've places to go, people to entice."

"I just want to be there for you."

Grace shook off Franklin's grip with such force he took a step back from her. "I know you went to see your Uncle Paulie. What did you promise him? Huh? Because I've got this, *we've* got this," she pointed at

Franklin who was raising his hands in submission. "Don't go making things worse, Aaron."

"I might have said *something*," Franklin quickly told his flatmate apologetically. "But, Aaron, in my defence, you know I'm utterly terrible at keeping a secret."

"Don't you worry about Paulie," he said this to Grace and then to both of them, "let's go."

"No." Grace stubbornly refused to move. Aaron's sudden desire to accompany her to the club was strange and worse than that, it was confusing. They'd still yet to discern what was even going on between them. How was she expected to dance erotically for strangers with her maybe boyfriend in the room? And was going back to Aaron the right move? She'd been so deeply wounded when they broke up and—

"We're leaving *now*," Franklin grabbed her forearms and began bundling her towards the door. "Stiles is a stickler for good time keeping and I'm not about to be late for him because of some bloody domestic."

Aaron followed and the three of them walked in silence to the tube station. The rain had eased from a torrent to an icy drizzle. Umbrellas still bobbed along the street and Grace tugged up her hood, knowing that she needed to keep her wig as dry as possible.

Once on the train the uneasy silence endured as they were ferried underground towards their next stop. It was only when they surfaced in Menthol Tiger's district that Aaron spoke. He tugged on Grace's arm, drawing her to his side.

"I won't go in if you don't want me to." He sounded so calm, so logical. "I'll just wait outside until you're done."

"No," Grace shook off his touch, "you'll just go and sit in some bar and drink the night away."

He grunted like he'd just stepped on something sharp. "I'm trying," he told her sincerely. "This is new territory for us both and I'm not going to fuck things up again."

This wasn't the kind of conversation Grace needed to be having before her final performance. Her heart was already clenching with the agony and the ecstasy of it. He was talking about trying again, but to try again meant opening herself up to all that had come before, all the pain.

"Fine, come in and just sit with Franks."

"Ooh," Franklin clapped his hands together. "Some company for little old me in there, how novel."

"What do you take off?" he tilted his head and lowered his voice as he delivered the words directly into her ear, raising his hands to peel back the edge of her hood.

"I… uh…"

"Because I need to know how much to drink to get through this."

"I keep on my underwear," Grace told him briskly. "I just dance."

I just dance.

Since losing Peter that had been her one goal in life. As she moved through the years she unquestioningly chased her goal, always telling anyone who was interested;

"I just want to dance."

But tonight her stage was a podium, her soundtrack the booming base of a club stereo system. This was not the dream.

"But you're still dancing." She could almost hear Peter, hear his boundless ability to always try to see the best in a situation.

"Well, then," Aaron coughed nervously. "That shouldn't be too bad."

"And we get to catch up all night," Franklin enthused as they approached the main entrance to Menthol Tiger.

"Great."

"That better not be sarcasm I hear."

"It's not; it's pure, unadulterated joy."

"Nope, definitely sarcasm."

"Come on," Grace pushed her way between them both. "Let's just get tonight over with."

27

Thursday marked the busiest night in Menthol Tiger that Grace had experienced so far. She did her best to ignore the faces that peered up at her and just focus on the music, her movements. With each pivot around the pole she battled not to think about Aaron, about where he might be sat with Franklin. Was he watching her? Or was he facing the bar, his back towards the podium?

Grace kept dancing, kept letting the music guide her limbs. Time became viscous; slow and stubborn. As a new song came on she wondered how long was left, how long until she'd earned all the money she so desperately needed.

The men who bordered her podium wore suits along with their stares. Leaning back in their chairs they surveyed her like she was there for their entertainment and theirs alone. Bank notes were thrust against the edge of the podium, notes Grace knew better than to pick up. Since she wasn't a regular at the club she wasn't working for tips. When her stint was over someone else would come and collect up any money adorning her podium and distribute it between the other girls.

You're not good enough. You need to go home. You need to give up.

Alone on the podium it was all too easy for her mind to inflict pain.

"But I'm still dancing," she told herself, calling upon the hope which had loomed so large in her twin brother. Had he still been hopeful as he faced death? Or did it ebb away along with his final, strained breaths as he looked up at the watery image of his mother holding him down?

"Hey!"

An objection, from close by. Grace realised she'd lost her footing. She landed rump first at the base of the podium, feeling the shock of the fall bouncing up her spine.

"At least stay on your feet," a man scorned, his thinning brown hair revealing a glistening central bald spot as he leaned down to adjust the buttons on his shirt. "I'm not paying to watch you fall."

Clutching the pole Grace stood back up and resumed dancing but now her palms were slick with sweat and her back ached. Her audience had thinned since she'd let herself get distracted, let herself fall. But the brown haired man remained. He wore an ill-fitting navy suit and the plumpness of his face made it difficult to estimate his age. When he spoke it was with a haughty, condescending air.

On the other side of the club people were excitedly gathering near a booth. Keeping a tight hold of her pole Grace craned her neck to peer at the action. She saw several men dressed in black with ear pieces coiling down towards their thick necks; bodyguards. She instantly envied whoever was in the booth. They'd paid for protection, didn't need to walk the streets of London checking over their shoulder since they had someone to do that for them.

"Hey," with a click of his fingers the blue suited man caught Grace's attention. His lips were puckered in anger. "Never mind that fucking Spencer Daniels just walked in. He's not going to want to watch your shoddy show. Now dance, love, come on."

Spencer Daniels.

The name chimed with recognition. Grace searched her memory and realised that during her time in possession of a Mac book his name had been flashed across all the gossip sites. There were rumours circulating him like vultures, rumours of rape and abuse and a court date had been set where he could plead his case. Clearly he wasn't overly concerned since he was now sat in a high end strip club on a Thursday night.

Grace was still glancing over, still wondering if the millionaire playboy was as terrible as the media painted him out to be. The blue suited man stood up and scoffed at her.

"Fine, fuck it," he snatched back the money he'd previously placed on her podium and slumped over to the next dancer.

Two more hours slowly slid by. Most people in the club had gathered around the booth housing the infamous VIP, orbiting him like planets drawn to a star. When Stiles came to tell Grace her time was up she could have wilted in relief. She clambered down off the podium and followed him through the hidden door in the wall and into the back corridor.

"You did okay," he handed her a stack of bank notes with no objection. "But if you ever want to do this professionally I suggest you maybe take some classes or something. You can dance, sure, but you don't move like the other girls do."

"I'm too aware." Grace already knew the flaw which would forever prevent her from dancing as seductively as the other girls.

"Maybe, whatever," Stiles shrugged and began to walk away. Pressing a finger to his lips he suddenly spun around. "Just," he let the finger fall along with his gaze which lingered on his faux snakeskin loafers. "Tell Franklin we're even, okay? And if he wants to call me he can."

"Sure." As Grace nodded, Stiles was already loping his way up the corridor seemingly desperate to remove himself from her presence.

*

"Well, you're a free lady now," Franklin helped Grace into her coat. "No more working the stage. It's like the end of *Flashdance*. How do you feel?"

"Exhausted." She looked to Aaron who was stood at Franklin's side, head bowed. "I really just want to get home."

"Well, I thought you were fabulous," Franklin discreetly accepted the money which she passed to him, which he then left in Aaron's more capable hands. "And did you see who came in?"

They stepped outside. The street sparkled with the glow of streetlights and neon signs, the rush of the wind silenced by the swelling murmur of voices within nearby pubs and clubs.

"Spencer. Daniels," Franklin stated as he sidled out, arm in arm with Grace. "He's got some nerve to show his face in public considering what I've read about him lately."

Aaron hung back, separating himself from the duo. Grace tried to twist to glance at him but Franklin was pulling her along at a brisk pace, adhering to her request to head straight home.

The tube station was in sight when a shadow emerged from the shadows and blocked their path. Grace instantly edged closer to Franklin as she locked eyes with the stranger. Her first instinct was to scream, or maybe run. She wondered if the man had been sent via the thug who'd come to their door. But they still had a day to repay. She was about to tell the stranger as much when she realised that she recognised him. Though he was now clad in a long woollen coat, he bore the same plump face and angry eyes which gave him away. Raising her chin and clenching her jaw Grace stared down the blue suited man from the club.

"You're in our way," she told him defiantly.

"Bitch, you owe me a dance. A *proper* one." He managed to lean a little too heavily on his own words, almost losing his footing.

"She's no longer dancing at Menthol Tiger," Franklin told him with a grandiose air. "Go get your kicks somewhere else. And take that shabby estate-agent-esque excuse for a suit with you."

"I paid good money." The man shoved Franklin hard, revealing force unbecoming to his portly build. Grace reached for her keys in her coat pocket, ready to swipe them across the man's chubby cheeks if she needed to. She wasn't about to be accosted by some drunk. But she needn't have reached for her keys. Aaron swung into action, emerging from behind her like a deadly tsunami. He crashed straight into the man, his fist connecting with his lower nose. They all heard the unsettling crack of something breaking.

Arms rushing to his face, the man staggered back as his nose became a fountain of blood.

"Fuck!" he screamed at them all. "Fuck you, you bunch of fucking pricks. You broke my nose."

"I'll break your entire face if you don't get out of here," Aaron threatened.

Grace sensed a crowd closing in around them, tapping into their phones. Was someone going to call the police? Aaron had over three thousand pounds in cash on his person, he couldn't spend the night in a cell.

"We need to go. Now." Grace grabbed the hand which had thrown the punch and began dragging Aaron along the street. Franklin followed, his long coat sweeping out behind him like a cape. They raced into the station, down the escalators and thankfully just caught their train. As it thundered through darkened tunnels Grace took a moment to try and control her breathing. She saw Aaron studying his hand, his knuckles reddening.

"You didn't need to do that," she told him quietly. He said nothing.

Aaron didn't speak until they were back at the flat. Then he threw the front door open so hard that it shook fearfully upon its hinges.

"Fuck the money!" he roared, turning to face Franklin and Grace who'd nervously entered in his wake. "Fuck it, all of it. I should never have let you do this—"

"Wait, just—"

"No," he pawed at his head with his wounded hand. "This isn't you, Grace. Fuck the fucking money. When that thug shows up here tomorrow, if we're short I'll just… I'll just…"

"I danced for you," Grace told him sternly. Then, turning, "and for you," she eyed Franklin. "And for Jasper. And for myself." Now she was again staring at Aaron. "You don't own me, you never did. I can look out for myself. It was my decision to dance," she gestured to his bulging coat pocket, "and it was worth it. That money will go a long way to help us pay off the bloody creep harassing us."

"Grace—"

"I just want to go to bed," she shouldered her way past Aaron and headed for her bedroom. It felt good to shake off her coat and shoes, to climb out of her clothes and pull on her soft flannel pyjamas. Curling up against her pillows she hoped that sleep would soon find her. She wanted to distance herself from the events of the night with dreams and—

Aaron walked in, a bag of frozen peas clutched against his knuckles. "Can we talk?" He sat on the bed and peered at her tentatively.

"I just want to sleep."

"Okay then, can we sleep?"

"You have a temper." Grace stated as she rolled onto her side.

"I know," she felt the mattress shift as Aaron wedged up beside her. "But I'm working on it. It's just... the way that guy was talking to you... I saw red."

"You could have broken his nose."

"I hope I did."

"Aaron—"

"I keep trying to shield you from the world," he ran his good hand along her back. "I keep thinking you're as delicate as you look but you're not. I understand that. But I'm still the same stubborn headed guy who is trying to get better. Can you be patient with me?"

"Why did you even come tonight?" with a sigh Grace dropped onto her back, tracing the cracks in her ceiling as she spoke. "I mean, you'd not bothered the other nights."

"I guess... I guess I wanted to see."

"Me making a fool of myself?"

"You being so beautiful." Grace twisted her head to look at him, convinced he must be taunting her but she saw only sincerity in his gaze. "Yeah, you weren't throwing out the same moves as the other girls but you were beautiful and so... so alive. You have this connection to music through dance which I've always been in awe of."

"You didn't need to punch that guy."

"I know."

"Although in fairness he's got a face you just want to punch."

"See," Aaron playfully poked her.

"But really, now I just want to sleep. These last three nights have really taken it out of me."

"Okay," Aaron nuzzled against her pillows. "Let's sleep."

Grace closed her eyes but they quickly fluttered open. "What is this even?" she demanded.

"Sleep. It's what most people do at night."

"I mean, us," her body began to ache with regret. What if she was just repeating past mistakes? What if things once again turned toxic between them? She wasn't sure she had the strength to endure that a second time.

"Grace—"

"Is this how it is now? You sleeping in my bed all the time?"

"I'd like to," he leaned up and kissed the tip of her nose. "I know I've got a lot of making up to do. But, like you said, for now let's just sleep, okay?"

Exhaustion made it easy to agree. "Okay." Grace let Aaron spoon her as her eyes finally closed and stayed that way. Her breathing slowed as she listened to the gentle rattle of the wind against the window. In Aaron's arms she felt safe. No matter what came the following day, knowing they would face it together gave her enough comfort to drift off into a deep, dreamless sleep.

28

"With what we've already paid we're at eighteen thousand." Aaron was stood behind the counter in the kitchenette, his palms resting on either side of the stacks of money and loose change which adorned it.

"Eighteen?" Franklin massaged the back of his head as he stood close by. "That still leaves us pretty short."

"I know."

"And how long do we have?"

Aaron checked the time on his phone. "Just a few hours."

Friday had arrived. For most people it brought with it the excitement of the impending weekend but for the group it brought only a sense of dread.

Grace was on the sofa, her legs curled up beneath her as she leant against the back and looked over at her friends, at the vast amount of money Aaron had spent the afternoon meticulously adding up several times. She'd pulled the hood of her jumper up, concealing hair still damp from a shower underneath.

"There's no way we can make several thousand in just a few hours," Franklin stated with dismay.

"We just need to give the guy what we have," Aaron began stacking the money together into more manageable piles.

The radiator against the wall hissed but the flat still felt cold. Grace shuddered within her oversized hoodie. If they failed to pay the thug who was hounding them the full amount a second time what would he do? Her mind swiftly began to wander down a darkened path. Would he take a finger for every thousand he was still owed? What if that still wasn't enough? The thought of ending up in a watery grave made Grace want to retch.

"I used to feel so safe even in this crummy flat," Franklin muttered despondently. "Now I feel like I took that safety for granted."

Grace didn't share his concern. She'd learnt at a young age how it felt to feel unsafe and alone, to feel the sharp press of danger's blade against your back.

"Fuck," the expletive was carried as a long, drawn out sigh as Franklin landed on the sofa beside her. "This truly sucks. I'm so wound up I don't even want to make a cup of tea."

"Fine, I'll make it," Aaron grumbled from where he remained over by the kitchenette.

"You're too busy playing Scrooge in his counting house."

"Someone has to."

They were bickering. Grace recognised the sharp back and forth, the barbed looks. She didn't want the mood in the flat to descend any lower than it already had.

"I'll make tea," she straightened and left the sofa. "I'll make dinner too if you want."

No one objected.

Together they ate beans on toast and tried not to notice the inevitable passing of time.

"What time did he show up before?" Franklin asked once his plate was clean.

"Huh?" Aaron wiped at his mouth.

"Thug loving, you were here alone when he made his last appearance a week ago. What time was that?"

"Around ten."

It was quarter past nine. Grace shuddered and decided to busy herself with tidying away plates and mugs, anything to keep herself occupied. As she thrust her hands into a sink full of soapy warm water she heard her friends discussing the potential outcome for their evening.

"If he's pissed it's not the full amount?" Franklin ventured.

"Then he's pissed."

"And if he decides to take out his anger on one of us like he did with Jasper?"

Aaron lowered his voice but not enough so that Grace couldn't hear him. "Franks, we have no choice here. We bled ourselves dry getting this money. I'll explain that it's all we have, that there won't be any more. You and Grace, you can leave if you want, let me deal with it."

"This is not the time to play hero," Franklin countered sharply. "We're in this together. Moreover," his voice grew thin, like it was being painfully stretched to its limits, "this, truly, is my fault. I brought that damn briefcase here."

"You didn't know what was in it."

"I still spent it. I let greed blind me and…" he sighed and Grace felt the ache in his tone reach into her own chest. "This is on me more than anyone else. I need to be here, okay?"

"Okay."

The plates were washed and stacked on the draining board. Grace's hands still smelt of lemon but lacked the softness the washing up liquid adverts promised her they'd have. It was twenty to ten.

"How punctual do you think he'll be?" Franklin wondered, leaning back on the sofa and kicking his feet up onto the empty television stand.

"Reasonably." Aaron was stalking into his bedroom. He emerged a few minutes later brandishing a cricket bat.

"Woah!" Franklin instantly raised his hands in protest. "I don't feel like we should be answering the door with *weapons*. Surely that will only escalate things further?"

Grace fingered the sharp end of the knife she'd concealed up her sleeve when she'd been washing up earlier.

"It will be to the side of the door," Aaron marched across the flat as though he were striding towards the wicket. He placed the bat near the front door, just out of sight of any potential visitors. "It's there if we need to use it."

Franklin leapt to his feet. "Do you think we will?" Fear drained all colour from his face. "I mean, how bad do you anticipate things will get?"

"I…" Aaron looked between the wooden bat and his friend. "I honestly don't know."

There was a knock at the door. It was slow yet deliberate, delivering power with each connection of fist on wood. Franklin yelped and hurried towards Aaron's side. Grace joined them as they edged towards the door.

"Wait in your room," Aaron ordered tersely.

"No," Grace reached for the latch on the door and turned it. "We're all in this together, remember?"

The door swung back towards them and there he was. Only this time he wasn't alone. The thug who'd placed the order for the money was flanked by two equally large men, all dressed in black and wearing matching scowls on their faces. Grace noticed that the man to the right had a thick scar which ran down his cheek and died on his lips.

"So," the man in the middle addressed Aaron first. "Here we are again. We're getting awfully tired of having to drag our arses out to this neck of the woods. You best have my money."

Aaron briefly left the doorway and doubled back towards the kitchenette to grab the piles of cash carefully piled up on the counter. Franklin nervously eyed Grace while managing to keep his features set in a calm, flat expression.

"This is all we have," Aaron handed the money over. "Coupled with what we've already paid that puts us at eighteen grand."

"Eighteen?" the thug handed the money to his acquaintants and stared hard at Aaron. Grace could feel her blood rushing to her head, burning beneath her cheeks. If someone lurched forward she knew she'd need to fight, there would be no running, no abandoning her friends. Her fingertips grazed the end of the knife she was holding up her sleeve, praying she wouldn't need to use it. "Eighteen is short. We agreed on twenty-two."

"Well, like I said, it's all we have. Look around," Aaron stepped aside to allow the men in his doorway a glimpse into the flat. "We don't have much at all. We can't give you any more money."

This was it, the part where it would all come crashing down. Grace braced herself, imagining the scarred man breaking forward first, swinging for Aaron. Would there be time to grab the cricket bat? How would it sound as it's varnished wooden surface connected with a skull? Her palms were so damp that Grace began to wonder if she'd be able to grip her knife or if it would merely slide from her reach, clatter to the floor and leave her completely unprotected against the ensuing attack.

The thug who'd originally knocked on their door scratched his chin and then shrugged. "Fine, your debt is paid. I believe we have a mutual acquaintance in your Uncle Paulie. He put up five big ones for you kids, you owe him a solid."

Aaron nodded, seemingly unsurprised by this snippet of information. Grace tried to study him in her peripheral vision, wondering how much he now owed his uncle. Favours for favours he'd said before.

"Well, then, shouldn't you, you know, jog on," relief was making Franklin overly confident. He pointed down the corridor and frowned. "Pretty sure you're done here, gentlemen."

"Hope you kids learnt your lesson," the spokesman for the trio stared at them each in turn. "Don't take what isn't yours."

"In fairness I took the *briefcase*," Franklin clarified with an air of indignation. "I thought it'd add some pizazz to my look, I never set out to take your money." He exhaled sharply as Aaron elbowed him squarely in the ribs in an effort to silence him.

"You still spent it though," the thug who was familiar to Grace was backing away from the door. "Temptation has a way of finding us all. Learn from this, I don't want to be seeing any of your faces again, you get me?"

Franklin, Grace and Aaron nodded in unison. The men departed and the front door was thrown shut, the latch secured. For a moment no one spoke. Thoughts hurtled through Grace's mind like asteroids intent on colliding with one another.

The debt was paid.

It was over.

But Jasper was still in the hospital, in a coma, so what did it all mean?

"Well," rubbing his hands together Franklin drifted towards the sofa. "That felt like an anti-climax. If television has taught me anything it's that there should have been a shoot-out or at least some punches thrown on both sides."

"I'm just glad that they're gone," Grace dropped down next to him and then snuggled into his side. "I'd almost forgotten how creepy that guy was."

Aaron was the only one who didn't move. He remained at the front door, staring at it.

"But thug loving is gone," Franklin kissed her forehead. "Gone, gone, the witch is dead. Now we're free to be…" he raised his hand towards where Tina had once stood. "Poor and miserable. Great."

"Aaron?" Grace turned to look over at the door, at the forlorn figure standing beside it. "Are you alright?"

"I… just…" slowly he dragged himself over to the sofa. He looked utterly exhausted. "We all but killed ourselves getting that money together. And now… now it's paid, just like that."

"I don't think he was ever going to throw us a party," Franklin quipped.

"This isn't a time for jokes," Aaron scolded.

"Isn't it? Then what is it a time for? Being morose? Because God knows you make more than enough time for that as it is. This flat could use a bit of levity. Maybe we should throw a party."

"Jasper is still in hospital, still in a coma."

"And what? You thought that in paying our debt he'd somehow miraculously wake up? I don't think comas work like that, Aaron."

Grace felt something stir in her pocket, a gentle vibration. She reached for her phone and then jumped to her feet as though she'd just received an electric shock.

"You're talking about having a fucking *party*, like we have something to celebrate," Aaron growled.

"We're debt free! We're not going to be sleeping with the fishes! I'd say that's ample cause for celebration!"

"Shut up both of you," Grace yelled as she stormed away from them, her phone pressed to her ear. "Jasper's mum is calling me."

As she pushed her way into her bedroom Grace reminded herself to stay calm, that Jasper was surely okay.

But then why was his mother calling so late on a Friday night?

She choked against the clotting lump that had already formed in her throat, knowing she couldn't stand losing him. Jasper was gentle, kind. He was so like Peter that it both broke and mended Grace's heart at the same time. She saw in her flatmate the man her brother might had been had fate dealt him a kinder hand, a more stable mother. If Jasper was gone then—

Grace banished all dark thoughts from her mind and answered the call.

"Hi. Is… is everything okay?"

"It's Jasper," the old woman sounded like she'd just been yanked back from the edge of despair. There was exhaustion in her tone and something else that Grace couldn't quite decipher.

"Is he alright?"

"Can you get to the hospital?"

"Like… right now? Tonight?" Grace felt her heart rate rising with every word she uttered into her phone.

"Yes, yes right now."

"Of course. I'll be there within the hour."

"All of you," Jasper's mother added. "You should all come."

*

"Just stay on the line." That's what the call handler had told a six year old Grace as she stood in the kitchen with the phone in her hand. "Stay on the line, sweetie, can you do that?"

Grace had confirmed that yes, she could.

"Peter, he'll be okay, won't he?" she'd asked in a nervous whisper. In the nearby bathroom she could hear water gurgling down a plug hole as the bath was emptied. Did that mean he was alright? Once he breached the surface would his lungs fill with air, his cheeks with colour? Would he be able to open his eyes and look at her?

"Just stay on the line," the handler kept calmly repeating her single order. "Can you see your Mummy, is she there?"

Grace stared in the direction of the bathroom. "She's still with my brother."

"Okay, sweetheart. Don't worry. Help is on the way. Any minute now people are going to come through your front door. They may have to force their way in but don't be scared."

"Who is coming?"

"People who are going to help. So stay on the line. Are you safe? Where is mummy now?"

"Still in the bathroom."

"Okay, good girl. The police will be there any second."

Squeezing her eyes closed Grace counted out several long seconds.

One Mississippi.
Two Mississippi.
Three Mississippi.

"Grace, you still there, sweetheart?" the handler asked.

"I'm still here. Where is help?" The sound of the draining water was gone. With a creak the bathroom door opened and her mother staggered out, leaving droplets on the carpet as she cradled Peter in her arms. His head was turned towards the ceiling, hiding his expression. Grace wanted to run to him but she didn't dare abandon the phone. Her mother didn't even seem to register her presence as she hobbled over to the centre of the floor and squatted down, holding her pale son against her bosom and then opening her mouth to howl like a dog.

"It's coming, Grace. I promise. Just hang on a little longer."

"My mummy… she's here now, holding him. Will my brother be okay?"

"Just stay calm, Grace, you're being so brave. Nearly there. A despatch team have just arrived at your building. They'll just need to get up the stairs to your floor and then they'll be with you, okay? So stay on the line with me until then."

"What happens when they get here?"

"They'll help you, help your brother."

"So, everything is going to be alright?" Grace began to feel hopeful. She could hear the distant thunder of footsteps rushing along the corridor towards her door.

"Yes, Grace," the handler confirmed. "Everything is going to be alright."

She lied.

29

"Is that all she said?" Franklin had been reissuing the same set of questions throughout the entire train journey. Now they were walking across the darkened hospital car park where the lights from reception shone out like a welcome beacon.

"That was all she said, just that we should get here."

"Oh no, you don't think—" Franklin ceased walking and reached for the scarf snaked around his neck, hands trembling.

"I don't know," slowly Grace turned to him, her footsteps already heavy with apprehension. She had no idea what awaited them in the hospital. Outside, beneath the subtle glow of the floodlights that covered the car park she could at least pretend that it was good news. But once they passed through the sliding glass doors at the front there would be no more ambiguity.

"She wants us there so we should be there," Aaron remarked gruffly, hands deep in his jacket pockets, head bowed as he kept progressing towards reception. Grace looked at Franklin and offered him her hand.

"Whatever happens in there we're in this together, okay?"

He took her hand and squeezed. "Okay."

The hospital felt like a ghost ship as they walked the long corridors which led to the ward where Jasper was being held since his move from the HDU. Occasionally nurses and orderlies appeared from behind sets of heavy double doors, drifting like flotsam in the current towards their next destination. Everything felt subdued, quiet.

As Grace walked, she ground her teeth together. Her senses were at odds with themselves; a part of her was hopeful for good news but another, more prominent part kept remembering how it felt to have the police barrel into the flat, to pry her dead brother out of her mother's arms. Peter's head had briefly lolled back, eyes glassy and open. Grace had just stared at him and screamed. In that moment, seeing his gaze devoid of kindness, of love, she knew he was gone and that all the policemen were handing to the waiting paramedics was a shell.

What if Jasper was now that vacant in his bed? Grace reached for Aaron's arm and brought him to a halt.

"Can I do this?" she wasn't sure if she was asking him or herself.

"Yes," Aaron confirmed, resting a hand atop hers. "You can do this, Grace."

The ward was just as still as the rest of the hospital. Within the bay areas which each housed half a dozen beds the lights were dimmed and the figures beneath the thin blankets were still. The sandman was now king. Machines chirped and bleated but against the stillness and the darkness even their shrill sounds seemed subdued. The trio rounded a corner and reached Jasper's room. Aaron reached for the door handle but it snapped down before his fingers could connect with it and Jasper's mother hurried out to greet them. She looked flushed and there was a trace of a smile on her face. Wasn't there? Or was Grace just hoping that there was?

"Sorry for asking you to get here so urgently," the old woman looked between each of them. Only she didn't look quite so old any more, there was a glow beneath her papery skin, a light in her tired eyes. "But he was desperate to see you all."

"Wait, what?" Grace wasn't sure she trusted what she'd just heard.

"You mean?" Franklin stepped forward and peered through the little window within the door. "He's awake?" The elation in his voice made it real for Grace. With her friends by her side she burst into the little room.

Jasper was sat up in his bed, still the centre of machines and wires but the tube that had been breathing for him was gone. A discarded oxygen mask hissed at his side and the bruises on his face had softened to shades of red.

"Holy shit," Franklin shrieked as he hurried to Jasper's beside. "You're awake, you're actually awake."

"Yep," Jasper's voice was so raw but so unmistakably his. "That's me, wide awake." Grace knew he must still be sore but this wasn't the time for delicacy. She threw herself towards the bed, wrapping both arms around Jasper's slender shoulders.

"Oh, my God," she told him breathlessly, "I was so, so worried about you."

"We all were," Aaron confirmed, keeping a stoic vigil at the foot of the bed as the others clamoured over the patient.

"When? How?" Grace stepped back and looked into Jasper's blue eyes. He was clearly tired, but he was present, there was nothing glassy about the stare he returned to her. Hot tears of joy began to slide down her cheeks as she hugged him again.

"You really had us worried," Franklin told him. "We kept rooting for you to wake up."

"I'm just so glad you're okay," Grace wasn't sure she'd ever be able to let him go.

The friends talked, joked. Filled Jasper in on what they'd been up to, what he'd missed whilst in his coma. He tried to keep up with their mirth but as midnight approached his head began to droop down to his chest.

"It's been a big day for him," a nurse began ushering them out of the room. "He needs to rest. You can return during normal visiting hours tomorrow."

"How long—" Grace wasn't sure if the time was right to ask the question but it was there on the tip of her tongue because she wanted him back, wanted him home.

"How long until he's on his feet?" Aaron asked more pragmatically. Jasper undoubtedly had a long road of recovery ahead of him. He may not even want to return to the flat.

"We'll see," the nurse told them. "So far the doctor is pleased with all his vital signs but there's a lot of tests that need to be run."

Grace followed Aaron and Franklin through the maze of corridors that twisted through the hospital and soon they were back outside, standing in the deep shadows of the car park.

"He woke up," Franklin stared at the few vehicles which were parked up close by. "He really woke up."

A door closed with an elegant click and Grace turned in the direction of the car which belonged to Jasper's parents and hurried towards it, letting the beam from the headlights illuminate her as she lifted her arms to get their attention.

"Grace," Jasper's mother opened her window and leant out. "It's late dear, you should be heading home. Do you need a lift to the station?"

"What happened?" She knew that sleep would never find her if she didn't ask the question which had taken up residence in her mind since the day of Jasper's accident.

"What happened?"

"To the car that Jasper was driving. Why did it crash? Did the police ever find out?" As she fired off her questions Aaron and Franklin came and stood at her side.

"Actually," Jasper's mother glanced at her husband and he turned off the engine, killing the car's lights. The sudden darkness was jarring but only for a moment. With a soft click the passenger door opened and Jasper's mother climbed out, leaning against the roof of the car for support. Grace didn't like keeping her out in the cold when she too needed rest as desperately as her newly awoken son. But she needed to know the truth. Whilst Jasper lay in a coma it didn't feel right to keep asking but now that he was awake it—

"The police got back to us yesterday," his mother confirmed. "And their conclusion makes for grim hearing."

Grace felt Aaron's hand slide into her own and Franklin's arm loop around her shoulders. So the verdict was in. Did the police suspect foul play? Was this the part where Jasper's mother asked them if there was anyone who would want to hurt her son? How would they respond? If she knew that they might be somehow responsible surely she'd—

"Negligence." She said the word and then took a breath. "It turns out that Jackson had failed to have the car MOT'd last September. Ellen, then his fiancée, had mentioned a fault with the steering wheel failing to align correctly and he'd intended to get it looked at but then with the whirlwind of the wedding he…" she dropped her head. "He forgot. And he feels utterly responsible for the accident and completely wretched. But of course Jasper won't press charges against his own brother, he's too sweet a soul for that."

"So the police said it was just an accident? Some sort of malfunction?" Aaron sought confirmation.

"That's right," Jasper's mother began to dip back inside the car. "As you can appreciate it's a difficult truth for us all to swallow. The main thing is that Jasper is alright but," she pursed her lips and blinked back tears. "If only we'd known what a death trap that car was we'd never have let him get in it."

"Well," Grace broke away from her friends and reached into the car to embrace the woman who was now gently shaking with repressed emotion. "Thank you for letting us know. At least the police figured it out."

"Thanks for coming to see him tonight, you lifted his spirits no end. No doubt we'll see a lot more of you as he recovers."

Stepping back, Grace watched the headlights burn bright again and the car slowly eased out of its space. And then Jasper's parents were gone, taking their uncomfortable truth with them.

"So all along it was an… accident?" Grace turned to the others and saw her own confusion written on their faces. Franklin threw his arms up to the moon which was partially hidden behind a veil of thin clouds.

"A bloody accident!" He cried. "A faulty fucking car. And we…" he dragged his hands against his chest. "I believed that someone did this to him, that it had been malicious, that—"

"That the guy at the door was behind it," Aaron concluded flatly. He walked towards Grace and draped an arm around her, letting her tuck into the nook beneath his left shoulder, a place where she always seemed to fit just perfectly, as though they were both pieces of the same puzzle. "But the fucked up thing is that he wasn't behind it, had nothing to do with it. We let a bunch of empty threats scare us shitless."

"Your uncle," Franklin snapped his fingers in his friend's direction. "Uncle Paulie believed the threats were legit, didn't he?"

"He did."

"So maybe we're not such a complete bunch of idiots for believing the words of a most menacing man. Maybe this sense of humiliation will pass," looking dejected, he dropped his head and kicked at a stone, sending it skittering across the car park.

"I feel pretty humiliated too," Aaron agreed. "But also relieved."

"Relieved?" Grace peered up at him. Of all the emotions currently flooding through her, relief wasn't one of them.

"Yeah, relieved," he nodded at her. "So, the guy at the door wasn't behind Jasper's accident but that doesn't mean he wouldn't have roughed us up if we hadn't paid. Giving him the money was the right thing to do, it removed the target off our backs."

"You know, over the last few weeks we've been in possession of almost forty thousand pounds in total," Franklin remarked. "That's a hell of a lot of money."

"And now we have none," Grace noted softly. "We're back to being skint."

"Skint but alive," Aaron gave her a squeeze. "And Jasper woke up, that's huge."

"I know."

"Then why do we feel so bummed?" Franklin vocalised how they all felt. "I mean, I feel like I've been tricked, but that I let myself be tricked. I was so willing to believe that the prick from the door put Jasper in hospital. Too willing."

"Don't beat yourself up about it," Aaron urged. "We all thought the same thing."

"So, what now?" Grace wondered.

"We go home," Franklin decided, "and pray that Lady Luck hasn't completely turned her back on us because right now we could really use some of her love."

30

It was raining. Grace listened to the steady drum beat of it against the windows of the little flat as she plunged her fork into her cup of steaming noodles. Franklin was on the sofa next to her and Aaron was perched on the vacant television unit, each consuming their own meagre meals.

Saturday had already arrived as they trudged back to the flat, weary but elated over Jasper's recovery. After managing to catch a few hours' sleep Grace awoke to a stream of messages from her newly conscious friend. Even in text form he sounded so much like himself that it made her heart ache in a really wonderful way.

I can't wait to see you guys again x

As soon as I'm better I'm coming home x

Did you all miss me? Xx

"So much," Grace smiled to herself as she'd looked down at the last message.

Franklin drained the last of his noodles and slammed his empty cup down in a show of authority. "Okay," leaning forward he clasped his hands between his knees and looked at his friends. "I know we're riding a wave of awesomeness right now but I'm about to be the bearer of bad news."

Aaron groaned loudly but didn't stop eating.

"Rent."

The word ricocheted between them like a bullet. Grace straightened and dropped her fork into her cup.

"We're good for a couple of months, right?"

"Right," Franklin nodded at her. "But the future will probably arrive sooner than we'd like and if these last few weeks have taught me anything it's to be prepared."

"But we've got a few months," Aaron reiterated as he wiped a hand across his mouth.

"Yes," Franklin cocked his head at him, "*but* what if nothing changes? What if we remain the unemployed hopefuls that we are? And we can't rely on Jasper coming back anytime soon and bailing us out."

"He is coming back, though," Grace interjected. "He told me so."

"It'll be great to have him back," Franklin pinched the bridge of his nose, "to be the whole gang again will be brilliant. But, rent. It has to be paid. And we've literally nothing left to pawn," he gazed sadly past Aaron at where Tina used to preside.

"Feels like we've come a full circle," Aaron grumbled as he stood up. "We're back to worrying about the rent."

"At least we're predictable."

"Or just hopeless."

Grace checked out of the conversation and withdrew to her bedroom, unsure if she could stomach the boys bickering over money just yet. She knew that Franklin was right, that once the next few months had passed they'd need a plan for how they were going to pay the rent.

The few hours' sleep she'd snatched hadn't been enough. Grace dropped onto her back on her bed and sighed as the mattress eased the ache in her limbs. She thought of money, and briefcases, and at some point she drifted off to sleep.

A pulse. Prominent and then gone. It roused Grace from her dreams and forced her to sit up. Running her hands through her tangled hair she felt it come again, a strong and certain pressure, vibration at her side. Sleep was making her sluggish and it took several long seconds for her to realise that it was her phone. Grabbing it she looked down at the unfamiliar number on the screen. It was a London number.

Dread washed over her. Upon hitting the green accept button would she hear the deep voice of the thug from the doorway? Was he suddenly demanding more payment? But there was nothing left to give, the only thing of value Grace still possessed was the phone she was currently staring at and she needed it to remain connected with the wider world, with possible jobs.

As every muscle in her body tensed Grace answered the call.

"Hello?" she could hear the nervous uncertainty in her voice and wished she sounded bolder.

"Hi, is this Grace?" The woman on the other end of the line sounded chirpy and completely non-threatening.

"Yes, um, it's me."

"Great, I'm calling about your audition the other week."

Grace held her breath and felt the knots in her muscles tightening. To which audition was the woman referring? She'd struck out an epic four times at her last bout of auditions.

"For Matthew Bourne's company?" the woman prompted, and Grace didn't dare release the breath she was currently holding. "I apologise for the delay in getting back to you but we had quite a number of candidates to get through. But the good news is that we love your classic style and natural elegance and would love to offer you a permanent place in the company."

She was going to faint. Grace squeezed her eyes closed and gasped, letting all the air rush out of her. She wondered if this was all really happening or if she was curled up in a ball on her bed sleeping soundly and this was just some bittersweet dream.

"I… wow… that's… that's brilliant. Amazing. Thank you."

"I'll send the paperwork to the email address provided in your application and we'd like to get you started in the studio as soon as possible. How does a week on Monday work for you?"

"That… that absolutely works."

"Wonderful, we'll see you then, Grace."

The woman hung up and Grace looked down at her phone and realised that she was shaking. She didn't know what to do; should she shout to the others or just embrace her inner child and start jumping up and down on the bed for joy? Carefully placing her phone on the floor Grace opted for the latter. Standing tall atop her mattress she began to jump, with each bounce she felt lighter, more liberated. The bed springs groaned but Grace didn't care, she just kept jumping gleefully.

"Hey," the door opened and Franklin was peering in, cheeks still bearing the crease of the sofa cushions as he'd clearly been enjoying a nap of his own. "Some of us are trying to sleep in here." His head bobbed up and down in time with Grace's jumps as he took in what she was doing. "Ooh," he hurried towards the bed, "you should have said we were spending the afternoon reliving our misspent youth. Make room."

With two people bouncing on the bed it sounded as though it might snap. The noise drew Aaron's attention; he hovered in the doorway, watching the pair jumping up and down whilst frowning to himself. "What's all this in aid of?"

"Who cares?" Franklin laughed.

"I got… a… job," Grace explained between bounces. "A… real… one." She stopped jumping and looked straight at Aaron. "The Matthew Bourne company called and offered me a place." She wasn't on her feet for long.

"Holy shit," Franklin threw himself against her in a bear hug and they both dropped against the mattress. "Grace," he kept pressing her against his chest like she was his most precious toy, "that's so bloody wonderful. I can't believe it."

"I'm proud of you." She twisted within Franklin's embrace to see that Aaron's green eyes were shining. "I knew you could do it," he added. "You're such a beautiful dancer."

"And now at least one of us can pay rent!" Franklin released her and resumed bouncing. "Now I get why you were so giddy with joy!"

"Franks," Aaron clicked his fingers at him, "off the bed, you've worn it out enough."

Pouting like a disappointed child, Franklin stopped bouncing and positioned himself at the foot of the bed. "It really is such wonderful news though," he twisted to glance back at Grace. "Maybe the tide is turning for us all, perhaps this time next year we'll all be stars!"

"I hope so," Grace smiled.

"Until then, drinks," Franklin clapped his hands together. "Time we celebrated not just how children do but adults too. We'll go out and get well and truly rat arsed. We'll toast to your fabulous new job, to Jasper—"

"Wait a minute," Aaron held up a hand in objection. "Is a night on the town really the best idea?"

"Of course," Franklin insisted grandiosely. "I'll even order champagne. Okay, maybe Prosecco, but still, it will be fabulous."

"We can go out," Aaron approached the bed with slow, heavy steps. "On one condition."

"And what's that, *Dad*?" Franklin joked.

"No dumpster diving."

Grace felt reels of laughter come bubbling out of her.

"Oh, killjoy," Franklin threw up his arms in dismay, "but if I don't go dumpster diving where will our next adventure come from?"

"I'm serious, Franks, you see something in a skip you bloody leave it there, you got it?"

"Scouts Honour."

"You were never a scout, were you?"

"No," Franklin admitted, "but I can still embody their sense of honour."

"Right, okay," Aaron was now looking only at Grace. "A night on the town it is. A night to celebrate all things Grace."

"Does this mean you'll be in one of those wonderfully modern ballet performances?" Franklin asked her as he lay on his back and looked up at her ceiling. "I so hope you get to be in *Edward Scissorhands,* I'd love to go and see that."

"You'll come to any shows I'm in?"

"Of course," Franklin replied like it was a reflex, unquestionable that he'd do anything other than support her. "I'll be there front row centre if I can be."

"We all will." Aaron added.

"And by all he means me, him and Jasper. You've got your three musketeers back, Grace." Franklin raised his head briefly to blow her a kiss. "I told you that everything would work out alright in the end."

"You were quoting Mrs Potts then and you're quoting her now."

"Well, me and that old piece of china are both right. Things have worked out, enjoy it."

"We were just lucky." Grace looked to her window, listened to the steady patter of rain against the glass. She was staring absently as Aaron's warm hands looped around her waist as he sat down beside her but not before planting a soft kiss on her lips.

"We make our own luck in this world," he told her softly. "You worked so hard to get to this point, enjoy it."

"Right, I'm off," the mattress shifted as Franklin rolled off the bed. "You two have that gooey look in your eyes which tells me that I need to make myself scarce. Besides," he leaned forward to give Grace a final hug, "you've inspired me to grab a copy of *The Stage* and literally spend next week auditioning for every damn part in it. We're here to chase our dreams and that's what I intend to do."

"I'll buy you your guitar back," she whispered, looking into Aaron's eyes as the door closed behind Franklin. "As soon as I have enough money I'll go get it."

"No, you won't," he murmured as he began softly kissing her neck.

"Yes, I will," Grace insisted as her eyes closed with delight. "Franklin is right; we're here to chase our dreams. And we're all in it together, remember?"

"Stop talking about Franklin," Aaron instructed as he eased her further across the bed. The rain kept falling but Grace didn't care. She let herself become fully enveloped in the moment, the pain of her past no longer weighing her down.

Acknowledgements

Thanks so much to the wonderful team at Aria for their continued support and enthusiasm for myself and my work.

To my husband, Sam, for always listening when I have my inevitable mid-manuscript melt down.

Fudge - I developed an unhealthy addiction to it whilst writing this book and so big thanks to my Mum for being an enabler and always bringing me a pack of it whenever I needed perking up.

Rollo, as always you are the biggest constant in my writing life. Thank you for keeping me on track, even on the days when I didn't feel like writing you'd take yourself up to the pink room and patiently wait, whilst giving me a guilty look that made sure I sat myself down at my laptop and got some words down. For such an adorable dog you can be a hard task master.

Finally, huge thanks to you, awesome reader. Maybe this is the first book of mine you've read or perhaps you've been with me on my writing journey for some time, either way, thank you so much. For me there is no greater feeling than knowing that my books are being read and enjoyed. I hope that you'll stay with me as I continue writing.

xoxo

About Carys Jones

CARYS JONES loves nothing more than to write and create stories which ignite the reader's imagination. Based in Shropshire, England, Carys lives with her husband, two guinea pigs and her adored canine companion Rollo.

Find me on Twitter
https://twitter.com/tiny_dancer85

Find me on Facebook
https://www.facebook.com/CarysJonesWriter/?ref=ts

Visit my website
http://www.carys-jones.com/

A Letter from the Author

Dear Reader,

Thank you so much for reading my latest book, I hope you enjoyed it! If you did, please let me know by leaving a review online or getting in touch with me on social media – I'm on Twitter and have an active Facebook page – just follow the links below. These are also the places where I'll promote new releases if you want to keep up to date with me and my work.

Writing is quite a lonely pursuit, though I do have my handsome dog, Rollo, for company. Hearing from readers truly does brighten my day so do reach out, don't be a stranger!

Until next time. Happy reading!

Love,

Carys xoxo

Find me on Twitter
https://twitter.com/tiny_dancer85
Find me on Facebook
https://www.facebook.com/CarysJonesWriter/?ref=ts
Visit my website
http://www.carys-jones.com/

Also by Carys Jones

Find out more
http://headofzeus.com/books/isbn/9781786692481
Find out more
http://headofzeus.com/books/isbn/9781786692498
Find out more
http://headofzeus.com/books/isbn/9781786692504

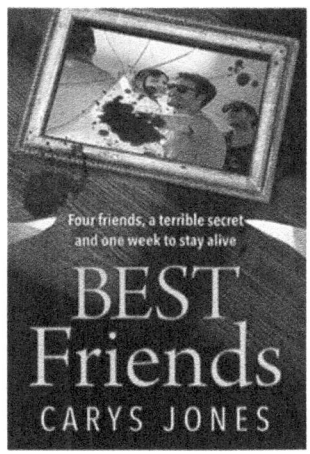

Find out more

http://headofzeus.com/books/isbn/9781788543286

First published in the UK in 2018 by Aria, an imprint of Head of Zeus Ltd

Copyright © Carys Jones, 2018

The moral right of Carys Jones to be identified as the author of this work has been asserted in accordance with the Copyright, Designs and Patents Act of 1988.

All rights reserved. No part of this publication may be reproduced, stored in a retrieval system, or transmitted, in any form or by any means, electronic, mechanical, photocopying, recording, or otherwise, without the prior permission of both the copyright owner and the above publisher of this book.

This is a work of fiction. All characters, organizations, and events portrayed in this novel are either products of the author's imagination or are used fictitiously.

9 7 5 3 1 2 4 6 8

A CIP catalogue record for this book is available from the British Library.

ISBN (P) 9781035906239
ISBN (E) 9781788543286

Printed and bound by CPI Group (UK) Ltd, Croydon, CR0 4YY

Head of Zeus
First Floor East
5–8 Hardwick Street
London EC1R 4RG

www.headofzeus.com

Printed and bound by CPI Group (UK) Ltd, Croydon, CR0 4YY
20/03/2026
02075568-0006